again—for today we become Women of The Code. The Girls' Twenty-
Ex ever again. Take his name off your en... not
You must not write The Ex letters or te... m.
5: You must not date anyone until you c... ng
ility. Do group activities with friends—both girl and guy friends.) Rule
Ex's pictures and any gifts that he gave you. Following the ritual: Rule 7
ight eating popcorn as you and your girls laugh over a fifty-page list of The
You are not to accommodate any male for any reason. Rule 9: Don't allow
th cooling-off period. You must not be his friend. Rule 10: Do not think
er band against your wrist. Rule 11: You must never date your girls' Exes.
er sleep with The Ex. Rule 14: The Ex's name can't be mentioned unless
or something you are passionate about. Rule 16: Do not call The Ex's
p you through the breakup, because they can't and they won't. Rule 17: Do
ted to The Ex's family. Rule 18: Do not ask anyone what The Ex is up
you see your girl's Ex, you must never mention it to her. Rule 20: You
, no more tears. (The twenty-four hours can be broken down into chunks—an
nother thirty minutes Tuesday night—then another four hours the next
out The Ex. Keep track of the twenty-four-hour timeline in a journal that
u of each rule in The Breakup Code.) Rule 21. You must always look
llow The Ex nor ask his friends to put in a good word for you. Rule 23:
ou must let him know what he has lost by flirting with him, touching him, and
King of the Jungle. Once you have built his ego up, crush it by telling
—the whole idea here is to reestablish your "single" self—you don't need
—not pettiness!!!! This is the most important rule of The Code, mean-
sk or beg The Ex to date you again, nor should he ever see you cry about
eave? His loss! Who's next? If he can't appreciate you, then some other
ourselves. There is nothing wrong with being alone. In order to be happy
son. Two wholes = One healthy, happy relationship. Rule 25: Do not
Ex, because you will—just give yourself the chance by letting The Ex go.

The Heartbreakers

The Heartbreakers

Pamela Wells

Point

Acknowledgments

A special thank-you to Abby McAden for letting me into the enchanted gates of publishing. I would like to thank Jen for getting this book into Abby's hands.

I would also like to thank Amber Silverstein for her contribution to this book.

Library of Congress Cataloging-in-Publication Data available on request.

ISBN-13: 978-0-439-02691-8
ISBN-10: 0-439-02691-1

12 11 10 9 8 7 6 5 4 3 8 9 10 11/0

Printed in the U.S.A.
First edition, December 2007

The display type was set in Liberty and NotMaryKate.
The text type was set in Horley Old Style.
Book design by Steve Scott

Dedication

To all the girls who have gone through heartache—
may this book be an inspiration to you

The Heartbreakers

ONE

Sydney Howard picked at her nail while she waited outside the locker rooms after a Friday night basketball game. Her thumbnail had caught on the zipper of her jacket and tore off, leaving it jagged. She flipped open her purse and dug inside, except the nail clipper she always carried wasn't there. Probably because her boyfriend, Drew, took it and left it somewhere that was obviously *not* her purse. He never put things back where he found them.

The girls' locker room door opened and cheerleaders started filing out. A few said hi to Sydney as they passed until Nicole, the head cheerleader, came out, her makeup reapplied in a thick mask on her face.

Nicole glanced over at Sydney and whispered something to her three friends, which made them all laugh.

Sydney rolled her eyes as they left. *Whatever.*

A few minutes later Drew emerged from the locker room in jeans and a sweatshirt, his black hair still wet from the shower.

"Hey," he said, readjusting the strap of the bag on his shoulder.

"Hi." She fell in step beside him as they left the school through the back doors. The freshly fallen snow crunched beneath their feet. Sydney pulled the collar of her jacket up around her neck when the cool air hit her skin.

"You should have worn a heavier jacket," Drew said.

She glanced over at him. "I didn't think it was going to be this cold." Even in the half-darkness of the night, Sydney could still see the blue of his eyes. Although every inch of him was good, she always thought of his eyes as his best quality. They were such a bright blue they were almost neon. She always teased him, saying if they were ever stuck in a cave, his eyes would probably glow and light the way out.

Together they followed the sidewalk down to the parking lot.

"I was wondering—" Sydney started.

"So listen—" said Drew.

Sydney tipped her head. "You first."

"Well, there's this party tonight," Drew began, flipping the zipper on his bag up and down, up and down, "over at Craig's. It's to celebrate the end of the semester and getting through exams. He really wants us to come."

"I don't know. I was thinking we could just go hang out at your house."

He groaned. "We do that every night, Syd."

A car stereo thumped bass beats somewhere in the parking lot. Sydney looked out and saw several football players and cheerleaders in a group around a few parked cars. She didn't fit in with them. Not that she tried or even wanted to. She was the junior class president and in the Honor Society. Going to a "kegger" wasn't her idea of fun.

"But do you really want to drive out there?" she said. Craig Thierot's house was on the outside of Birch Falls, a good thirty minutes away. She was hoping that would sway Drew. He hated driving and *she* certainly wasn't going to drive out there.

"Yeah. Totally," he said.

Okay. Maybe not.

"I don't think I want to go."

He hung his head to the side. "Come on, Syd—"

A squeal sounded behind Sydney. She turned just in time to see a flash of blonde hair as Nicole ran up to Drew and threw her arms around his neck.

"Awesome game!" she yelled, pulling away to touch Drew's chest.

Sydney knew every line of that chest, like the tiny crescent scar on his left pec where his older brother had chucked a rock at him when they were little. It didn't seem right that Nicole Robinson should be able to touch his chest so freely.

In the last year, Drew had gone from skinny, unknown basketball player to the insanely hot starting forward on the team. It did not escape Sydney that her shy, somewhat dorky boyfriend had transformed into the "It Guy" at Birch Falls High.

Or that every other girl in school wanted him. Two years ago, when he and Sydney started going out, no one really knew he existed.

Drew smiled, clearly glowing from Nicole's attention. "We couldn't have won without the cheerleaders."

"Oh, you," Nicole cooed, giving his bicep a playful thump. "Stop."

Sydney tapped her foot on the sidewalk. Come on, Drew, she thought, catch the hint.

"So," he said, after making quick eye contact with Sydney, "I'll see you at the party."

Nicole nodded. "Sure. See ya there." She waggled her fingers in a wave, ignoring Sydney, and headed off toward the parking lot.

"What," Sydney put her hands on her hips, "was that all about?"

Drew cast his gaze aside, pulling his dark brows together. "She was congratulating me on the game."

"I think it was more than that." Sydney took in a long breath and shifted from one foot to the other. She trusted Drew, but it was hard pretending that she didn't notice the other girls flirting with him. Or that the other girls looked at Sydney as merely an obstacle in their way.

Sometimes Sydney wished Drew was still the dorky Drew; the one that thought doing homework on a Friday night was fun and that keggers were for morons.

"I think Nicole has a thing for you," Sydney said.

Drew shrugged. "So what if she does?"

Sydney sighed and shook her head. "Whatever. Let's just go. Did you take my nail clipper? I can't find it."

"What about the party?"

She was hoping he'd forgotten about the party. "Can we talk about it in the truck? I'm freezing out here."

"Fine." He headed for the parking lot, and Sydney walked fast to catch up with his long-legged strides. He unlocked the passenger door of his truck then went around to the driver's side.

Sydney frowned. "You don't want me to drive?"

"No," he said, and climbed inside.

What was his problem? She always drove, mainly because Drew hated wearing his glasses. He only used his contacts for basketball games because they irritated his eyes. When she slid in next to him, he reached over and undid the latch on the glove compartment, taking his glasses out.

On the way out of the school parking lot, Sydney turned the heat on full blast and positioned the vents on her face. Her cheeks were freezing. "So, did you take my nail clipper?"

"Check the ashtray."

She pulled the ashtray open. Her nail clipper spilled out with several safety pins and a tube of chapstick. "Dang it, Drew." She ducked down to scoop up the mess.

"Just leave it," he said.

"It's all over the floor."

He flicked his eyes to her as they sat beneath a red light. "So? It's my truck."

She groaned and crossed her arms over her chest. "Fine. Whatever."

Drew shifted into second gear after pulling away from the stoplight. He didn't say anything and silence took over. He drove through the middle of town, past the darkened stores. Gold Christmas lights hung in the trees even though Christmas had passed weeks ago. Birch Falls kept the gold lights up year-round as "ambience." At least that's what the mayor said when a citizen questioned him in the *Birch Falls Gazette* editorial section.

Drew turned left on Palmer Street and pulled up to the curb in front of Sydney's house. With the truck idling, he turned to her. "Are you going to the party or not?"

Sydney fell against the back of the seat, letting a sigh out past her lips. He wasn't going to let it go. Why couldn't he just let it go? "What are you doing if I don't go?"

"I'm going to the party."

She raised an eyebrow, incredulous. "You'd go without me?" They always spent their weekend nights together. And if they weren't together, there was a good reason. Like a family reunion or something. The thought of Drew showing up at some party alone . . . it made Sydney's stomach knot.

There would be a ton of girls at the party. Nicole Robinson, for one. Out of all the girls in the junior class, Nicole was the girl Sydney loved to hate. It was the platinum-blonde hair, the acrylic French-manicured nails, the overdone bronzer. But most of all it was the way Nicole treated Sydney, as if Sydney was beneath her notice, as if she couldn't figure out why Drew would be with someone like Sydney.

Nicole was obviously clueless to the fact that Drew and Sydney had been together longer than Nicole had been blonde.

Maybe Sydney should just go. Maybe she should just swallow her discomfort and stubbornness and go.

"Syd." Drew picked at the crumbling leather of the steering wheel while he avoided looking her in the eye. "I don't want to hang out at home. I want to go out and do something."

"Hanging out used to be good enough for you."

"Yeah, well, it's not anymore."

She leaned forward, hoping to catch his gaze. Her face flamed with the beginning of anger and fear. "What are you trying to say, Drew? That hanging out, just the two of us, is boring?"

He turned in his seat, leaning against the driver's-side door. "Why do you always put words in my mouth?"

"You're the one who insinuated that I was boring."

Lately they'd been fighting like this a lot. It seemed like everything caused an argument, from the color of Drew's shirt to the mustard that wasn't supposed to be on Sydney's burger.

Sydney couldn't explain it. When she found herself in another argument with Drew, she couldn't stop. It was like a car crash in slow motion. She could see it coming but couldn't do a thing to stop it.

Drew was just so pushy lately, bugging her to go to those stupid drunk-fest parties with his friends from the team. They were all idiots if you asked her. Evolution had somehow missed them. They acted like cavemen.

She didn't want to go.

"I'm not saying you're boring," Drew said. "I'd just like for us to go out and do stuff instead of sitting inside watching TV."

"But it's not that we're watching TV. We're being together, Drew. That's what couples do. They *be* together. They don't go out to parties to separate and get drunk."

He clenched his jaw and took a deep breath. "I never said we had to get drunk."

"But you want to drink, and then I'll have to drive home in the middle of the night from the middle of nowhere."

He threw up his hands. "You know what, Syd, I'm done."

She froze. "What?"

"I'm done."

"Done with what?"

Sighing, he lowered his voice. "With us."

Sydney's mouth dropped. "Are you . . ." She swallowed hard, feeling bile rise in her throat. "Are you breaking up with me?"

He shifted again and stared straight ahead at the street. The absence of an answer told her more than words would have.

The shock burned into anger. "Fine!" She got out of the truck and slammed the door behind her. She stomped up the shoveled sidewalk, the snow making wet slapping noises beneath her shoes.

On the front porch, she stopped and turned back to the road, hoping that Drew was running after her. But he drove off, the transmission shifting through gears quickly. She watched as the red taillights of the truck disappeared around a corner.

What in hell just happened?

She felt the stinging of tears behind her eyes but took a deep breath to stop them. A hunk of jet-black hair flew in her face. She grabbed it and gave it a shove over her shoulder.

This was just another fight in a long list of many lately. But they'd never broken up before . . . not like this.

Tomorrow they'd make up, she told herself as she trudged inside. Tomorrow they'd fix this, and everything would be fine.

TWO

The rock music blasting from the St. Bernard–sized speakers on the back wall was so loud, Raven Valenti could barely hear her own breathing. And it was a bad song, too. The drumbeats drowned out the guitar riffs, making the song sound something like a drummer boy leading an army.

Her father, a has-been singer, had taught her how to read music for beauty and flaws. Now it was almost habit to analyze it, to pick apart a song like an English student picking out grammar and punctuation mistakes in a book. Sometimes it was almost impossible to sit through her band class. Not that she was a master flutist, but, well . . . some people just *aren't* musicians.

She elbowed her way out of the living room's makeshift dance floor and headed for the billiards room. Her boyfriend, Caleb, was there, hunched over to line up a shot on the table. He pushed the stick forward and the cue ball sailed down the length of the red felt, cracking into a striped ball. It clattered into the corner pocket.

"Caleb," she said.

"Shhh." He frowned. "Eight ball in the left side pocket," he called out. After several seconds, he sunk the eight ball exactly where he said he would. He straightened up and grinned at Kenny, who was standing behind him. "Pay up, dude."

Kenny forked over a twenty-dollar bill. Caleb slid it into his jeans pocket.

"Caleb," Raven said again, and motioned him over with her finger.

He came up and slid his arms around her waist. His breath smelled like beer, his dark brown hair like Aussie hair gel. "Did you see me kick Kenny's ass?"

She rolled her eyes but smiled. "Yes, but I wouldn't exactly call you a pool shark."

He laughed and bent down, kissing her neck. "You want to go upstairs for a while?" He raised his eyebrows suggestively.

"Not right now." Raven's mother was right about one thing (if *that* was even possible), boys thought about sex *all* the time. Raven slept with Caleb for the first time a few months ago. Since then he was constantly bringing it up.

"Let's go get something to drink. My throat is raw from all this cigarette smoke." She waved away the air around her. Not that it would do much good. The party had been in full swing for an hour now. There was a smoke haze in every room. It wasn't just in the air, it *was* the air.

"I'm going to watch the next game." Caleb tipped his head toward the pool table. "Grab me something though? A beer?"

She sighed and said, "Fine," then made her way to the kitchen. The song on the stereo had switched to something a little more appealing but still not quite there. She wondered if this was Craig's CD collection or if someone else had brought the music. If it was the former, Craig had really bad taste, which, now that she thought about it, was not surprising.

In the front foyer, Raven dodged the door as it opened. Drew walked in. Alone. "Where's Sydney?" she asked, checking the doorway for her friend.

Drew grimaced. "I don't want to talk about it."

Raven frowned. That was bizarre. Drew and Sydney were always together, they were like two halves of a whole. Maybe she should text Sydney after she grabbed a drink. Something was definitely up.

Drew scanned the dozens of people hanging around the front room. "Have you seen Todd?"

Raven shook her head. "I just talked to Kelly a little while ago. She said he was on his way."

Drew cursed and shut his eyes as if annoyed. He pulled out his cell, dialed, and put the phone to his ear. "Todd? Where the hell are you?" Drew nodded a good-bye at Raven before disappearing back outside.

Raven headed off to the kitchen. It was just as packed as the living room. People were filling up red plastic cups at the keg. Figuring that's what Caleb wanted, she got him a cup then searched the refrigerator for a bottle of water. Finding one, she turned and rammed into someone. The beer sloshed inside the cup. She quickly set it down on the counter before it spilled all over her vintage Firebird T-shirt.

"Hey!" she shouted, then recognized who it was. "Oh, Horace, hi."

Her heart sped up instantly seeing his green eyes pinned on her. Horace was in the school band with her. He was in the percussion section . . . but they'd shared more than music recently.

"Hey, Ray."

An elbow jabbed her in the ribs. "Oww."

"Come on," Horace shouted. "It's safer over here." He grabbed her hand and pulled her out of the throng of drink-seekers and into the darkened mudroom.

"Thanks."

"No problem." He smiled and butterflies zinged in her stomach. Horace always had this look in his eyes, and a warm tone in his husky voice, like he knew things about Raven she hadn't told him.

Realizing that she was now alone with Horace in a darkened room, she flushed and looked away. The last time she'd been this close to him, they'd kissed. It was just a month ago, when they'd gone to regionals for the school band. Earlier that day, she and Caleb had gotten into a fight, and then the band lost at regionals. Raven had been in a crappy mood and Horace was good at cheering her up. She'd kissed him in a moment of weakness, nothing more. Since then, she'd avoided him at school and in her mother's shop, where he worked nights.

Raven didn't want things to be awkward between them. Like now . . . when she could think of nothing *but* that kiss. Or how his breath smelled like the cinnamon mints he ate like candy.

The butterflies grew incessant and she edged away. She had a boyfriend, dang it. She was trying to make it work, unlike all the boys in her past.

"So, uh," she began, wanting to fill the silence. "I'm sorry I didn't answer that text message a while back. I just—"

"It's all right, Ray."

Lots of people shortened her name, but it didn't sound half as good as it did coming from Horace.

"No, it's not okay," she said, pulling her eyes back up. "I should have explained. Or something . . ."

"Maybe." He shrugged. "I kind of figured it out though."

Right. Of course it was obvious. He probably thought she was a bitch. Probably she was, for kissing him and then avoiding him. "I should go."

She turned but Horace grabbed her arm. "Wait."

She stopped, liking the feel of his hand on her skin. Goose bumps popped on her forearm. "Horace, I—"

He kissed her. Just like that. Nothing forceful or gross, just a soft, innocent lip-lock, as if he worried that he'd scare her away with anything more aggressive.

"Raven!"

She pulled away from Horace and turned back to the kitchen, the sound of her name carrying over the din of the party.

Caleb.

Lips pursed, face red, he shouted, "What in the hell are you doing?"

"I'm sorry," Horace whispered.

"It's not your fault."

"Yes it is."

The drinking crowd parted, letting Caleb through effortlessly. He stalked into the mudroom, putting his nose in Horace's face.

Raven put her hand on Caleb's arm. "Let's just go."

He yanked out of her grasp. "Don't touch my girlfriend," he said to Horace.

While Horace had more muscle, he was a good five inches shorter than Caleb. Raven didn't want to see them fight. She didn't want Horace getting hurt because of her.

"Just stop, Caleb." She tried pulling him away, but he pushed her. Horace reached out as she fell back. Caleb took the opening and punched Horace in the face, sending him down on top of Raven. His lower lip started bleeding, swelling up instantly.

"Caleb!" Raven shouted as Horace rolled over and wiped his lip with his shirt. "I can't believe you just did that."

Caleb leaned over her. "That makes two of us, Raven, 'cause I can't believe you cheated on me with a freakin' band geek."

"I didn't cheat on you!"

"Oh, yeah, what do you call kissing him, then? Just an innocent gesture between band geeks? Is that something band geeks do?"

"Quit saying that."

"What? Band geeks!" His voice rose every time he said it.

Raven tried to ignore him and helped Horace to his feet. "Are you okay?"

"I'm alive."

"Oh, sure, Raven. Baby him," Caleb retorted.

"You punched him in the face."

"You know what?" He spread his arms out. "We're over."

"Caleb!" She ran after him. "Stop." When she reached the living room—the stereo having been muted for the "live" show—Caleb grabbed Tina Strong, a blonde sophomore in the crowd, and kissed her. When he pulled away he said, "How do you like that, Raven?" then disappeared into another room leaving two stunned girls behind.

Frozen in place, Raven's mouth hung open, her arms limp at her sides. He did *not* just do that! Was she partially to blame? She had, after all, kissed Horace first. Maybe she deserved it.

Maybe.

Head hanging, she made her way back to the mudroom. She wasn't surprised to find Horace gone. She leaned against the wall and closed her eyes, wishing she could take the entire night back.

Why was her love life so screwed up all the time? Her best friend, Alexia, would probably say it was because Raven cycled through guys too often, *and* she picked the wrong ones to go out with in the first place.

But Raven liked Caleb. So, okay, maybe he had a temper and maybe he was too much of a "guys' guy," but when they first started going out, he'd bought her flowers and called her every night to say good night. He'd *felt* like Mr. Right. She'd thought maybe he'd become her first serious boyfriend. That's what she wanted—to find someone she could fall in love with. She had tons of guys to pick from. Why couldn't she find a great one?

Probably because he didn't exist. Either that, or she was just destined to be alone. The thought made her nauseous. Alone. She hated being alone. She didn't want to end up like her mother, who sat home on Friday nights with scrapbooking as her only hobby.

Lame!

Raven's cell rang in her pocket. Her heart sped up. Maybe it was Caleb calling to apologize. She checked the screen. It was Sydney.

"Hey."

"Ray?" Sydney's voice cracked through the phone.

"Are you crying?" Raven asked.

Sydney sniffed. "Can you come pick me up? I don't want to be home right now."

Something *had* happened with Drew. Raven just knew it. She set aside her own drama to focus on Sydney. "Of course. I'll be there in thirty minutes. Okay?"

"Thanks."

"I'll see you soon." She flipped her phone closed and left.

THREE

Kelly Waters checked her reflection in the darkened windows of a closed shoe store. Hmm. She pulled her coat aside to see her figure better. There was a little bit of pudge beneath the back strap of her bra, but otherwise it was a skinny day for her.

Up ahead, light shone on the sidewalk through the windows of the Birch Falls Art Gallery. Kelly gave her watch a glance and cursed, realizing the opening reception had already begun. She quickened her steps, suddenly thankful that she'd gone with flats instead of high heels. Not only did she leave her house ten minutes late, but the parking downtown was brutal. Though most of the stores were closed, Fredrick's Restaurant—just down the block from the gallery—was always busy Friday nights. Lots of people from school hung out there this time of year since there was nothing to do in Birch Falls during the cold months.

Inside the gallery, Kelly slid off her fleece gloves and shoved them in her purse along with her matching scarf. She couldn't wait for spring. Winter was not her season. Not that it was anyone's season, really. Well, maybe if you made a living by snowboarding.

She recognized a few faces from school and smiled, nodding at them as she went farther inside. She found Will in the far corner, pointing to a framed canvas on the wall as he talked to Brittany, a girl from school whose thin figure and height screamed couture model while Kelly was more Oprah-ish. She felt skinny one week and downright fat the next.

A twinge of jealousy furrowed her brow and she hesitated, wondering if it was her right to interrupt their conversation, since she and Will were a sort-of couple, or if it would be rude. She took tentative steps across the gallery, her flats clacking on the hardwood floor.

As Will talked with his hands, he saw Kelly waiting on the periphery. "Excuse me," he said to Brittany.

Relief overtook the worry, and Kelly smiled. If he'd rather talk to her than Brittany, he must like her more, right? Maybe she should get back to the gym. And stop eating so much chocolate. It was her diet kryptonite. It didn't help matters that her older brother, Todd, was always talking her into late night fast-food runs because their mother couldn't cook. And Raven's mother was always making those awesome Italian dishes and insisting Kelly stay for dinner. . . .

"Hey," Will breathed into her ear, then kissed her cheek delicately. "You're late," he said, the smile on his face slipping away.

"Sorry." She tucked a stray hair behind her ear and cast her eyes to the floor.

"Well." He took a breath. "You want to check out my pieces?"

"Sure."

He led her to the far wall where he'd been talking with skinny Brittany. "This is it. My favorite one is *Kites*."

He inclined his head toward the abstract painting done in bright, childlike colors. Were there actual kites in there somewhere?

"And this one," Will went on, "took me weeks to finish. Every time I put the brush to canvas, something changed." He put his index finger to his chin, musing over his own work. "I like how it came out though."

Kelly glanced over the second piece. It was a blue face in the middle of something green. Trees maybe? Honestly, she didn't get the whole art thing. Especially the way Will did art. Sure, she could appreciate the *Mona Lisa* or the fantasy art that was so popular lately. But that was art. There was something to see and look at. You didn't have to think hard about it, or analyze it, or interpret it. But she wasn't about to say that out loud to Will.

"Wow," she said, making her voice sound breathy. "It's all great, Will."

"Yeah." He nodded, his mouth quirking. He flicked his eyes to her. "You look great tonight, by the way."

"Thanks." She smiled again and bit her lower lip to stop herself from squealing. At least being late had paid off in some way. "Can we walk around? I want to see what the other people did."

"Sure." He threaded his fingers with hers and led her away from his collection. The gallery was bigger than Kelly had first thought. She'd never been in here before tonight. Even farther back than Will's wall was a little room filled with black-and-white photography.

When they went inside, Kelly found the room empty. Perfect opportunity to tell Will about her Valentine's Day plan. It was just a few weeks away. She was planning on V-Day meaning more than *V* as in *Valentine.* If all went as planned, it would mean *V* as in the day she lost her virginity.

She and Will had been together—or sort-of together—for several months now. They weren't official, but Kelly wanted to make it official. What better timing than the day of love?

"This guy," Will was saying, "is really good though his style is a little out there. He doesn't fit normal conventions. And he has a lot of tattoos."

"Tattoos are bad?" Kelly asked.

"Art is for canvas, not skin." He put his arm around her shoulders and drew her in. "At least that's what I think."

"Yeah, I get that." She snuggled in close to him. He smelled like licorice and soap. It was an interesting mix. "So," she said, wondering how she should bring up Valentine's Day. She was so excited about it. She was afraid talking out loud would somehow jinx the whole thing.

Finally, she said, "I've got a surprise planned for us."

"Yeah?" he said, keeping his eyes on the wall of photographs.

"I was thinking, for Valentine's Day, we could make reservations at a hotel restaurant and then maybe we could—"

"Wait." Will pulled away so he could look her in the eye. "You're making special plans? For Valentine's Day?" Confusion furrowed his brow. "I can't. I thought I told you I had plans already."

"Plans?" No, he hadn't told her. "What are you doing?"

He ran his hand over his hair, probably checking that it was still perfectly styled. "Brittany asked me out to dinner. I can't back out after agreeing."

"Brittany?" Kelly's voice hitched on the name, sweat beaded on her forehead. This was exactly why she didn't want to talk about it out loud.

"Kelly," he said, using that adult tone of his. "You know we're not exclusive."

"I know, I thought . . ." Well, it didn't really matter what she thought now. She forced her lips into something she hoped resembled a casual smile. "I know we're not exclusive. I just thought it'd be fun to hang out."

"Yeah," he said, visibly relaxing. "We could maybe do something that Sunday?"

"Yeah. Maybe." She managed a false sense of cheerfulness. She did not want Will knowing what she really felt right now—crushed. She'd been hoping they could spend the whole weekend together. She wanted them to be a real couple. Finally. After waiting so long. She figured that if she stuck around and showed Will how much she cared about him by complimenting and supporting him in his endless list of extracurricular activities, that he'd eventually make the relationship serious. At least that's what the astrology article in *Seventeen* had suggested for sweeping Capricorns off their feet.

Will did all the talking as they went through the rest of the gallery. Kelly didn't feel like saying anything. What she wanted to do was go home and get out of these stupid clothes and put on some sweatpants. Suddenly she wasn't feeling so skinny.

After seeing all of the exhibits, people started drifting into groups in the middle of the gallery. Will dragged Kelly over and introduced her to Brittany. She knew Brittany; *everyone* knew

Brittany. Why make it a point to introduce them? Why didn't Will just stab her in the heart and save himself some trouble?

"We've never really talked," Brittany said, shaking Kelly's hand.

"Yeah. It's nice to finally talk," Kelly lied. Brittany was even prettier up close. She had delicate features, rosy-red cheeks. How was Kelly going to compete with her?

"Are you coming to the dinner after this?" Brittany asked.

"Um . . ." What dinner? Kelly looked at Will for clarification.

"I forgot," Will interjected. "We're all going to dinner at Bershetti's. You can come."

It didn't sound like he wanted her to come. She'd bet he'd withheld the info, not forgotten.

Feeling like she was going to vomit, Kelly excused herself before answering and hurried to the bathroom. Finding it empty, she allowed a few tears to slide down her face. She swiped them away angrily and faced herself in the long mirror on the wall.

Maybe she was making more of this than she needed to. Was it such a big deal that she and Will wouldn't hang out on Valentine's Day? She'd been trying to have a serious relationship with him for months now. It wasn't time to give up yet. Maybe Brittany, for all her physical attributes, was a huge bitch, and after hanging out with her, Will would dump her.

With renewed determination, Kelly left the bathroom and headed into the main part of the gallery, except it was quieter now, and looking around, she saw fewer people. She scanned the faces, searching for Will. When she didn't see him, she made a circle around the gallery and still didn't find him.

She went up to the first person she saw—a guy with thick, black-framed glasses—and said, "Excuse me?" He turned. "Do you know Will Daniels?"

"Uh, yeah, I know *of* him," the guy said.

"Have you seen him?"

"Yeah." He pointed toward the front door. "He just left, not even five minutes ago."

"You're sure?"

"Yup." He turned back to the wall of photographs.

"Thanks," she muttered and hurried outside. She'd seen Will's car parked across the street when she came into the gallery, but looking over there now, she saw an empty parking spot where his black BMW should have been.

She pulled her cell from her bag and dialed his number. It rang and rang and then finally someone picked up.

"Will?" she said.

"Uh . . . no, this is Ben."

Kelly frowned. She dialed Will's twin brother's phone?

"Will left his cell at home," Ben explained. "Is there a message I can forget to tell him? 'Cause I really love forgetting his messages and watching him blow up when I remember to tell him days after. His face gets all red and—"

Kelly gave a half-laugh and interrupted Ben. "No, it's all right. Thanks anyway."

"'K. Later."

Kelly hung up and slipped her cell back in her purse. Will had left her at the gallery. And he didn't even say good-bye. How could he do that?

Then tears came for real. She wiped them with her hands and saw mascara come away. Great, now she was crying *and* looked like hell.

Two hours ago, she'd been excited and hopeful that she and Will would be boyfriend and girlfriend after Valentine's Day. Now everything felt wrong. Will had broken up with her, and the worst part was that they weren't even really together in the first place.

Time for some Chunky Monkey, aka "Woe Is Me" ice cream. Ben & Jerry should rename it. It'd sell like crazy.

FOUR

Alexia Bass dipped a tortilla chip in mild salsa as *Best Week Ever* played on the TV. Christian Finnigan was her favorite commentator: 1) he was cute and 2) he was funny. Both were great qualities for a guy to possess.

At the next commercial break, she got off the couch to grab more tortilla chips but stopped when she heard her cell phone playing Beethoven's "Für Elise" in the den.

"Ohh!" she shouted to the empty house and ran in to grab her cell, hoping voice mail didn't pick up before she got there. How long had it been since her cell rang on a Friday night? She couldn't remember. That translated to *A Really Long Time*.

"Hello?"

"What are you doing?" Kelly asked.

Alexia smiled, hearing her friend's voice. "Watching *Best Week Ever*."

"Can I come over? With my Chunky Monkey?"

Alexia walked back into the living room and plopped down on the couch. "Chunky Monkey usually means you're upset. What's wrong?" There was an extended pause. "Kel?"

"It's Will. Kind of."

Best Week Ever came back on. Alexia dove for the DVR remote and paused it. "What happened?"

"How about if I come inside and tell you? I'm sitting in your driveway."

Alexia went to the front window and pulled up the Roman blinds. Kelly's blue Honda Prelude sat in the driveway. She waved and hopped out of her car, tugging her jacket hood down to block her face from the onslaught of snow and wind. Clutching a brown paper bag to her chest with the other hand, she ran up to the porch.

Kelly had only been friends with Alexia, Raven, and Sydney since seventh grade. Lately, Alexia had been hanging out with Kelly more than the other girls because Raven and Sydney were more serious with their boyfriends.

It was weird, the genesis of friends. Alexia and Raven had been best friends since second grade. Sydney joined them two years later, when her parents moved from Hartford to Birch Falls. The three of them had a tight bond. Back then, Alexia never would have thought they'd eventually add another. Three friends had always seemed like a big enough group.

But then, Alexia met Kelly in seventh grade and invited her to join Sydney, Raven, and her for a night at the movies. Kelly had been a part of the group ever since. It certainly helped that Sydney had a huge crush on Drew, who was Kelly's best friend back then. Sydney *always* wanted to hang out at Kelly's house.

Sometimes when Alexia hung out with Kelly, she could *almost* forget that she was the only one of the four girls who didn't have a boyfriend. Kelly was crazily in love with Will Daniels. Unfortunately, it didn't seem like Will was crazily in love with Kelly, which left her a lot more free time than a full-time boyfriend would.

Alexia flipped her cell closed and pulled the front door open.

Kelly brushed her hood aside and ran her hand down her strawberry-blonde locks. "I can come in, right?"

"If you promise to share your Monkey."

"Deal," Kelly said. She held up the paper sack. "I supply the Monkey, you supply the spoons?"

"Follow me, my dear." Alexia walked to the kitchen, Kelly trailing behind, her wet boots squeaking on the cherry-wood floor.

"Your parents here?" Kelly asked.

Alexia shook her head. "They're out of town for a seminar."

"All weekend?"

"Yeah. They should be home on Sunday." Alexia set her cell on the kitchen island and dug in the silverware drawer for two spoons. She handed one to Kelly when she heard Beethoven playing again.

Two phone calls in one night?

If you asked her an hour ago which was more likely, being struck by lightning or receiving two phone calls on a Friday night, she would have picked the lightning.

The cell phone screen said it was Sydney.

"Hello?"

"Lexy, you need any company?"

"Uh . . . " she looked across the kitchen island at Kelly. "Kelly's already here and she brought Monkey."

"Oh, God, that sounds so perfect. We'll be there in five."

Alexia said, "bye," and hung up, realizing afterward that Sydney had said, "We." Was she bringing Drew or something? Drew and Sydney sometimes hung out at Alexia's house, but not on Friday nights. They usually did their own thing.

"Syd's on her way," Alexia said. "Looks like we'll need more spoons."

Five minutes later, as promised, Sydney showed up, but with Raven, not Drew.

Sydney shuffled into the kitchen in terry cloth pants and a hooded sweatshirt. Her messy ponytail bobbed behind her. Her eyes were glassy, lids heavy with exhaustion.

Raven, too, looked . . . different. Her usual caramel complexion was closer to a milky latte and there was a permanent scowl on her Angelina Jolie lips.

"Something wrong?" Alexia asked.

Raven grabbed a spoon and took a seat in the breakfast nook with Kelly. "Tell them," she said to Sydney, then took a spoonful of ice cream.

Sydney sat down, too, and Alexia took the seat next to her.

"Drew and I got into a fight."

"A fatal fight," Raven said.

Kelly gasped. "He broke up with you?"

"Not really," Sydney argued. "I mean, we'll make up tomorrow and everything will be fine."

Raven shrugged, cleaning her spoon off. "Well, Caleb *did* break up with me."

Alexia frowned. "What?"

She got another scoop of ice cream. "I don't want to talk about it."

"This is really weird," Kelly said, heaping her spoon with ice cream. "Will sort of broke up with me, too. Not that we were together in the first place. It's just . . . it's over."

Alexia looked around the table. Sydney's eyes and nose were red from crying. Kelly shoveled more Chunky Monkey in her mouth than Ben & Jerry could have ever hoped for. Raven avoided eye contact, probably hoping that her stoic expression masked the real heartbreak she felt at being dumped.

Their boyfriends had broken up with them all on the same night.

"Maybe lightning did strike," Alexia muttered.

♥ ♥ ♥

An hour later, the Chunky Monkey was gone and all four girls were in the living room. The TV played a commercial for a Hallmark Valentine's Day teddy bear. Raven groaned and flipped the channel to Fuse. "It's a dumb holiday," she muttered as she settled back into the crook of the couch.

Sydney sat at the other end of the couch hugging an Asian throw pillow to her chest. Her knees were drawn close as if she was trying to fold into herself. She sucked in several sharp breaths, almost choking herself with them. Fat tears rolled down her flushed cheeks. "I just can't believe he went to the party without me."

Raven pulled the rubber band from her ponytail and shook her hair out. Long, ink-black waves covered her shoulders. Alexia had always been jealous of Raven's hair.

"If it makes you feel better," Raven said, "he didn't appear to be with anyone."

But Sydney just cried more and Alexia reached over to the end table to grab another wad of tissue.

"I shouldn't have let him leave."

Alexia crossed her legs beneath her as she sat on the couch. "Begging for him to reconsider would have been bad. You would have regretted giving him that much power over you."

While Alexia sympathized with Sydney—with all three girls—she couldn't relate because she'd never had a boyfriend. Let alone one that stuck around for two years. It wasn't for a lack of good looks. She had a heart-shaped face, wide, caramel-colored eyes, and vivid red hair.

All three of her best friends said she was a rare beauty. She was just too shy to show it off. Maybe they were right, but while physical attributes were easy to change, introverted tendencies were not.

Having no boyfriend was like getting picked last in gym class. She felt like such a loser. And feeling like a loser only made her shier.

Sydney grabbed a tissue and blew her nose, which was red and raw from too much wiping. "I wish there was some quick fix to all of this. We've been fighting so much lately. I just want the feeling I had when we first got together. You know? That good feeling?"

Alexia shook her head. She had no clue what Sydney was talking about, but she could take a guess at what the answer should be. "Your relationship will never be the same way it was when you guys were a new couple."

"Why not?"

"It just won't."

Raven picked at some split ends. "You could get a new guy."

Sydney shook her head. "I don't need a new guy."

Kelly said, "I think Will has a new girl already. That really skinny girl, Brittany?"

Raven groaned. "She's taking AP English and all those other college-level classes." She threw aside the lock of hair she'd been picking at. "How do you know he's with her?"

Kelly shrugged and then rubbed her stomach as if she felt sick. Probably she ate too much ice cream. "He's going out with her on Valentine's Day."

Sydney wiped at her face again, the tears slowing now. "Are you serious?"

Alexia wanted to feel for Kelly, too, but her sort-of-boyfriend was worthless. They all thought so, but the only one honest enough to speak her mind was Sydney, which lessened the overall effect.

"Will" — Sydney always said his name like it was a piece of spinach stuck between her teeth — "is a total jerk. Not to mention he's a sucky class president."

That had nothing to do with the breakup, but Sydney hated that Will was technically in charge of the student council because he was the senior class president. She always used that against him as if it was a bad character trait.

Kelly curled into a ball on the other couch. Her usually clear, peachy-toned skin looked splotchy.

Maybe it was time for Alexia to back Sydney up. She ran through Will's imperfections. "Now you don't have to put up with his whining. 'I ordered this with ketchup. Not mayonnaise. What, do you want to give me a heart attack?' "

This made them all laugh, even Kelly, who usually defended Will against everything.

"I wish I were you right now," Kelly said, giving Alexia a serious stare.

"Why?"

"Because you're happy and not nursing a broken heart."

"Second that," Sydney said. "You have no idea how lucky you are."

"Lucky? To never have had a boyfriend?" Alexia raised her eyebrows in question. "I think I'd rather be heartbroken and know what love felt like rather than always wondering."

Raven dug in her bag and pulled out her iPod. "I'm not even sure I loved Caleb—and I'm still heartbroken. A boyfriend is no guarantee."

Sydney shrugged. "Love is great. But heartbreak sucks." She slouched farther into the couch.

"You guys!" Alexia said. "Have you forgotten that women cannot be defined by their men? You're letting your state of mind suffer because of something a guy did to you. You need to stop."

"It isn't . . . that . . . easy," Kelly said, sniffing.

"No. It isn't," Sydney agreed. "And I need a coping mechanism."

Alexia's parents were both psychologists, so she knew that term well. When she was seven and her tabby cat, Gypsy, ran away, her parents told her to make a coping list. When she got sad about Gypsy being gone, instead of dwelling on it, she played with the dog. Instead of laying her head in Gypsy's old cat bed and crying, she donated the bed to a pet charity. And when she saw a cat, she stayed away for a while, until she got over Gypsy, because playing with another cat would just make her miss her cat even more.

Thinking of the coping list gave her an idea.

"Wait here a sec," she said and got up. She went into the den and rummaged through a few desk drawers searching for the candles her mother always stored. She wanted to help her best friends with their heartbreak. It'd been so long since they were all together like this.

Their boyfriends took up all of their free time. In the last six months, Alexia had felt like they were all drifting apart. Maybe the breakups were a good thing. She wouldn't tell them that, but as she went back into the living room, she grew excited that maybe, just maybe, three breakups would create a whole new bond of friendship.

A rekindling of *best* friends.

Alexia lit the four candles she'd found and, within a few seconds, the melting wax threw a vanilla scent around the four girls. With the TV and ceiling light off, the living room glowed and the waving candle flames cast odd shadows around the group as they settled in on the floor.

"So what, exactly, are we doing?" Raven asked.

Alexia folded her notebook open and poised her pen over the blank page. "When I was little, my parents had me make a coping list when I lost my cat. I thought it might help you guys cope with your breakups if we made a coping list. Or more like a code to follow."

Raven didn't look so convinced. "I don't know."

"I can barely cut three hundred calories a day," Kelly said. "How am I going to follow a code?"

Sydney brought her knees to her chest and wrapped her arms around her legs. "I'm not even sure I know what's going on with me and Drew."

"Well, if you guys make up tomorrow," Alexia said, "then you don't need to follow the code. But it might help Kelly and Raven."

Kelly shrugged. "It's worth a try. Who better to advise us than the daughter of psychologists?"

Raven blew a long breath out past her lips. "All right, you got me there. But if this gets hokey, I reserve the right to extricate myself." She held up her iPod to illustrate her point.

"That's fine," Alexia said. Raven was usually hard to convince. Alexia was just glad she was there at all. She glanced down at her blank notebook. "Rule number one . . . "

♥ ♥ ♥

We hereby instate the following code to ensure that we will never be hurt by a boy again—for today we become Women of The Code.

The Girls' Twenty-Five Breakup Rules for Exes:

Rule 1: *You must not email or IM The Ex ever again. Take his name off your email list.*

Rule 2: *You must not call The Ex's answering machine or voice mail just to hear his voice.*

Rule 3: *You must not write The Ex letters or text messages saying you miss him.*

Rule 4: *You must forget The Ex's birthday. Forget that he was born.*

Rule 5: *You must not date anyone until you can go two weeks without thinking about The Ex. (Take this time to find yourself & focus on your emotional stability. Do group activities with friends—both girl and guy friends.)*

Rule 6: *You must perform a ritual with the help of your girls to rid yourself of The Ex's pictures and any gifts that he gave you.*

Following the ritual: Rule 7 should be enforced.

Rule 7: *You are required to stay up late on a Thursday night eating popcorn as you and your girls laugh over a fifty-page list of The Ex's flaws.*

Rule 8: *Take three months and only do the things you like to do. You are not to accommodate any male for any reason.*

Rule 9: *Don't allow The Ex to talk to you for longer than two minutes during the initial three-month cooling-off period. You must not be his friend.*

Rule 10: *Do not think about your past with The Ex. If you feel yourself thinking about it, snap a rubber band against your wrist.*

Rule 11: *You must never date your girls' Exes.*

Rule 12: *You must never date a friend of The Ex.*

Rule 13: *You must never sleep with The Ex.*

Rule 14: *The Ex's name can't be mentioned unless the person who broke up with him brings up the name.*

Rule 15: *Find a hobby or something you are passionate about.*

Rule 16: *Do not call The Ex's parents to tell his mom or dad why you broke up, hoping the mom or dad will help you through the breakup, because they can't and they won't.*

Rule 17: *Do not keep in touch with The Ex's parents, sister, brother, or cousins or anyone related to The Ex's family.*

Rule 18: *Do not ask anyone what The Ex is up to. Who cares! Your only concern should be what you are up to.*

Rule 19: *If you see your girl's Ex, you must never mention it to her.*

Rule 20: *You have twenty-four hours to mourn the loss of The Ex. After the twenty-four hours, no more tears.*

(The twenty-four hours can be broken down into chunks—an hour on Monday—then another two hours on Tuesday morning—then another thirty minutes Tuesday night—then another four hours the next week—but once you reach twenty-four hours, no more tears or conversations about The Ex. Keep track of the twenty-four-hour timeline in a journal that holds The Breakup Code, which you must carry around with you to remind you of each rule in The Breakup Code.)

Rule 21: *You must always look beyond extraordinary in the company of The Ex.*

Rule 22: *You can never follow The Ex nor ask his friends to put in a good word for you.*

Rule 23: *I know you can't wait for this moment: If you come face-to-face with The Ex, you must let him know what he has lost by flirting with him, touching him,* *and doing whatever the situation calls for. In other words, make him feel like he is the King of the Jungle. Once you have built his ego up, crush it by telling him you're so happy that the two of you broke up.*

♥ ♥ ♥

Just Kidding: Don't do that—the whole idea here is to reestablish your "single" self—you don't need an ego boost of toying with your Ex. You should exert confidence and poise—not pettiness!!!!

♥ ♥ ♥

This is the most important rule of The Code, meaning under no circumstances is it ever to be broken:

Rule 24: *You must never ask or beg The Ex to date you again, nor should he ever see you cry about the breakup. Your attitude must be:*

Good riddance! What took you so long to leave?

His loss!

Who's next?

If he can't appreciate you, then some other guy will.

Remember, girls, no guy can complete you—you must do that for yourselves.

There is nothing wrong with being alone.

In order to be happy in your relationship, you must be a whole person and the guy must be a whole person.

Two wholes = One healthy, happy relationship.

Rule 25: *Do not ever think that you will never meet or love a guy the way you liked or loved The Ex, because you will—just give yourself the chance by letting The Ex go.*

♥ ♥ ♥

Alexia capped her pen and looked up. "Okay, girls, time to enforce The Code."

FIVE

Rule 1: *You must not email or IM The Ex ever again. Take his name off your email list.*

Sydney stared at Drew's user name on her Instant Messenger, willing the little yellow smiley face to light up. Where was he at eleven on a Saturday morning if not on his computer?

Usually Saturday mornings she and Drew were either on the phone or Instant Messenger, planning what they would do after he finished playing poker with his friends. Drew liked to have a plan. He had a plan for everything: college, graduation, marriage, and children. He knew he wanted to marry around the age of twenty-six and have children by the time he was twenty-nine.

Not having a plan for tonight was probably killing him. It was killing her. She'd been with Drew so long, his habits had become her habits.

But the absence of an itinerary was hardly the worst thing running through Sydney's mind. Last night *was*. Forget the fight. What had Drew done at the party? Did he stay the night at Craig's? What if he hooked up with someone? Like Nicole?

Sydney's stomach turned over. Drew knew how much she hated Nicole. That would be the ultimate deception. And if he did hook up with Nicole, would Sydney be able to forgive him? Would their relationship be ruined? She didn't even want to think about it.

To keep herself busy, she clicked on Yahoo's horoscopes and looked up hers.

Dear Aries,

Patience is an unfamiliar word to Aries, but the time calls for it. Take a deep breath and relax. What you're waiting for will come eventually. In the meantime, focus on that major project you've put off.

Major project? Sydney wrinkled her nose in confusion. She didn't have any major projects. And if she did, she certainly wouldn't have put it off. The new semester at school started Monday. A new semester meant new classes and no major projects.

She hoped she and Drew had study hall together. They'd specifically asked for the same hour so they could sit with each other. Unless he hooked up with Nicole. In which case he should change his name and move across the country because Sydney would kill him.

Sighing, she closed Internet Explorer and lolled her head back against the chair. She stared at the ceiling, noting the canopy of cobwebs in the corner. Ever since her mom became an executive at SunBery Vitamins, she'd been practically living in Hartford. Which meant Sydney and her dad had to fend for themselves. Probably those cobwebs would start to grow their own cobwebs before Sydney's mom either cleaned them herself or hired a housekeeper.

Sydney would put money on the latter because her mom was barely home enough to sleep in her own bed let alone clean house. And lately, money seemed to be her easy solution.

The Instant Messenger chimed as someone signed in. Sydney lurched forward. It was just Alexia. She was probably checking on her. Sydney gritted her teeth against the frustration. She right-clicked on Drew's user name and opened a message box.

> Syd17: *where r u???? call me when u get this. . . . we need to talk.*

She closed all the windows on her computer and got up. It was a Saturday morning and she had nowhere to be and no one to be *with*. That was a first. She hoped Drew would call soon and they could go out to breakfast or something. Well, lunch, now, she thought as she glanced at the clock on her wall.

As she got up to leave her bedroom, she noticed her copy of The Code on her dresser. Alexia had typed the rules up last night and printed out several copies.

"Rule number one: You must not email or IM The Ex ever again," she read. If she was supposed to be following this thing, she just broke the first rule.

But she and Drew were good at fixing their problems. That's why they were "The Couple" at Birch Falls High. In high school terms, a two-year relationship was like marriage. They'd probably be voted Most Likely to Grow Old

Together for yearbook mock elections. No way had they broken up over some stupid party.

Now, if only Drew would call her so they could fix this problem.

Sydney threw The Breakup Code in the trash. It wasn't like she really needed it.

♥ ♥ ♥

Raven heard a soft rapping on her bedroom door. She groaned and opened her eyes, quickly regretting it. It was so bright in her room with the blinds off the windows. When the hell was her dad coming over to hang up the new ones?

It'd been at least three weeks since he'd taken the blinds down, promising to replace them that weekend. But he'd been so flaky lately, focusing on his latest condo development, she'd probably have to hang them herself. Ever since her parents divorced, her dad had been doing things around the house to fix it up. He just wasn't very good about finishing them.

The knocking came again.

"What?" she croaked, and opened one eye to peek at the door.

Raven's little sister, Jordan, came in, shutting the door behind her. She was already dressed in jeans and a pink stretchy shirt. Her black hair was curled into perfect ringlets, which she'd pulled back into a ponytail and topped with a pink headband.

"What time is it?" Raven asked, flopping back against the pillow and closing her eyes to the attack of the too-cheery sunshine. Had she slept all day? She'd stayed up late going over the events of the night before in her head while listening to My Chemical Romance on her iPod. She should have been obsessing over the breakup and the scene Caleb made, but no matter how hard she tried, her mind kept wandering to Horace.

And kiss number 2.

"It's eleven thirty," Jordan said. "Mom told me to wake you up."

"If Mom told you to throw away your Milo Ventimiglia collection, would you do it?"

When there was no response, Raven looked over at her sister. Jordan stood at the end of the bed, wringing her fingers.

"Come here." Raven waved her sister over and Jordan climbed on top of the grape-colored blanket. "I'd fight Mom off with a broom," Raven said, "if it meant saving your Milo collection."

Jordan laughed. "Thanks."

"You still have it hidden?"

"Yeah, in the back of my closet under an old blanket."

Their mother was against anything pop culture—she said it was a waste of time. Teen magazines were out. MTV and The N were blocked by parental controls, and if she had her way, the Internet would be a foreign word to both girls. But when Raven got into middle school, it became apparent that homework could not be done without some Internet. Of course, there were parental controls on that, too.

So Raven and Jordan hid their forbidden pop culture. Jordan was obsessed with Milo (circa *Gilmore Girls*, not *Heroes*). She cut out all his pictures from magazines and put them in a binder. Raven usually bought magazines like *Bop* and *Teen Star* for Jordan to devour.

Raven's secret stash was usually comprised of *Spin* and *Blender*. And stuffed beneath her mattress, like a boy's porn stash, was a poster of Three Days Grace. That Adam . . . yum.

Yawning, Raven pulled herself into an upright position. "Mom save me anything for breakfast?"

Jordan shook her head. "She didn't make anything today. I just had granola."

"Serious?" Raven's mother was the poster woman for Mom of the Year. She always made breakfast. Always packed their school lunches. Always had the laundry caught up and put away.

"When I got up, she was scrapbooking," Jordan said. "She's working on a new design for tonight's class."

Well, that explained it. Raven's mother, while still Mom of the Year, had backed off her mom duties in the last several months since she opened the scrapbooking store/café called Scrappe. Scrapbooking was her life now.

"Well, I gotta go pack. Cindy's mom is picking me up at noon," Jordan said.

"Are you staying there tonight?"

Raven got out of bed as Jordan picked up The Breakup Code from the trash. Ignoring the question completely, she turned to Raven and waved the papers in the air. "What's this?"

"Something Alexia came up with last night."

Jordan fingered a ringlet with her thumb and index finger. "So, you're supposed to follow this if someone breaks up with you?"

Raven sighed. "Someone did break up with me."

Jordan's mouth hung slack. "Caleb broke up with you?"

Raven hated the sound of those words. Like she was somehow damaged goods. "Yes, he broke up with me and no,

I don't want to talk about it." Talking about it would mean admitting defeat. Raven had told her little sister just a few weeks ago that she thought Caleb was The One. The one that Raven could fall in love with. The one that liked her for more than popularity and a pretty face. The one that would never leave her like her dad left her mom.

"All right," Jordan said, "I won't ask." She brought the rules closer and read, "Rule number one: You must not email or IM The Ex ever again. Take his name off your email list." She looked over at Raven. "Did you do that?"

"No."

"Well, why not? It's the rule, isn't it?"

Raven grabbed the papers out of her sister's hand and threw them back on her desk. "Yes, it's the rule. I just haven't gotten around to it yet."

Jordan sat in Raven's desk chair and shook the mouse so the screen woke from sleep mode. She double-clicked on the Instant Messenger icon on the desktop and Raven's friend list popped up. "There you go." Jordan stood up. "Time to ax him."

Raven hesitated. If she worked really hard at it, she could probably get Caleb to take her back. But did she want him back? Would she want him back because she seriously liked him or because he'd broken up with her and that drove her nuts? Or because she'd failed a relationship and wanted another chance to prove she could make it work?

"Ray?" Jordan raised her brow and cocked her hip out to the side. "Are you going to follow the rules or what?"

Raven plopped down in the computer chair and scrolled through her friends list. She right-clicked on Caleb's user name and chose the delete option.

Are you sure you want to delete "Calball"?

Raven clicked on YES.

"See ya later, sucker," Jordan said, snickering.

Standing, Raven put her arm around her little sister's shoulders and led her out of the room. "You're really starting to sound too much like me, you know?"

"And what's so wrong with that?"

Though Jordan was only fourteen, Raven couldn't help but see herself in her little sister already. She just hoped Jordan didn't follow her footsteps where relationships were concerned. Because it was a really lame road to travel.

SIX

Rule 1: *You must not email or IM The Ex ever again. Take his name off your email list.*

Rule 16: *Do not call The Ex's parents to tell his mom or dad why you broke up, hoping the mom or dad will help you through the breakup, because they can't and they won't.*

Kelly lay on her queen-sized bed curled into a ball. She clutched her stuffed koala bear, Mr. Jenkins, in her hands, his matted white hair pressing into her face. Will had given it to her last August when they officially met for the first time.

They'd gone to school together for years, but they talked for the first time when Kelly started volunteering at the animal shelter. Her second day there, a dog came in who'd either been lost or abandoned. He died later that day from being malnourished. Kelly remembered locking herself in the shelter's bathroom and crying. She loved animals, and it was hard to see one so unhappy and emaciated.

When she came out of the bathroom, Will was there with Mr. Jenkins in his hands. The shelter had a whole closet full of stuffed animals that they gave away when people adopted an animal. While Will obviously hadn't gone to much trouble to acquire Mr. Jenkins, it was the thought that counted.

He'd handed over the stuffed koala and said, "I remember the first time I saw a dog die. It was so hard."

Kelly had cast her eyes to the floor and said, "But I bet you didn't lock yourself in the bathroom and cry."

"Actually . . ." He shrugged and said, "I threw up, which made me want to cry." He nodded at the koala. "I commemorated the dog's life with one of the stuffed animals. I still have it at home. His name is Bear."

Kelly had laughed, trying to picture a stuffed animal sitting on Will's bed. She'd had no idea he was so sweet. She knew about Will Daniels, of course, since they'd gone to the same school. A lot of people thought he was too preppy. Kelly had been guilty of thinking the same thing. But after that day at the shelter, she realized there was a lot more to him.

That same night he'd taken her out to dinner. And a few weeks later, she was practically in love with him. It helped that he was incredibly smart, which Kelly thought was super sexy. And just watching him interact with the animals put a huge smile on her face.

She smiled now, too, as she took a big whiff of Mr. Jenkins. He smelled like her Karmala perfume—Will's favorite—and the smile morphed into a sob.

God, this sucked.

She rolled over onto her back and stared at the sunbeams shining across her white ceiling. She just wished there was something she could do to make Will commit to her and only her. Why couldn't he just be her boyfriend? Was there something wrong with her? Was it because she wasn't smart enough? Pretty enough? Skinny enough?

She felt that she'd done everything she could to be the right girl for him. She was supportive of everything, all the extracurricular activities he did. She didn't call him constantly asking where he was and what he was doing (which she knew drove him nuts because his brother, Ben, had told her so when she'd asked for some pointers).

She'd done everything she thought she could to be the perfect girl for Will and still he hadn't asked her to be his official girlfriend.

And then he left her at the stupid art gallery!

Like, seriously, what did she have to do?

She wasn't the type to become just another girl in the harem. So how did she get that role in Will's life? Blind pursuit. She didn't want to believe he was seeing other girls. She didn't want to believe he *wanted* to see other girls.

Sighing, she rolled off the bed, intent on scavenging for some kind of chocolate in the kitchen when she heard the familiar ding of a new email sound from her computer speakers.

She jumped in the computer chair and shook the mouse to bring the screen out of hibernation. The screen lit up, and a picture of her and Will from Christmas stared back at her. Her little sister, Monica, had taken it, and Kelly had made it her computer's wallpaper. Will's arm was around her shoulders and she was smiling happily. Her eyes were lit by the flash and looked as though they were twinkling.

Will had always been more affectionate when there were fewer people around. That night it'd just been Kelly's family. Will had held her hand practically the whole night. She'd thought for sure they were headed toward a serious relationship, which was exactly why she started thinking about losing the big *V* to him and planning the Valentine's Day surprise.

Thinking about the upcoming holiday made Kelly's chest heavy. She did not want to be alone on the holiday of love. That would totally suck.

She double-clicked on the Internet Explorer icon and waited for a window to open. She signed into her email account, excitement and hope making her bite her lip.

I hope it's Will, emailing to apologize, she thought.

She clicked on her one new message and saw Will's name in her inbox. Yes! Quickly, she opened it and took in one long breath to settle herself.

Hey, Kelly,

Where did you go last night? I thought you were coming to Bershetti's with us. Just wanted to make sure you were all right.

—W

That was the Will she loved. The one that sent her emails wondering how she was. Last night must have been some huge misunderstanding. She checked her Instant Messenger to see if he'd signed in there, too. The smiley face next to his name was dark. She hit REPLY on the email and typed in a quick message, hoping to catch him online.

I thought you left me at the gallery on purpose! I wasn't sure what was going on, so I just went home.

Should she write more? Maybe tell him how much she wanted him to be exclusive with her?

Will, I have to tell you something that's been on my mind lately.

No, no, no. She deleted the last sentence and started over.

Will, I really think we need to talk about our relationship.

No, that was too serious! Maybe she should be honest with him. And if she was going to be honest, it would be better to do it through email because she wouldn't be subjected to laughing or grunting or eye rolls if he thought what she wrote was ridiculous.

Without editing or rereading, she typed in exactly what she was thinking.

And I was upset because of the whole Valentine's Day thing with Brittany and thought you were leaving me behind at the gallery to spend time with her. Were you? What's going on with you guys?

Kelly clicked SEND. She jumped out of the computer chair and flung her arms in the air, silently saying Yes! She got it out and there was no taking it back now. She grabbed Mr. Jenkins from her bed and sat back down in front of the computer, minimizing Internet Explorer so she could look at the picture on her desktop again.

Will was so darn cute. He had chestnut-brown hair that was always neatly combed. His face was clean-shaven. He had perfect skin, too, better than hers. She was always breaking out.

The email ding sang again and Kelly opened Internet Explorer, refreshing her inbox. She clicked on Will's new email.

> *I waited around for you and when you didn't show up, I thought you left ahead of us. I'm sorry. You know I'd never leave you on purpose like that.*

The more she thought about it, the more she realized it was true. When they'd gone to Will's extended family's Christmas party at the Marriott, he'd never left her side because she'd told him she was nervous and slightly intimidated. Both his parents were top attorneys in Birch Falls, and his grandfather had been the flippin' mayor! Will had promised to make her as comfortable as he could, and he'd kept that promise.

If he'd invited her to the art show, he would never have left her without saying something. She realized this now, all too late.

She read the rest of the email.

> *Brittany and I are friends like you and I are friends. You know I hate to get in a serious relationship right now. I have too much to focus on with school and extracurricular activities, etc.*
>
> *I'm sorry if you're upset about Valentine's Day, but I can't break the agreement. That would be unfair*

to Brittany. We'll hang out later that weekend.
I promise. Call me later.
Will

He just wanted to be friends. The word ran through Kelly's head like an annoying little cricket chirp. Didn't he know that she'd give him space to work on homework and all the extra things he did after school? They'd been hanging out for months now. That proved he had the time for a girlfriend. She was practically his girlfriend already! They were always together.

Will wanted all the perks of a girlfriend without any of the commitment.

Kelly closed Internet Explorer and dropped her head onto the desk. What could she do to get Will to commit to her and only her? Maybe if she got Mrs. Daniels on her side, she'd have an easier chance of getting Will on her side. It was worth a shot.

♥ ♥ ♥

Kelly picked up her cell and dialed Will's home number. As the line rang, she sat down on her bed and crossed her legs in front of her. She watched out the window as snowflakes blew in a whirlwind. The sun had just set so the sky was a washed-out indigo. It reminded her of last winter when she, her brother, Todd, and Drew all went hiking at Birch Falls Park. Halfway through the two-mile trail, it started snowing and blowing. It was practically a blizzard and Kelly hadn't dressed for a flippin' blizzard. Drew ended up giving her his coat. He was such a great guy like that. Todd probably would have left her out there in the half-darkness to freeze.

"Hello?" Mrs. Daniels answered the phone, snapping Kelly out of her reverie.

"Oh, Mrs. Daniels . . ."

In the background, Kelly could hear Will's younger brother, Samuel, screaming about a stuffed toy. His nanny shushed him, and soon after, music played, tinny and tinkly, as if it were a music box.

Kelly switched the phone to her other ear. "Uh . . . is Will there?" She figured it was a good idea to pretend like she'd called for Will and not his mother. She wanted to be sly about this.

"No, he just left. He's covering an extra shift at the animal shelter."

Kelly wished she were working, too. The urge to see Will hatched butterflies in her stomach. Somehow it seemed like everything would be fine if she could just see him.

"Oh." Feeling a bit bold, she said, "I thought for sure he'd be with Brittany."

"Brittany?" The confusion in Mrs. Daniels' tone said she hadn't yet met Brittany.

"Yeah. She's this girl Will's been seeing."

A long pause. Kelly began to wonder if Mrs. Daniels had hung up. But then she took in a breath and said, "What's this Brittany like?"

"Well . . . she's . . ." Super-skinny, cultured, smart, classy. All the things Mrs. Daniels wanted in Will's girlfriend, which Kelly knew because he'd told her. Well, maybe not the skinny part.

There was one thing that Kelly could use against Brittany. "I think she's a smoker."

"Ewww," Mrs. Daniels said.

Score!

"And Will is, like, two-timing us," Kelly blurted. "He's seeing me and Brittany at the same time."

Samuel started screaming again. Chopin, their Maltese dog, barked as the doorbell rang. "Michelle, will you get that?" Mrs. Daniels said, then pulled her attention back to Kelly. "You knew Will was never exclusive, Kelly. For now it's best if he focuses on school."

Kelly winced. That was not what she wanted to hear. Kelly had thought the "focus on school" stuff had come from Mr. Daniels, but apparently Mrs. Daniels was in on it, too.

Why had Kelly said anything in the first place? What had she been thinking?

Well, she'd been looking for a sympathetic ear, obviously hoping Mrs. Daniels would say she'd talk some sense into Will.

Ha! Yeah, right. Kelly should have known better.

As a matter of fact, wasn't that one of the rules? That she wasn't supposed to talk to The Ex's parents about the breakup? Or whatever it was that was going on between her and Will?

Great. Just great. It hadn't even been twenty-four hours and already she'd broken a rule.

Way to go, Kel.

"I have to go," Mrs. Daniels said. "Michelle!" she yelled away from the phone. "Grab Samuel, please, before he makes a mess."

The line went silent.

Kelly pulled the phone away from her ear and stared at it. Mrs. Daniels had just hung up on her!

Wonderful. Her day was going from bad to worse and there was only one thing that would take the crap quota up a few notches.

Chocolate cake.

But chocolate cake was like six hundred calories or something.

I don't care, she thought. It sounds so good.

God, what was she going to do when Valentine's Day came around next month? All the stores would overflow with chocolate candy hearts painfully reminding her that she was single. And what better way to deal with the pain of a broken heart than to eat those stupid chocolate hearts?

Ugh!

Kelly headed out of her bedroom but froze in the hallway when she heard a chorus of male voices coming from the kitchen.

She'd forgotten tonight was Todd's night to host the Saturday poker game.

She looked down to survey her appearance. She was still in her frog-print pajama pants and a stained white tank top. She just hadn't had the energy to shower yet, and she couldn't let all of Todd's friends see her like this!

She hurried back to her room and rifled through her closet. She threw on her gray American Eagle slub hoodie and a pink skirt. She checked her reflection in the mirror on the back of her bedroom door.

There, now. Her outfit was better than pajamas, but still inconspicuous enough to look like she'd been lounging in it all day and hadn't thrown it on just to impress. She ran her hand over her messy ponytail. Thankfully, it wasn't greasy yet and the pony would do.

She made her way to the kitchen and found Todd at the counter pouring a bag of Cheetos into a plastic bowl. Matt and Kenny sat at the table discussing a car they'd seen on TV recently. Drew popped up behind the open refrigerator door with a two-liter bottle of cola in his hand.

"Hey, Kel," he said.

"Hi." She went over to the counter and pulled herself onto it. She grabbed a handful of Cheetos from the plastic dish. Todd tried smacking her hand away but missed.

"The snackage is not for you," he said, and moved the bowl to the table.

"I just wanted a few." She wrinkled her nose at him. Sometimes he was such a pain in the butt.

Drew brought the soda over to the counter and grabbed four glasses from the cupboard to Kelly's right.

Kelly wanted to be mad at him for breaking up with Sydney. She wanted to snub him or tell him he was a jerk, but Drew had been Kelly's friend far longer than she'd been friends with Sydney. And besides, Drew just *wasn't* a jerk. If he broke up with Sydney, there had to be a good reason.

He was incredibly kind and caring and super-smart. Add in his total hotness and that made him practically perfect in guy terms.

As a matter of fact, Drew had been Kelly's first crush. She was eleven when he started hanging out with Todd. He was over at their house all the time. Kelly had just been too shy to say anything. Todd probably would have freaked out anyway.

Then Sydney met Drew through Kelly, and before Kelly knew it, Sydney was going out with him. Kelly knew the crush was useless after that, but that didn't stop her from still admiring Drew.

"Want a glass?" Drew said.

"Huh?"

He laughed. "You're just staring at me. I thought maybe you were trying to send me a subliminal message that you wanted a glass, too."

"She's staring at you because she's trying to read your brain waves," Todd said. "Didn't I tell you I found out she was an alien?"

"Shut up, Todd!" Kelly gave him a shove, but he only budged an inch and then laughed at her.

Drew grabbed a fifth glass out of the cupboard and poured cola into it. "Here." He handed the glass over.

"Thanks."

Cola didn't really go well with chocolate cake, but she didn't want him to think she was a huge pig, so she'd just wait until they all went downstairs. For now, she took small sips of the soda.

"Anyway," Todd said, "we're outta here." He rolled the Cheetos bag closed and grabbed one glass of soda. "Kenny, grab the snacks, dude."

Kenny pushed his chair back, stood up, and took the Cheetos bowl. Matt came around the counter, nodded a hello/good-bye at Kelly, then took two glasses of soda and disappeared downstairs.

"Time to kick butt," Drew said. "You should come downstairs with us."

Kelly shook her head. "Nah. It's guys' night. Besides, Todd would probably chase me out."

"I'll make sure he doesn't."

It was tempting to hang out with a bunch of guys like she did when she was a kid, but her mom's famous chocolate cake was sitting over on the stovetop, calling.

"I can't," she said. "I have to get ready to go to Alexia's in a little bit, anyway."

"All right. See ya." He grabbed his soda and left.

Kelly hopped off the counter and went to the stove. She smiled, suddenly giddy. "Well, chocolate cake, it looks like it's just you and me."

After serving herself a slice, she sat down at the kitchen table, pushed aside the morning's newspaper and Monica's homework, then she took her first bite.

Mmmmm.

SEVEN

Rule 6: *You must perform a ritual with the help of your girls to rid yourself of The Ex's pictures and any gifts that he gave you.*

Alexia was used to being home alone. Her older brother, Kyle, had been out of the house for four years now. He was finishing his senior year of college in Hartford. Her parents were always at some function. They owned a small practice in Birch Falls, but their self-help books made them famous. Now their lives were nonstop. Seminars here, book signings there, radio shows all over the nation. This weekend they were . . . where were they again? Illinois or something. Alexia couldn't keep their schedules straight.

They lived in the same house, but Alexia hardly saw her parents. She'd gotten used to entertaining herself when they were gone and her friends were out with their boyfriends. She'd seen every season of *America's Next Top Model* (Kahlen was still her favorite, why did that girl *not* win?). Veronica Mars seemed like her best friend, and she was a *Best Week Ever* aficionado.

She'd never been the type of person to need social interaction in order to have fun. She was often quite happy being alone in the house. When she was alone, she could do whatever she wanted, whenever she wanted.

If she wanted to watch *Zoolander* for the fiftieth time while eating popcorn covered in pepper, then she could. But now she could hardly wait for some company as she set out lit candles and bowls of chips and salsa. Eventually, hanging out by yourself gets old, and everyone needs some company every now and then to stay sane. What better company than your best friends?

Last night, they'd all decided the ritual for laying The Ex to rest had to be performed right away. The sooner the better, Raven said. As always, she was ready to move on from the ex-boyfriend, but in her old style, she would have moved on to another boy. Now it was The Code. Alexia wasn't so sure Raven could do it. She was the boy-crazy one out of the four of them.

For some reason, Raven thought being alone was a sign of lameness. Alexia suspected her neediness had something to do with her parents divorcing a few years ago. With her dad gone all the time, Ray kept looking to boys to fill that void. Hopefully, with The Code as her aid, she'd realize she didn't need a guy to be happy.

The doorbell rang and Alexia grinned. She opened the front door and the night air slipped in, chilling her skin. Goose bumps popped on her forearms.

"Hey, guys!" she said, seeing Raven and Kelly on the porch.

Kelly, as usual, hid in her fur-trimmed hood. Even standing on the enclosed porch out of the chilled wind, she was moving constantly as if trying to get her blood pumping faster.

If you looked at Raven standing next to Kelly, you'd never guess both girls were from the same climate. Raven's jacket was only a black hooded sweatshirt, a pink skull printed on the front. Her hands were bare, two plastic bags hanging from her wrists.

"Warmth!" Kelly shouted, barreling past Alexia.

Alexia looked over Raven's shoulder and to the driveway. She saw only Raven's red Nissan Sentra. "Sydney come with you guys?"

"Sydney," Raven said, "is a no-show." She walked in, and Alexia shut the door. They headed to the kitchen. Raven set her bags down on the kitchen island, shoving aside the bowl of fruit. "I called Syd and she said she wasn't coming."

"She hasn't talked to Drew yet," Kelly explained, pulling out one of the bar stools at the island. "And he's been at my house half the night." She slid out of her coat and set it on a stool next to her. "I think Syd's hoping he'll call and they'll make up and everything will be okay."

Alexia sighed. "Well, hopefully they *will* make up, but they've never broken up before. This seems serious."

"I tried telling her that," Raven said. "But she didn't want to hear it."

"You guys still want to do the ritual, then?" Alexia couldn't keep the hint of disappointment out of her voice.

"Of course." Kelly pushed her ponytail off her shoulder. "I want to lay Will to rest as soon as I can."

"And I made us all Ex tombstones out of paper," Raven said. "I figured we could burn them." She pulled three tombstones out of an envelope and laid them on the table. One said

Drew, one Caleb, one Will. They were made out of heavy black cardstock and the names were done in gothic lettering with silver glitter.

"These are so cute!" Kelly picked up Will's and fingered his name. Some glitter came away, sprinkling onto the moss-colored countertop.

"They aren't supposed to be cute!" Raven said.

Kelly shrugged. "Well, they are."

"Leave it to Kelly," Alexia said, "to find something cute in something that's supposed to be slightly morbid."

"She would think a demon was cute if he had good hair," Raven added.

"Hello, I'm right here." Kelly waved her hands in the air.

They all laughed.

"Come on, I figured we'd do this in the sunroom." Alexia led them to the back of the house. The walls and ceiling in the sunroom were made entirely of glass, so the sky was overhead, stars shining brightly in the clear night. There were candles lit all over, the flames reflecting off the glass walls. Alexia had moved all the wicker furniture back to make a place for a roasting pan in the center of the room. She'd taken the big floral cushions off the wicker chairs and set them around the pot.

"For burning things," Alexia explained, nodding at the roasting pan.

"Of course." Kelly smiled.

Raven sat on one of the pillows. "Well, let's get started." She grabbed her two grocery bags and started unloading them. There was a whole gift box full of letters, a hair scrunchie, a T-shirt, an envelope full of photos, and a sock.

"What is all that stuff?" Kelly asked, grabbing the envelope of pictures.

"Everything that Caleb gave me. Or, if it reminded me of him, I threw it in the bag."

Alexia poked the sock with her finger. "And this reminded you of him?"

Kelly snorted a laugh.

"He left it at my house," Raven explained.

Alexia raised her eyebrows. "Oh, I see."

"What did you bring?" Raven asked Kelly.

Kelly grabbed her purse and dug inside. She pulled out a brochure to the high school's last art show and one picture of Will speaking at a school assembly that she had obviously taken herself.

"I know," she said, looking at her pile, then Raven's. "I had a pathetic relationship with Will."

Alexia shook her head. "I think the boyfriend was more pathetic than the relationship."

"Any guy would be lucky to have you, Kel," Raven said.

Kelly gave an unconvinced smile and nodded. "Thanks, you guys."

Alexia was pretty sure Kelly suffered from the I'm-not-good-enough syndrome, what Alexia's parents called self-criticism. But no matter how many times Alexia or Raven or Sydney told her how pretty she was, she always thought she could be thinner or have better skin.

Of course, Alexia's friends were constantly telling her how pretty she was, and she never seemed to have enough confidence to talk to guys. Maybe she was suffering from self-criticism, too.

Alexia shook a box of matches in her hand. "I'll start the fire. I have the fire extinguisher close at hand, just in case something goes wrong."

“I’m so flippin’ ready for this,” Raven said.

“Throw your letters in,” Alexia said to Raven. “That’ll get the fire going.”

Raven dumped the letters out of the box and into the roasting pan. Alexia struck a match, the sulfur filling her nose. She threw it in and the flame burned a hole into one of the letters. Soon they all were lit up. “Now, throw in everything else,” she said. “We’ll do the tombstones last.”

Raven didn’t hesitate. She chucked things in without looking and was done within a minute. Kelly threw in the brochure first but then dwelled on the picture of Will.

“Come on, Kel,” Raven said.

Kelly gave Will’s picture one more look and threw it in.

♥ ♥ ♥

Sydney stared at her computer screen. She refreshed the window to see if she had any new emails.

You have 0 unread mail messages.

She let out a long sigh. Why hadn’t Drew called or emailed or something? Was he deliberately avoiding her? She picked up her cell phone and double-checked her messages. Still nothing. She called his cell and voice mail picked up right away.

“You reached Drew. Leave it after the beep.” *Beep.*

“Drew, call me!”

She flipped the phone closed and went out to the kitchen. Her mother was at the table, clicking away on her laptop. The laptop and her BlackBerry were permanent tools at her side now that she was an executive at SunBery Vitamins. It’d taken her ten years of hard work but she finally got to the top. Sydney was proud of her for reaching her goal, but it didn’t really feel like she had a mother anymore. Or any parental unit for that matter. Sydney wondered if her mom's new position was putting a rift in her parents' relationship.

She watched her father pull a pan of meat loaf out of the oven, floral oven mitts on his hands. He'd taken over the role of Mr. Mom in the last two years. He was getting better at it, but occasionally he forgot to buy toilet paper or misplaced the cable bill, which resulted in an hour's worth of searching the house. That is, until Sydney logged into their account online and printed out a new bill.

His dinners were improving, too, but Sydney hated meat loaf. It was her mother's favorite, though, so she couldn't fault her dad for making it.

Sydney came up beside him. His silver-framed glasses slipped down the bridge of his nose. She noticed more gray hair on his head than black. A year ago, she might have poked fun at him for it, but now he wouldn't laugh or make fun of himself. He'd just shrug and probably say, "I'm not going to stay young forever." He was rarely in a good mood anymore.

"Need any help?" she asked. She didn't really feel like helping, but it was something to get her mind off Drew's flakiness.

"No," he said as he set the pan on the stovetop and poked the meat with a knife. Sydney swore she saw it breathe. "Thanks for asking though." He turned to his wife. "Honey, dinner is done."

"All right." She clicked in a few more things on her laptop. "I'm almost finished. Just five more minutes."

Mr. Howard nodded and got plates out, then started slicing up the meat loaf. Sydney groaned, seeing the moist meat on her plate. She didn't want to be here right now—certainly not eating that. Her house had become this silent, half-living thing. She could predict exactly what would happen over dinner.

Her dad would serve the food. He'd pour the drinks. He'd try to make small talk with his wife until her cell would ring, or her email alert would go off. Then she'd bury herself back in her work, ignoring Mr. Howard and Sydney.

"Dad, I think I'm skipping dinner tonight."

He pushed his glasses back. "You have to eat."

"But not meat loaf." And not at the table, either. She'd take her food to her room. At least there she'd have the TV to keep her company instead of two bodies that moved and breathed but had somehow forgotten how to communicate.

"Well," her dad said, "I haven't gotten groceries yet, so there isn't much else."

Sydney opened the fridge. There was leftover spaghetti from three nights ago on the top shelf. Grapes and sour cream were on the second. She grabbed a carton of blueberry yogurt and read the expiration date in the fridge's light. OCT 10. *Way* overdue for the trash can.

Throwing the yogurt away, she went on to the cupboards and found them in the same sad shape.

Correction: Her house had become this silent, half-living, *empty* thing.

The thought of spending her Saturday night like this made Sydney want to cry for another two hours. Or sleep for a month.

"I'm going to Alexia's," she announced. There was always food at Alexia's. She got the groceries herself and her food tastes were the same as Sydney's, which meant lots of junk food.

"All right, then," Mr. Howard said. "Drive carefully. Love you."

"Love you, too." She glanced at her mother. "Bye, Mom."

Mrs. Howard's fingers tapped incessantly on the laptop keyboard. A deep frown etched her forehead into wrinkles. She didn't look up as she said, "Bye, honey."

Sydney rolled her eyes and left.

♥ ♥ ♥

The first thing Sydney noticed when she walked in the front door of Alexia's house was the smell of something burning, then the scent of cinnamon and apples. She ran through the house, checking every room until she got to the sunroom. There were candles all over the place and a fire burned in a big blue roasting pan that her friends sat around.

Sydney froze over the threshold and took it all in. "Are you guys practicing witchcraft or something?"

They all looked at her and laughed.

"Yes, we're putting a hex on Drew," Raven said.

"Don't do that!" Sydney shouted, hurrying into the room. Not that she believed in witchcraft or magic or anything. She was all about science and facts, but with Raven, anything was possible.

A boy Raven really liked dumped her in middle school and, to retaliate, she bought a spell book from a used bookstore and cursed him. The next day at school, he fell in a mud puddle before lunch and then sprained his ankle in gym class. If she were being honest, Sydney found it a little suspicious.

"She was kidding," Alexia said. "Raven."

"What?"

Raven was always goading Sydney. If anyone was a pain in her butt it was Raven, but she loved the girl. It was like having a love/hate relationship with the sister she never had but always wanted. Being an only child sucked. Sometimes.

Pulling her coat off, Sydney sat on one of the pillows in front of the roasting pan and peered inside. Pictures crinkled from the fire. There was a sock smoldering and a T-shirt burning in two places.

The burning smell was coming from the pot, and the apple and cinnamon must have been the red candles around the room.

"So what exactly are you doing?"

"Laying The Ex to rest." Kelly licked her glossed lips. Sydney would bet the lip gloss was chocolate flavored. It was Kelly's way of satisfying her sweet tooth without eating too many calories. "Did you come to lay Drew to rest?"

Sydney got that weak, tingling feeling in her throat as if she were about to cry. She swallowed hard and pulled a breath in through her nose. Why hadn't he called her? He never went this long without returning her phone calls. She felt helpless and restless. She just wished she could fix it, like *now*.

Raven held up a tombstone-shaped piece of paper that had Drew's name on it. "We wouldn't leave you out of the fun. Here."

Sydney took the paper. "This is dumb." She stood up.

"Sit down," Alexia said. "You don't have to do it if you don't want to."

"We aren't technically broken up yet, you know." But the more she talked about it the more she doubted her own words. They'd never fought like this before. Or uttered the "we're done" words. They weren't the on-again/off-again kind of couple.

And the longer the silence between them stretched, the more she began to believe they were, in fact, broken up. It seemed wrong, though, to burn a tombstone with his name on it. Doing so might jinx them and they'd never get back together even if there was a chance.

Tears started beneath her lids and a few slid out. Darn it, crying again? And in front of her friends?

"Why don't you keep it for now?" Alexia said. "If you get back together, throw it away. If . . . well, just keep it."

Sydney nodded and slid the paper in her purse. She'd throw it away when she got home, after she finally talked to Drew. Because he had to call, *didn't* he?

EIGHT

Rule 10: *Do not think about your past with The Ex. If you feel yourself thinking about it, snap a rubber band against your wrist.*

Raven pulled her crumpled schedule out of her jeans pocket to check her next class. It was the first Monday after the breakup and the first day of the new semester at school. Could things get any worse?

Yes, they could, if she had any classes with Caleb. Hopefully, her day would be Caleb-free.

She perused her schedule. The only thing that'd crossed over from last semester was band. Next hour was US History.

Boy did that sound like fun. Yeah, right.

Although, she had to admit, it was kind of sexy that George Washington was a colonel in the US Army and led 300 men by his early twenties. There was just something about a man in a position of power. Like Caleb being the captain of the football team.

"Aw, crap," she muttered, remembering the breakup and The Code.

I just broke a rule, she thought.

Which rule was it? She pulled her new Breakup Code journal out of her locker. She'd bought the white notebook yesterday at the dollar store then decorated the cover with some of her mom's scrapbooking stuff.

She'd cut a cardstock heart in half and glued that on the front. Then, using a purple acid-free marker she wrote, *The Breakup Code* in curvy letters. It was simple but cool.

Inside the front cover, with the same purple marker, she'd copied the code. Running down it now with her finger, she stopped at Rule 10. *Do not think about your past with The Ex. If you feel yourself thinking about it, snap a rubber band against your wrist.*

After checking her backpack and her locker, she came up empty-handed, which wasn't surprising. She hardly ever wore her hair up. It was either messy and down or half up in a barrette. She always thought her ears looked too big when she wore her hair in a ponytail.

"Hey," Kelly said, coming up behind Raven, green plastic bangle bracelets clanking on her wrists.

"I broke a rule," Raven said, slamming her locker shut as Sydney sidled up. "I need a rubber band to snap when I think of Caleb."

Sydney leaned against the bank of lockers, hugging her bag to her chest. "The only one I have, I'm using," she said, as she tucked a loose strand of black hair behind her ear. She pursed her thin lips, which accentuated her high cheekbones.

It was unlike Sydney to look so disheveled for school. Not only was her hair in a bumpy ponytail, but she had on sweatpants and a hoodie. There was nothing wrong with that; Raven saw Sydney in those clothes all the time, but *out* of school. In school, she was strict with her appearance and wore polos and sweaters and stuff. As if college recruiters were lurking around every corner waiting to catch her out of the prim character she portrayed at Birch Falls High.

"I have one," Kelly said. "I bought us all special rubber bands, actually. For this very rule, since it seemed absolutely impossible not to think about The Ex." She pulled a small Wal-Mart bag from her purse and dug inside. She handed a green hair tie to Raven. "Here."

Raven took it. There were four-leaf clovers printed on the thick material.

"For good luck," Kelly added.

"Right." Raven slid the hair tie on her wrist and pulled it back, then let it go. "Ahh, God, that flippin' hurts." She rubbed the already red skin.

"I know," Kelly said. "I've already snapped it like fifteen times since Saturday. But I think it's starting to work."

Sydney snorted and pushed away from the lockers, straightening her back. "You're going to have welts if you keep doing that."

"Not if I stop thinking about He-Who-Shall-Remain Nameless," Kelly said. "Which is the point, right?"

"I guess."

"Here, I have one for you, too."

Sydney took her rubber band and shoved it in her pocket.

"You talk to Drew yet?" Raven asked tentatively. Guessing by Sydney's bad attitude and appearance, she probably hadn't.

"I'm going to talk to him today," Sydney said matter-of-factly. "He just needed time to cool off."

"Yeah." Raven wished Sydney would just open her eyes and see the truth. They were broken up and, from the sounds of it, Drew was in no hurry to make amends.

"I should probably go before the bell rings." Sydney hoisted her bag higher on her shoulder. "See you guys later." She headed in the opposite direction and disappeared around a corner.

"I gotta go, too, see you at lunch?" Kelly said, veering off in another direction.

"Yeah, see ya."

Raven headed for the C hallway where the history classrooms were and nearly ran into someone as she rounded the corner.

"Oh!" the girl said, then, "Ray-Ray! I've been looking everywhere for you."

"Hey, Lori," Raven said.

"I heard what happened at Craig's party the other night." Lori scrunched up her nose as she pulled on her long, sandy-brown braid hanging down her shoulder. "Sometimes my brother can be such a jerk."

Raven shrugged. She totally agreed, but she didn't feel like discussing Caleb right now or his lack of respect. Especially with his little sister. Lori was a good friend of Raven's, but Lori had a hard time keeping anything from Caleb. Those two were practically best friends, which was way weird if you asked Raven.

"Anyway," Lori said as Raven started to edge away. "I wanted to know if you could make a quick appearance at Simon's bar mitzvah reception this weekend. He totally wants you there. You know how Simon is. He's in love with you."

"I don't know." Raven shifted her weight from foot to foot. The bell was going to ring any second. "I don't know if it'd be a good idea."

Lori swatted the air. "Are you kidding? It's fine. Caleb is supposed to leave around six to go home to let the dogs out. You could come at six, say hi to Simon, and then bolt." She stepped closer and lowered her voice. "Do it for Simon, please?"

Raven was starting to feel coaxed, but she wasn't sure how to get herself out of it. Simon did seem to look up to her for some insane reason. Caleb always said Simon had a crush on her. She hated to let him down.

"Okay. A quick appearance, but I do not want to see Caleb."

Lori nodded emphatically. "Totally. I'll make sure he isn't there."

The bell rang overhead. Raven scowled at the annoying sound and the tardy that was sure to come.

"Oh, better go!" Lori hurried off, waggling her fingers over a shoulder. "I'll talk to you later."

"Yeah, okay," Raven muttered and ran to her history class.

The teacher, Mr. Banner, pushed his glasses back by the nose bridge and eyed Raven with irritation. "You're tardy."

"Sorry. First day, you know?" She shrugged and flashed the smile her dad had paid a fortune for.

Mr. Banner tipped his head toward the classroom. "Sit down."

She breathed a sigh of relief. She hated to start the new semester off with a tardy on her record. Two tardies earned you a detention, and Raven hated detentions. She'd had her fair share last semester because Caleb always made her late. The good thing about that, though, was he usually served detentions with her and they'd pass notes to each other.

Raven scanned the room for an available seat and saw one near the back. She moved to take it but froze when she noticed the person sitting in the next desk over.

Horace.

Her heart went from a silent-and-steady beat to a loud hammering in only two seconds. Suddenly she felt light-headed and clammy all over. This kind of thing *never* happened to her. Usually she was all confident and casual around guys. What was it about Horace?

She hesitated at the front of the room, searching for another empty seat even though she knew there wasn't one. Why did this room have so few desks? Her last-hour English class had five empty seats, giving people the option to choose.

"If you'll sit down," Mr. Banner said, "we'll get started."

Raven muttered, "Sorry," again, and hurried down an aisle of desks to slide in the empty one. The chair squeaked. She crossed one leg over the other and tried to regain her bearings.

"The spots you're all in now," Mr. Banner said, his voice loud and commanding, "will be your seating arrangements until further notice."

Several girls near the windows smiled and turned to their friends sitting next to them. Raven slid a glance to her left and looked at Horace. He smiled that sheepish grin of his and ran a hand through his messy reddish-blond hair.

His lip was still swollen and cracked from Caleb's punch, but it looked like it was healing. A knot of guilt settled in Raven's stomach and she quickly looked away.

She was used to being the center of attention, especially where guys were concerned. But she'd never seen someone get punched because of her. She used to like flirting with guys just to see what they'd do, but Horace . . . somehow that had gone all wrong.

She'd lost control of the situation somewhere, probably when they'd kissed on the bus. She still couldn't figure out what had gotten into her. Now she had to defuse the situation before it blew up in her face.

♥ ♥ ♥

Alexia loved books, which meant she loved the library. It was her favorite place to be. The high school library, the public library, it didn't really matter which library. They were all great.

So, when she got her schedule that morning and saw that finally she'd gotten the library assistant position as her fourth-hour elective, she was ecstatic. One whole hour of school spent in the library? Going through books, checking out books, reading back-cover copy? Could school get any better than that?

No, it couldn't.

Except, when she pulled back one of the double doors of the library and went around the front counter to announce her arrival to the librarian, she ran into Ben Daniels.

On first glance, she thought it was Will. They were identical twins, both with chestnut-brown hair, moss-green eyes, and a strong chin, but it only took a second glance to see all the other differences.

Will always combed his hair down, nice and neat. He wore button-up shirts and polos and jeans and khakis. Ben, on the other hand, wore cargo pants most of the time. Even now, in the dead of winter. His hair was uncut and unkempt, curling around his ears and down the back of his neck.

Ben was Will on a bad day.

"Hey," he said, his voice slightly hoarse. "Alexia, right?"

The bell rang and Alexia dropped her bag on a chair. "Yes."

He leaned an arm on the counter and crossed his legs at the ankles. "Do people call you Al?"

Sometimes her friends shortened her name, but it wasn't like it was a nickname or anything.

"No."

"Lexy?"

"No."

"Alex?"

Sighing, she sat down. "Just Alexia, thanks." Where was the librarian? And why was Ben here? He wasn't an assistant, too, was he?

Though she had no opinion of Ben—since she'd never really talked to him before—carrying on a conversation with him seemed traitorous. His twin brother just dumped her best friend four days ago. Wasn't Ben kind of guilty by association?

"Alexia, then," he said, and sat in the chair next to her. He slouched a bit, his long legs spread out in front of him. "I'm Benjamin, but people call me Jamin."

She snorted and glanced over at him. "They do not."

He groaned. "All right, so they don't. But it'd be cool if they did."

A smile crossed her face but she quickly squashed it. "I'll call you Ben, *if* I need to call you."

"I suppose you'll be calling me a lot when you fall head over heels in love with me. Yeah," he slouched more and slung his arm over the back of the chair, "the ladies really like me, so I hear. I can't blame them. What with my wit and stunning good looks."

Coming from anyone else, Alexia probably would have groaned and ignored the guy, but Ben's facial expressions and sarcastic tone of voice said he was just trying to make her laugh. It worked.

He straightened in the chair. "See, I knew there was a smile in there somewhere. Though I think it's unfair that you're laughing *at* me. You don't think I'm good-looking? Or witty?"

She smiled again. She just couldn't help herself. "Well, you're . . . ah . . ."

"Just say it," he teased. "I'm like the next Brad Pitt. I know, I know." He held his hands up as if stopping her from fawning. "I get that a lot."

Alexia scrunched up her nose.

"No?" Ben asked. "Not Pitt?"

"More like . . . mmm . . . Jensen Ackles."

"Yeah? Jensen?" He checked out his reflection in the librarian's office windows. "I never thought of that."

The library door opened and the librarian, Mrs. Halloway, hurried in, a coffee mug in one hand, a stack of books in the other. "Oh, sorry I'm late," she said, rushing past Alexia and into her office. She unloaded her things on her desk, grabbed a file folder, and came back out. "Ben," she said, looking over her glasses, "don't you have somewhere to be?"

"Right. I forgot."

"Mmhmm." To Alexia she said, "Give me two more minutes, dear, and I'll get you started. I have to make a phone call." She headed into her office.

"I guess that's my cue to go," Ben said.

Alexia stood. "I thought you were another library assistant." She tried to keep the disappointment out of her voice. "Aren't you going to get in trouble now for being late?"

"Nah. I'm a computer lab assistant this hour—this is my second semester doing it—and Ms. Fairweather has the hots for me, no lie."

Alexia laughed since the computer lab teacher was older than her mother and smelled like mothballs.

"And," Ben continued, "she's as blind as an armadillo. She's probably talking to the closet door right now, thinking it's me."

Frowning, Alexia said, "Armadillo?"

"Yeah, they don't have very good eyesight. See, hang out with me a little more and you're bound to pick up facts about important things."

"Such as animal sight?"

He smiled. "Right. Now, if you're ever running from an armadillo, you know to hide instead of run. He won't see you."

Alexia followed him from behind the counter to the computer lab door in the library. "I hate to think of how tragically my life could have ended if I hadn't talked to you just now."

"I can see the headline now, 'Death by Armadillo.' Tragic, yes."

"Benjamin," Mrs. Halloway said, "off to class now before Ms. Fairweather marks you absent."

"I'm going." He tipped his head toward Alexia. "Later."

"Bye."

He opened the door to the computer lab and went inside. Alexia moved to the narrow, rectangular window on the door and watched him walk up to Ms. Fairweather. She readjusted her glasses as she peered at him, then smiled and nodded. It seemed he was off the hook for being tardy. He left her desk and walked out of Alexia's view. She was about to turn away when he reappeared in the window and put a note up to the glass.

MS. FAIRWEATHER JUST ASKED ME TO MARRY HER. WHAT DO I SAY?

He had this panicked look on his face.

Alexia laughed. She mouthed, "Tell her you're taken."

He widened his eyes in mock exasperation. "Thank you."

"You're welcome," she said, face beaming as if she actually had been crucial to his fake dilemma.

When he disappeared again from the window, Alexia went behind the library counter to get her instructions from Mrs. Halloway. The short, curly-haired librarian went through the computer and filing system. Alexia nodded when she was supposed to and said, "Okay." "Sure." Except every few minutes she'd look up at the computer lab door, hoping to see Ben in the window again.

NINE

Rule 3: *You must not write The Ex letters or text messages saying you miss him.*

Sydney typed in a text message to Drew on her phone:

where were u this weekend? y didn't u call? we need 2 talk. i miss u.
syd
xoxo

She hit the SEND button and flipped the phone closed, sliding it into the front pocket of her bag.

There, he couldn't ignore that, could he?

Beneath her desk, Sydney's knee bobbed up and down. She put her index finger to her lips and started to try and chew on the already nonexistent fingernail tip.

She felt like she was wasting time by sitting here in the middle of Creative Writing, listening to the old and deaf Mr. Simon drone on in his monotonous voice about their next writing assignment.

She thought the first day of a new class was supposed to be laid back while the teacher explained a few ground rules and passed out textbooks.

Of course, that sounded boring, too. Particularly when she had somewhere to be. Or rather, someone she needed to talk to. Drew was still MIA, though if she believed the witnesses, he was somewhere within the walls of Birch Falls High. The problem was, he was everywhere she wasn't.

So far they hadn't shared a single class, which was disappointing, considering they'd scheduled their classes together. Mrs. Hunt, the guidance counselor, promised she'd do her best to get them in the classes they chose.

But Sydney's first-hour trig was a bust, as was her second-hour study hall. At first she thought Drew was absent, but then she asked a few of his friends if they'd seen or talked to him. They all said yes, though they were adamant about not saying anything more, as if they knew something she didn't.

The rest of class dragged on. She hoped it wasn't going to continue like that for the rest of the semester. She actually liked writing, but Mr. Simon was ruining the experience. Probably he could make skydiving sound as interesting as watching paint dry.

When the bell rang, Sydney scooped up her things and hit the hallway at a fast pace, heading toward B hall where Drew's locker was. She waited for him to show, but within minutes the hallways thinned out as the students headed to their next classes. There was still no sign of Drew.

Then she spotted Craig Thierot rounding the corner up ahead. "Craig!" she called, jogging to meet him. "Hey, have you seen Drew?"

"Yup. I just talked to him in study hall."

He had study hall fourth hour? What, did he purposely switch on her at the last minute?

"So, uh . . ." Uh, what! What was she supposed to say? How was she supposed to fish for information without sounding like a petty girlfriend? Unfortunately, the talent for prying for information was a mystery to her. Kelly was better at that. Probably because she was so cute and bubbly. It was easy for her to sound casual while asking for information.

"Hey, Syd, I gotta jet before the bell rings," Craig said. "I've already got a tardy today." He started running off, but turned halfway. "Hey, I'm sorry, you know, about you and Drew. It's a bummer. You're a cool chick." He winked. "Later."

She froze in the middle of the hallway, stunned.

What did he mean by that? What was a bummer? Had Drew said something? Or more importantly, done something that she didn't know about?

The thought made her nauseous.

As the bell rang overhead, she rushed to the bathroom and slammed the door into the wall behind it. She went into a stall and slid the lock in place. Kneeling on the floor, her face over a toilet, she breathed in deeply, trying to quell the nausea.

When it subsided, she came out of the stall and sat on the metal bench along the wall. Was Craig serious? Or was he kidding around? It'd be just like him to try and start something between her and Drew. He was a jerk.

But the more she thought about it, the more it made sense. Drew's avoidance and Craig's comment meant one thing: They were done.

D-O-N-E.

But they couldn't be done! The last four days of Drew-silence had practically killed her. There was no way she could go another day. As it was, she felt like she was going to explode with anxiety at any minute.

Just as the tears started rolling down her face, her phone vibrated in her backpack. She scrambled for it. It was a text message from Drew.

we'll talk during lunch. lets meet at my truck after this hour.

drew

"That's it?" she muttered. There was no, "I love you." No, "I miss you, too. This is a huge mess and I can't wait to see you."

He was so cold and impersonal in the message that she hardly wanted to leave the bathroom, let alone talk with him at lunch. Maybe she should feign being sick and go home. Drew had always taken care of her when she was ill. And she did feel like vomiting.

But what if he didn't come over? And he spent another four days avoiding her? Four days might as well have been a year. She couldn't go another four days! And if she wasn't at school, then Nicole Robinson would take the opportunity to follow Drew around between classes and lunch. . . .

Sydney scowled at the thought. No way was she going to let that happen. Drew was hers. He'd always been hers.

If he wanted to talk, then she'd talk, but she wasn't going to allow the conversation to end with them being broken up for real.

♥ ♥ ♥

Sydney slipped into her black peacoat and buttoned it up to hide the hooded sweatshirt she'd stupidly put on today. She looked down at her gray Old Navy sweatpants and her scuffed charcoal Nikes. What had she been thinking this morning when she got dressed? She should have worn those Lucky Jeans her mom had bought her last fall. The ones that actually gave her a butt. She'd been so tired and depressed this morning that she hadn't felt like putting in much of an effort getting dressed.

Outside, the cloudy sky gave the day a gray cast. It was drab and dreary, matching her mood. She plunged her hands in the front pockets of her coat. Her breath puffed out in front of her in a white cloud.

At the first aisle of cars, she stopped and scanned the vehicles for Drew's truck. A couple ran past her toward a red car. The girl laughed at something the guy said. He smiled over the roof of the car as he fidgeted with the lock.

What wouldn't Sydney give to be that happy again? She could still turn back. If she didn't talk to Drew, were they still going to be done? If she avoided it, maybe it wouldn't happen.

But then she felt a hand on her shoulder and she turned, electric blue eyes meeting hers.

"Drew."

"Ready?" he said, keys jingling in his hand. He'd used gel in his hair today so that the front of it stuck up in a crooked spike. She hated it when he gelled it. Maybe he'd done it on purpose, as if to say he didn't care what her opinion was anymore.

"Yeah, I was just . . . looking for the truck."

"Third row," he said, and ambled off, the snow crunching beneath his Doc Martens. She hesitated, dread knotting her gut. She breathed in and put purpose into her step as she caught up with Drew.

He unlocked the passenger side door then went around to the driver's side. He had his glasses on before he slid in next to her and put the key in the ignition. He drove to Rocco's, a drive-through deli that probably survived on the income it made during Birch Falls High's lunch hour.

Through the front windows, Sydney could see several of the tables were full. There was a line at the front counter.

Drew pulled around the sand-colored brick building and stopped at the speaker box. Two more cars pulled up behind them, engines idling.

A female voice came through the speaker. "Welcome to Rocco's. What can I get for you?"

"A Turkey Lavish and a Diet Coke," Drew said. He turned to Sydney. "What do you want?"

She shrugged. She wasn't very hungry, but if she refused food, Drew might think she was being dramatic. "The usual."

He turned back to the speaker. "And a tuna sandwich with a Diet Coke."

After paying for their food, Drew drove to the park where they usually spent their lunch hours. The playground in front of the parking lot was empty and iced over. The duck pond was frozen, too, and covered in snow. It was barely visible except for the slight dip in the landscaping.

Drew parked and let the truck idle, the heat blowing out through the vents.

"So," he said, sliding his straw into his drink, "what did you want to talk about?"

"You asked me here," she said, ripping off a tiny piece of her sandwich. She mashed it between her fingers then popped it in her mouth.

Drew let out a long breath through his nose before saying, "You texted me and said we needed to talk." He took a big bite of his Lavish and got cream cheese on the corner of his mouth. "Will you get me a napkin?"

She checked in the white deli bag. Finding none, she popped open the glove box and dug inside. She always stuffed napkins in there for emergencies such as this. She pulled out a wad and handed them to Drew.

"Thanks," he said around a mouthful of food. After wiping his mouth, he set his food down and sipped from his soda.

Sydney could feel his eyes on her as she picked at her sandwich. There was so much running through her mind, but she couldn't get anything past her lips. She wasn't one to pour her heart out—or ask questions she didn't want to hear the answers to. At the same time, her rational mind said she had to finalize this. Otherwise, it'd sit like a heavy weight on her shoulders. She hated leaving things unfinished.

"Are we broken up for real?" she finally asked, turning away from the fogged passenger window and to Drew. He pinned his eyes on her. She had the fleeting thought that, broken up, his eyes would be for someone else soon. He wasn't going to be single long. There was Nicole, of course, waiting on the sidelines to scoop him up. And about twenty other girls in the school.

Sydney couldn't let him get away.

"I'm sorry, Syd," he said, shifting his gaze to the windshield and what was beyond it. She followed and watched a squirrel bounce across the snow. Probably now, whenever she saw a black squirrel, she'd remember this moment: the pain and realization.

Stupid squirrel.

"Is there any particular reason why?" she dared to ask.

After a pause he said, "We're just not any fun anymore."

"You mean, *I'm* not fun anymore."

He cocked his head to the side. "I didn't say that."

"But that's what you were thinking."

"You're a mind reader now?"

"Don't be a jerk."

He dropped his hands in his lap. "There you go, reason number two."

"What?"

"This. The arguments. It's stupid. Every time we're together we argue."

"We do not."

Sighing, he shook his head and pulled the truck into reverse. He backed out of the parking lot and drove to the road.

"Where are you going?"

"Back to school."

"We still have fifteen minutes," she argued, nodding at the digital clock on the dash stereo.

He didn't say anything as he pulled through an intersection.

"Now you're not going to talk to me?"

"No."

"Why?"

"Talking leads to more arguing. If I don't talk," he flicked his eyes to her, "we don't argue."

"No, Drew. Stop. We need to fix this."

"There's nothing to fix."

"We've been together for two years! You call that nothing?"

"I call that a good relationship that has finally run its course."

She fell back into her seat and crossed her arms over her chest. "Is this about Nicole? Do you like her? Did you guys hook up?"

He slid to a halt in front of a stop sign and turned to her. "No! This is about us, Sydney. Me and you and no one else. Got it?" He groaned in the back of his throat and straightened in the seat. He stepped on the gas pedal, pulling through the deserted intersection. The truck's tires splashed through melted snow.

Heat flamed in Sydney's cheeks. Her chin trembled with wanting to cry. She sucked it up. "If it's just about us, then why can't we fix it?" Her voice hitched and she was pretty sure he knew she was on the verge of tears, but he ignored it.

"Because we just can't."

"You promise you don't like someone else?"

"I promise."

That relieved her fears, if only a little. Maybe he just needed a short break. She could deal with that, couldn't she?

The rest of the ride to school was silent except for the whir of the heater vents blasting out warm, dry air. When Drew parked the truck, Sydney got out without a word and, instead of heading toward the school, veered to the left.

"Where are you going?" Drew asked.

Right now, she didn't care about school, or work, or her bag still in her locker. She didn't care if her dad found out she skipped school and grounded her. It wasn't like she had anyone to go out with anyway.

At her car, she pulled the keys out of her jacket pocket and unlocked the driver's side door as Drew caught up to her.

"Syd, where are you going?"

"Home," she said, then climbed inside the car, shutting the door in his face. He grimaced, running a hand through his hair, messing the spike. The hair scattered, sticking up randomly like pins from a cushion.

"I'm sorry," he said again as she started the car up. She backed out of the parking spot, threw the car in drive, and never looked back.

TEN

Rule 19: *If you see your girl's Ex, you must never mention it to her.*

Kelly used to love Wednesdays. She and Will worked as volunteers at Birch Falls Animal Shelter. Kelly not only loved the animals but also the location. The shelter was on the edge of town on a quiet dirt road. It was just so peaceful out there, even if there were ten dogs barking in the background.

And, even more, she had fun working beside Will for a few hours every week. He was great with the animals. He'd been great with her, too.

At least she thought they'd been great, but they couldn't have been *that* great if he wasn't ready to make it an official, exclusive relationship.

This Wednesday, however, with the breakup fresh in her mind and silence continuing between her and Will, Kelly was dreading the end of the school day and her shift at the shelter. Would Will be a no-show?

As much as she hoped for it as she stuffed her books in her locker and grabbed her bag, she knew that Will wouldn't skip out on volunteer work even if his mother was in the hospital. He was so focused and determined. The work at the shelter was going to look good on his college application, and he wouldn't sacrifice that for anything.

Maybe she should be a no-show. College was just a misty dream, somewhere far off in the future. And it wasn't like she needed a Harvard degree in order to be a journalist for *Seventeen* or one of the other teen mags. She just needed creativity and energy, and she had plenty of both. The education could come from any journalism program. If the teachers were good, why did it matter what the school's name was or how much the tuition cost?

Alexia sidled up next to Kelly at her locker. Her red hair hung around her shoulders in natural waves. Kelly wished she had Alexia's hair. Kelly's straight hair wouldn't hold a curl even with an entire bottle of hair spray. And it was the color of a washed-out gourd.

"Walk me out to the parking lot?" Alexia asked.

"Sure."

Alexia zipped up her coat as they walked down the hallway. "So, uh, I saw Will today in the library."

"Alexia!" Kelly shouted, pulling a few stares her way.

Alexia looked alarmed. "What?"

"Rule nineteen? If you see your girl's Ex, don't mention it to her?"

Alexia scrunched up her nose. "Oh, right. Sorry."

Jeez! And she was the one who came up with The Code in the first place!

They pushed open the exit doors together and hit the cold outdoors. Instantly, Kelly shivered and pulled the hood up on her coat. "So, what was he doing in the library?" She did have a right to ask, didn't she? Besides, Alexia brought it up.

"He came in to see his brother in the computer lab."

"Oh." Well, at least he wasn't with a girl. Wait, was he? "Was Brittany with him?"

Alexia shook her head. "He was alone."

Well, good. At least he wasn't moving right past Kelly and on to another girl. Even if he had dated other girls during their sort-of relationship, she knew without a doubt he spent the most time with her. They were together every Friday night and most Saturdays. And there were Wednesday nights at the shelter, too.

Was he even sad they weren't, like, together now? Did he miss her yet? God, she missed him. She wouldn't admit to it out loud, but she did. She'd almost looked for him at lunch. They used to sit together. And right now, she was itching to call him on her cell to see what he was doing. Or if he was on his way yet to the shelter.

At her car, Kelly pulled out her keys and said bye to Alexia. She sat behind the wheel for a few minutes silently debating her options. She could skip out on the shelter. Or she could go and be an adult about all of this. The shelter needed the help. They'd have to work harder to make up for her absence and that wasn't fair.

With a sigh, she left the school parking lot and headed for the shelter.

♥ ♥ ♥

When Kelly pulled into the shelter parking lot, the first car she noticed was Will's two-door black BMW.

Kelly glanced at her watch. She still had five minutes before she was supposed to show up. She could still leave if she wanted. Make a fast getaway before the tension ruined her day.

But no. She had a responsibility to the animals and the shelter; she couldn't bail because of a boy.

Locking the car up, she went inside and instantly the smell of animals hit her. The dog food and cat dander and dirty dog hair. Morris, the head animal control officer, smiled as she walked in, his chubby cheeks growing plumper with the expression.

"Good afternoon, Kelly," he said, tipping his black hat her way. Morris was a man in his forties who loved dogs and reptiles. He was Birch Fall's reptile guy, not that there was a huge reptile population, which always made Kelly wonder why he studied reptiles in the first place.

She was more of a dog person herself. Especially the little ones. She was trying to talk her mother into buying a Boston terrier, but so far she'd been unsuccessful.

"Hi, Morris," she said as she came around the counter and headed down the hall to the bathroom. She changed into her work clothes: a pair of Gap yoga pants and a gray long-sleeved shirt that was quickly fading to eggshell. They were work clothes but *cute* work clothes.

After depositing her bag in the hall closet, she opened the holding door between the front lobby and the kennel room where the dogs were. Will was there, crouched over, cleaning the gutters with a hose. The dogs barked at each other or maybe at Kelly.

Will didn't look up to greet her.

The longer she stood there and watched him, the quicker her heart beat in her chest. Suddenly, her tongue felt like it weighed ten pounds. Speaking of pounds . . . she hadn't run on the treadmill that morning. She glanced down at her midsection to check for any signs of a belly roll. She tugged uncomfortably on her shirt, pulling it away from her hips.

Mental note: Run on the treadmill!

Kelly swallowed and sucked in a breath. "Hey," she finally said. There, that sounded casual.

Will stopped spraying and looked over his shoulder. "Hi." He straightened. "How come I haven't heard from you?"

Kelly fidgeted with her watch. He still had no clue? Maybe she should be honest with him. If he heard her concerns, maybe he'd realize how serious she was about an exclusive relationship, and he'd realize he really liked her and dump Brittany.

Internally, Kelly snorted. *Highly* doubtful.

"Will," she began, when an adult dog started yelping outside.

Will rushed through the exit door and to the outdoor kennels. Kelly followed closely behind him. The German shepherd that arrived yesterday had its paw stuck in the chain-link fence. Will carefully freed the dog, then, "I should take him for a walk. He probably hasn't been out for a while." His breath puffed out white. Already his pale cheeks were getting pink from the cold.

They went back inside and Will slipped into his coat. "Will you finish the gutters?" he asked as he grabbed a blue rope leash from one of the hooks.

Kelly wrapped her arms around herself. "Yeah, sure."

"Oh, and scoop the kennels?"

It was his week to scoop the kennels but she said, "Yeah," anyway. Will thanked her and left. When the door shut, she leaned against the wall and rubbed her forehead. She'd probably broken several rules just then. Wasn't there a rule against talking to The Ex?

Probably.

She went up front. "Hey, Morris?"

Morris set his book down. "Problem with the dogs?"

"No, they're fine. I just wanted to talk to you."

He swiveled his chair around to face her and propped one leg up on the other knee. His large ring of keys jingled at his side. "What's up?"

"I need different hours, like, immediately."

"Something come up?"

She nodded emphatically. More like, *someone.* "It's personal."

"All right. How about Sundays? I'm short for the visiting hours."

"That sounds awesome, thanks."

She felt better now that it was settled. No more Will meant no more stress. Or at least she hoped so.

♥ ♥ ♥

After slipping on her fleece gloves, Kelly started up the car in the shelter parking lot. She turned the heat on full blast, shivering at first as cold air hit her, but she was of the opinion that turning the heat on high made it warm up faster.

Usually time at the shelter flew by, but tonight it had dragged. There was a lot to do—dogs to walk, kennels to clean, cats to feed—but with Will on the periphery, Kelly couldn't focus. It certainly didn't help that he kept talking to her.

"When are we going to hang out again?"

"What are you doing tonight?"

"Did you get Jacobs for English?"

Answers: Never. Nothing. No.

For some reason, she couldn't get any of that out, though. It was like her brain didn't work right around Will. Probably because he sucked up all the hot air in the room.

She'd wanted to say, "Hey, Will, you're a sucky friend and I don't want to waste any more time with you." But, if she were being honest, that wasn't completely how she felt. He was a sucky friend, but she so *did* want to hang out with him, which was really the problem in the first place. He didn't want a relationship and she did. But he wasn't getting a relationship for free anymore. He wanted all the perks without the commitment. No way was she settling for that. No matter how much she liked him.

Before backing out of the parking space, Kelly called Alexia to see what everyone was doing.

Alexia picked up quickly.

"You busy?" Kelly asked. "I'm done at the shelter and I don't want to go home. My mom was making steak and potatoes tonight for my brother, and I hate steak."

Through the phone, Kelly could hear Alexia chomp on something before she answered. "There's a *Falcon Beach* marathon on tonight. Want to come over and watch it with me?"

"Would I ever. I'll be there in about ten minutes."

Alexia's mom answered the door when Kelly knocked. She was an older woman in her late forties and had passed her fiery red hair on to Alexia. Dr. Bass wore hers short, layered around her chin, while Alexia's was long and wavy. Both mother and daughter had the same tiny, perfectly straight nose and light dusting of freckles.

"Well, hello, Kelly!" Dr. Bass said. "I haven't seen you in a while."

Kelly's face heated up. Dr. Bass was right; after all, Kelly had been too busy with Will to give Alexia the time she deserved. Why was it, when a girl got a boyfriend the rest of the world faded away? Love sure was blind. And dumb.

"Yeah, I was . . . finishing up some projects," she lied.

A blender started up in the kitchen and Dr. Bass rolled her eyes. "My husband is trying to make a wheatgrass shake," she said. "I better go check up on him before I have it on my ceiling. Alexia's in the living room."

"Thanks."

Kelly found Alexia on the couch with a bag of Goldfish crackers in her lap, although, right now, she looked more involved with the hot guy on the screen than the fish in her hand.

"Hey," Kelly said, plopping down on the couch. The smell of Febreeze wafted up from the throw pillows. She reached over for the cracker bag and pulled out a handful. "Wow," she added, finally looking at the guy on the screen. He was blond and had an extremely nice body. A lot nicer than Will's. Will didn't really have a body. He counted his calories and exercised, but he didn't tone enough. His stomach was decidedly flat. But his twin brother, Ben . . . oh, boy, he had one rocking body. Kelly had seen him shirtless plenty of times while she was hanging out with Will at their house.

Ben was definitely eye candy.

"That's Jason," Alexia said, nodding at the TV. "He's the hottie of Falcon Beach."

Kelly raked her teeth over her bottom lip. "I'll say."

When a commercial came on, Alexia finally turned to Kelly, and popped the cracker into her mouth. "So, how was the shelter?"

Kelly sighed and pursed her lips. She was about to say she didn't feel like talking about it because it was too depressing, but then everything tumbled out. "I probably broke like a bamillion rules by talking to him. I just wish I could get over him already."

"Well, stop breaking rules and you should," Alexia suggested. "That's what The Code is for, after all."

Kelly licked cracker salt from her fingers. "Easy for you to say." Then, feeling like a total whiner, she changed the subject. Besides, if she talked about Will any longer she was liable to start crying again or get depressed enough to put herself in a chocolate coma. "So, how was your day? Have any cute guys in your classes?" She waggled her eyebrows.

Alexia shrugged and stole back the Goldfish bag. "Not really."

Except—Kelly was pretty sure Alexia was lying. Her cheeks were bright red—she always got red in the face when she was lying or avoiding something and her freckles seemed to change to this mossy green. Weird, right? But, as much as Kelly liked to dish about guys and crushes, she knew Alexia wasn't open with that kind of stuff. And prying it out of her would be über cruel.

ELEVEN

Rule 13: *You must never sleep with The Ex.*
Rule 17: *Do not keep in touch with The Ex's parents, sister, brother, or cousins or anyone related to The Ex's family.*

"Oh, I've been meaning to ask you," Raven's mom began as she spread her special lasagna sauce in a glass baking dish, "did you get into that precalculus class we were talking about?"

It had been a full week since Raven started her new classes. She was surprised her mother hadn't checked on her new schedule as soon as Raven got home from school on Monday. It was probably because Ms. Valenti was constantly working now that she owned Scrappe. The store was like a godsend to Raven. Scrapbooking kept her mother busy, which meant she spent less time nosing over Raven's shoulder.

"Honey?" Ms. Valenti said.

Raven gave the metal colander full of lasagna noodles a good shake over the sink. The water dripped out the bottom and slowed to a trickle. Maybe if she pretended to be busy, her mother would stop bombarding her with so many questions.

"Raven, did you hear me?"

Well. It was worth a shot.

Raven set the colander back in the pot the noodles had cooked in and turned to her mother. "No, I didn't. The class was already full," she lied. She hadn't even asked for precalculus. Who in their right mind would take that crap? She'd struggled through the required geometry. She certainly wasn't going to make things harder by taking precalculus. Instead, she'd asked for accounting as her last math credit. But she wasn't going to tell her mother that.

Ms. Valenti had dropped out of college her freshman year when her parents refused to pay her tuition. They refused to pay her tuition because she was pregnant with Raven and because Raven's dad was African American. The Valentis, a pure Italian family, had wanted their only daughter to marry a "good Italian boy," as they said. And when they found out she was pregnant and planning on marrying Raven's dad, they flipped out.

Raven's mom had dreams of becoming a pediatrician. And now, seventeen years later, it seemed like Ms. Valenti was either 1) punishing Raven for being one of the reasons she'd had to quit school (like Raven got her pregnant!), or 2) was living vicariously through her daughter.

It was no secret that her mom wanted her to take all the hard classes so she could get an Ivy League university acceptance. Raven would have all the things her mother never did. It was almost like she wanted Raven to make up for her mistakes.

Raven could only imagine what her mother would say when she admitted she didn't want to attend an Ivy League school. Like she'd get in, anyway. Actually, she wasn't really sure what she wanted to do after graduating, but going right back into school was certainly not high on her priority list. Kelly was constantly suggesting Raven try modeling, but she wasn't a huge fashionista like Kelly was. Clothes didn't get Raven excited.

She always thought taking a long road trip across the United States sounded like fun. Maybe with her friends—or whoever her boyfriend was at the time. She wanted to see California and New Orleans and Las Vegas, baby! She just wanted one year off to live and breathe away from her mother. Ms. Valenti was like a hawk, always hovering over Raven, asking questions, giving commands.

Now her mother looked across the kitchen at her with those you've-disappointed-me eyes.

Raven sighed and crossed her arms over her chest. "What?"

Ms. Valenti shrugged. "Maybe if you'd gotten into the counselor's office earlier, like I asked you to, you would have gotten in precalc." She nodded at the colander of noodles. "Will you hand me those?"

Raven grabbed the pot and hauled it over to the L-shaped counter where her mom was putting together the lasagna. She set the pot down, then said, "I'm going to get into the shower." She did *not* feel like arguing with her mother about classes right now. She had enough on her mind. Like Simon's bar mitzvah reception and the possibility of running into Caleb. She was so confused about him. Or, rather, about her feelings toward him.

One minute she missed him so bad, her chest hurt. And then the next minute she was overcome with shame for having gone out with him in the first place. Everyone said Caleb was wrong for her, that he was a jerk. But not everyone knew how Caleb was when he was alone with Raven. He could be really sweet.

"You're not going to help me with dinner?" Ms. Valenti unfolded a lasagna noodle and lay it in the baking dish.

"I'm going to Simon's bar mitzvah reception, remember?"

"So you won't be eating dinner with your sister and me? You know I like to have us all at the dinner table. That's when families are supposed to communicate."

Ms. Valenti loved to read the parenting how-to books and magazines, which was where she got the latter jewel of wisdom. If a doctor or psychologist recommended something, then she did it. It didn't matter how ridiculous the idea sounded. She'd read that overexposure to the media disconnected children from their parents and, since then, she'd cracked down on the amount of pop culture that came into the house.

She'd imposed a one-hour time limit per day on the TV. Supposedly, tabloids and fashion magazines were the reason so many teenage girls had body issues, so the girls weren't allowed to read them.

An expert's word was the gospel in this house. And Alexia's parents were practically elevated to godly status.

"I probably won't be home for dinner. Sorry."

"Well, I suppose we can make an exception." Ms. Valenti grabbed another noodle and laid it in the baking dish. "Just don't stay out too late, please."

"Mom, it's a bar mitzvah reception. I don't think they'll be up past midnight celebrating." Not that Raven was exactly sure what they did to celebrate bar mitzvahs, but something told her it wasn't that kind of party.

"Raven." Ms. Valenti looked up and breathed a long sigh. "Just . . . please be home by midnight, okay?"

Raven nodded. That probably wouldn't be hard to pull off considering she didn't have a boyfriend anymore. Her life was officially unexciting.

♥ ♥ ♥

Raven parked her Nissan Sentra in the back of Loon Cast Banquet Hall's lot. The sun was just setting, casting pinks and oranges in the sky off on the horizon. The snow had stopped falling earlier in the morning, but with the wind blowing it back and forth, it almost seemed like it was snowing.

Three Days Grace's "Pain" filled the small interior of Raven's two-door car. The chorus of the song said, "I'd rather feel pain than nothing at all." Alexia had said almost the exact same thing last weekend after the breakups. But that was easy for her to say, since she'd never been brokenhearted.

Raven wondered what it'd be like to feel nothing at all. On the one hand, she'd never be sad or angry or frustrated with guys. But then again, she'd never feel excitement or giddy anticipation like she felt right now as she looked at the large building in front of her, wondering if maybe Caleb was on the inside. Lori had promised Caleb wouldn't be around, but Raven was kind of hoping he was.

She wanted to see him because she looked good in her silky black dress and black flats. Also, her hair had cooperated nicely after her shower and now hung around her shoulders in inky black waves. Or rather, it would once she got inside and took off her gray leather jacket. She'd wanted to forgo the jacket, since it was hard to be sexy in winter wear, but it was just so cold out.

But mostly, she just plain missed Caleb. That sucked, because he'd treated her like crap at Craig's party last weekend, but still . . . her mind just wouldn't move past him.

She'd barely seen him in school all week. They didn't have any of the same classes together and their lockers were on different ends of the school.

Someone knocked on the passenger window of Raven's car. She jumped and brought her hand halfway to her chest.

"What are you doing?" Lori yelled. "Are you going to sit in your car all night?"

Raven turned the key and the car shut off. She popped a piece of Big Red in her mouth (she hated mints, it was gum all the way) and checked her teeth in the rearview mirror.

You look good, she thought. If Caleb was inside, he was totally going to drool.

She pushed open the driver's door and met Lori at the front of the car. Lori was wrapped in a raspberry Columbia jacket, her arms crossed tightly over her chest. A red dress hung from beneath the jacket. "Let's get inside where it's warm!" Lori jogged as best she could in her high heels over the snow-covered parking lot while holding her dress down with her arms.

Raven was glad she'd worn flats. She'd probably break her neck in heels, which was why she avoided them at all costs. Her mom had bought her a pair last year to wear to her grandparents' fiftieth anniversary. That was the first and last time she'd worn them.

Lori held the side door open for Raven. The wind followed them inside until Lori slammed the door shut on it. Lori shrugged out of her coat and hung it on one of the multitude of gold hooks on the wall. She ran a hand over her upswept hair as if to check for bumps. A few curled wisps hung along her heart-shaped face.

Raven pulled off her jacket and hung it next to Lori's. She shook out her hair and rubbed her glossed lips together.

"Wow," Lori said, giving Raven a once-over. "You look so hot!"

"Thanks. Is hot okay for a bar mitzvah reception?"

"Totally. It's fine. Come on." Lori took Raven's hand and pulled her through the closed door of the lobby.

Inside the main room, Raven was met with loud music sung in another language. Fiddles accompanied flutes and other stringed instruments. While it wasn't Raven's type of music, it did sort of have an inviting dance rhythm to it.

Lights flooded the stage where the DJ worked. The rest of the room was dark except for the flicker of candles on each of the round tables. The dance floor was packed with kids and their parents.

A girl no older than thirteen passed Raven with a huge cone of cotton candy in her hands. Raven spotted the cotton candy maker off to her right, next to the long table filled with Israeli food.

"My mom went all out for this reception," Lori shouted. "Probably because Simon is the youngest, you know. Later there's karaoke."

"Wow," Raven replied, taking it all in while also surreptitiously looking for Caleb.

"Simon's over here," Lori said. "Come say hi to him."

Lori made her way around several tables and stopped in front of a table along the wall. "Hey, Simon! Look who's here!"

Simon saw Raven and smiled wide. He got out of his chair and came around the table. "Thanks for coming, Raven!"

Raven couldn't help but smile back. The kid was so sweet and cute, especially tonight, in his black dress pants and white shirt. His red silk tie looked crisp and new. His dark hair was gelled down. Raven wondered if Caleb had done his brother's hair to help him out. He was extremely overprotective of his younger siblings. Even if he was a sucky boyfriend, he was one killer older brother.

"I had to come to see you." Raven squeezed Simon's shoulder and he blushed in response.

"So how come you haven't been over all week?"

Raven winced. What was she supposed to say to that?

"Later, Simon, okay?" Lori said. "Just be happy she's here now."

"But—"

"Simon!"

"Okay. Okay. Fine."

Mrs. Plaskoff, Caleb's mom, came up. "Honey," she said to Simon, "come say hi to your cousins from Illinois." She noticed Raven standing there. "Oh, Raven, honey!" She put her arms around Raven and squeezed. Mrs. Plaskoff always smelled like roses.

"I heard about it. I'm so sorry. My oldest boy, I swear, sometimes he just doesn't think. You know?" She shook her head, but her faux red hair, frozen in curls with tons of hair spray, barely moved an inch.

Raven smiled. She liked Caleb's mother. She was boisterous but extremely nice.

Mrs. Plaskoff leaned over to whisper in Raven's ear. "He's over by the punch bowl if you want to talk to him." She straightened and set her hand on Simon's shoulder. "Come on, Simon. Nice to see you, Raven." The mother/son pair disappeared in the crowd.

Raven turned to the food table where she'd seen the punch bowl. Caleb was there, a plastic cup in his hands. His eyes were locked on her, but there was another girl hanging on his shoulder.

He was in dress clothes, too, with a tie that matched Simon's. His face was clean-shaven.

Raven didn't recognize the girl. She was probably seventeen or so, but she was trying to appear older with tons of makeup and thick black eyeliner. Her thin lips were rimmed in red lipstick and her boobs looked pushed up with a bra, the cleavage sticking out of a low-cut black dress.

"Who's the girl with Caleb?" Raven asked Lori.

Lori looked in her brother's direction then groaned. "She's a friend of our cousin's from Tel Aviv. She's been hanging on Caleb since they got here."

Raven tried to breathe out the jealousy, but it burrowed deep into her chest. Although they'd broken up, she couldn't help but feel like she still had some sort of claim on Caleb. Certainly more than some Israeli girl from Tel Aviv did.

Raven threw back her shoulders, elongated her neck, and strutted across the oak floor, her flats clipping along as if cheering her on. She stopped in front of Caleb and slyly appraised the temptress now that she was up close. The girl's complexion was blotchy and there was a huge pimple at the corner of her nose. Her eyebrows were plucked crookedly and the foundation she used was two shades darker than her actual skin tone. Raven could tell because of the tide line along her hairline.

Raven plastered on a smile. "Hey," she said, hoping that Caleb's across-the-room eye contact had been a sign that he was still into her and wasn't about to blow her off in front of the enemy.

"Hey," he said. He set his cup down on the table behind him and shoved his hands in his pants pockets. "What's up?"

The song on the sound system changed to a classic rock song. Several adults hooted and quickened their steps on the dance floor, moving in time with the beat.

Raven clasped her hands behind her back. "Thought I'd come to wish Simon well."

The girl looked Raven over as if threatened.

Bet you don't even know who Simon is, Raven thought.

"Cool." Caleb nodded.

Raven noticed her black dress went well with Caleb's outfit. They would have looked like such a cute couple in photos.

"Can I talk to you for a minute?" he said, and shot the girl a look like, "Scram."

The girl curled her upper lip but darted away.

"Sure," Raven said, pleased with the outcome of that situation.

Caleb grabbed her arm gently and led her through a door behind the food table. They entered a kitchen where several people worked, packing away extra food and cleaning dirty dishes. The air smelled like salty fish and chicken soup.

Caleb headed through another door that took them into a hallway and then into an empty room that looked like a dressing room. He sat down on the couch along the wall and patted the cushion next to him. "Sit down for a second?"

She hesitated. He was being so nice, but at the same time, she was breaking a rule right now by being here, she just knew it. Still, she couldn't just leave things the way they were.

She sat down but was sure to keep some distance between them.

"So, uh," Caleb said, "I was totally buzzed that night and mad, too; you can't blame me. Ya know? You did kiss another dude."

Raven flicked her eyes to him. "It's not like I planned it. Or meant to hurt you." The bus ride home from regional band competition flashed in her mind. She saw herself and Horace in the back of the bus, with Horace's hands in her hair. Raven turned away from Caleb, afraid that he'd read the thoughts in her eyes.

"I know you didn't mean to hurt me." Caleb shifted so he could face her. "But you did."

He sounded sincere, but Raven would put money on the fact that he didn't technically have feelings, just pride. And that's what she'd bruised more than anything.

"Well, I'm glad we had this talk," she said, ready to get up. She was starting to get uncomfortable, as if her subconscious was trying to tell her how wrong it was that she was there.

"Me, too." He paused, then scooted closer to her, taking her hand in his. "I don't want us to hate each other."

"I don't hate you."

Maybe she'd gone too far with the black dress and the act she'd put on to drive the other girl away. Had she led him on?

Back here, away from the main room and the stereo, it was almost silent. She wondered if her breathing sounded too quick and whether or not Caleb was getting the wrong impression. She was feeling claustrophobic and definitely not excited.

She made a move to leave again but Caleb tightened his grip on her hand. "Wait." He pulled her into a hug. "I've missed you."

"Caleb."

He tilted her chin up with a finger and kissed her. At first she didn't stop him, mainly because she was frozen in place. She'd kissed him so many times before, that this just felt natural, like slipping into a comfy but holey sweatshirt she should have thrown out long ago. He wound his arm around her waist and guided her back against the couch so that they were both lying down.

Heat brushed her cheeks, while her mind screamed, "Stop!" as it tried to be rational.

She slid out from beneath Caleb and practically jumped off the couch.

"What's wrong?" he asked.

"We're not together."

"We can be together." He stood up, towering over her. "I *want* to get back together."

The only reason he was saying that now was because he wanted to sleep with her. That'd probably been his plan all along. That's why he'd pulled her all the way back here in the recesses of the party hall.

But she wasn't going to sleep with him. It not only broke a rule, it was just plain wrong. Her friends would never let her live that one down. Not that she'd have to tell them. But she would know she deliberately broke one of the more serious rules.

"I'm going," she said, straightening her hair with her fingers. She pulled open the door on the dressing room and hurried down the hallway.

Caleb ran after her. "Wait, Ray."

"Don't call me Ray." He made the nickname sound wrong.

"I've always called you Ray. Stop, would you?"

"There's nothing left to say!"

"If you didn't want to get back together, then why did you scare Yael away like you were jealous or something?"

Raven slowed. "Who's Yael?"

"The girl I was talking to when you came up."

She shook her head. She didn't have a good answer to that one. It was a huge mistake. "I'm done talking."

"Raven, damn it. Stop being a bitch." His voice had turned harsh, the same as it had last Friday night when he broke up with her. If Alexia were here right now, she'd say Raven didn't deserve to be treated like this.

Raven had no idea how she should be treated. She wasn't some princess that needed to be waited on—but she certainly didn't deserve being called a bitch.

She stopped at the door, hand on the knob, ready to bolt. She turned to Caleb, his face red with anger now. "If you weren't such an asshole," she said, "I wouldn't have to be a bitch."

She pulled the door open and ran.

TWELVE

Rule 15: *Find a hobby or something you are passionate about.*

Sydney was spending her second Saturday as a single girl in the attic. She should have been out shopping. Or maybe studying. Or getting her hair done. But she didn't feel like leaving the house, which was definitely saying something. She'd spent the last two years avoiding the house because it had become a hollow shell of what it used to be, with her mother gone ninety percent of the time and her dad trying to be Mr. Mom.

As a way to get her mind off Drew, Sydney was in pursuit of a Rubbermaid tote she'd lugged into the attic some six months ago. It contained several crammed photo albums, one ratty blanket, an empty journal, and a digital camera that had once been considered top of the line but was now sorely out-of-date.

The idea was, find the camera and take up a new hobby as a way of fulfilling the concept behind Rule 15.

Sydney stepped around a leather trunk, bumping into a tower of cardboard boxes. She stilled them with her hands before they toppled over, and moved farther into the room, which ran the length and width of the house.

Mostly there were cardboard boxes and Rubbermaid totes up here. Sydney's dad filled the boxes, but her mom had always said totes were more practical because they guarded against moisture and bugs.

The tote Sydney was looking for was clear with a top the color of flamingos. It should have been easy to pick out among the brown cardboard and the forest-green totes her mother always bought, but for some reason, Sydney was having a hard time locating it.

And it should have been right there by the door where she left it. Had her mother grabbed it? Maybe to take the camera?

Mrs. Howard used to be an amateur photographer. She would take Sydney out to Birch Falls Park on weekends to take photos of the swans and deer, and the duck pond near the back of the park, where people ice-skated in the winter.

Sydney used to love those outings. It was so routine that it almost became as familiar as the ratty blanket that was also in the flamingo tote. Sydney had slept with that blanket every night until six months ago when she decided she was too old for it. It'd been a gift from her now-deceased grandmother.

Part of her was searching for the tote, not only for the camera but the blanket, too. She'd lost the most familiar thing in her life: Drew. She felt like she was reaching for anything that would be familiar and maybe fill that hollow void in her chest.

Dust swirled in the muted moonlight pouring through the square window at the far end. Sydney wondered what time it was and whether or not she'd ever find this stupid tote. It had to be after nine if the moon was out.

She thought of Drew and wondered where he was and what he was doing. Hopefully, he wasn't with Nicole Robinson.

"Aha," she said to the silence when she spotted the pink tote lid peeking out from beneath a sheet. She pulled the sheet back. Dust spiraled in the air and she waved it away. When it settled, she sat on the floor with the tote in front of her and popped open the lid.

Sitting on top of the canary-yellow blanket was the digital camera, exactly where she'd put it six months ago. Did her mother miss those weekend trips to the park? Sydney had barely talked to her mother in weeks. And when they did talk, they didn't talk about the fun they used to have. Mostly it was about Sydney's schoolwork, and even then the conversations didn't last long. They usually went like this:

"How's school going?" her mom would say.

Sydney would reply, "It's good. I got an A in—"

Her mom's BlackBerry or laptop would start dinging with an incoming message. "I have to get that," her mom would say and then bury herself in her work for another two hours.

Sydney usually gave up at that point.

Now she took the camera in her hands and slid the power button over. The camera let out three chirps while the power light flickered green. The batteries were still good. The screen lit up with the last picture taken.

Sydney's mouth hung slack when she looked at it.

It was of Sydney and Drew on the back patio, sitting in the bench swing. Their backs were to the camera, but they were looking at each other so their faces were in profile, silhouetted by the flickering orange glow of a fire in the cast-iron pit.

That'd been two summers ago, when their relationship was still new and Sydney's mother hadn't yet received her promotion. Sydney never knew her mother had taken this picture. Or that she'd been there in the house watching them.

It was such a beautiful photograph. It reminded Sydney of how good her life was that summer.

I wish there was something I could do to get that back, she thought. *That perfection.*

But unless Drew took her back and her mother quit SunBery Vitamins, Sydney knew her life would never be that perfect again.

THIRTEEN

Rule 5: *You must not date anyone until you can go two weeks without thinking about The Ex. (Take this time to find yourself & focus on your emotional stability. Do group activities with friends—both girl and guy friends.)*

It was Wednesday, which meant the normal band instructor, Mr. Thomas, was at Lincoln Elementary leading band class for the little kids. The assistant band instructor, Ms. D, would be teaching the class today. She was a really, *really* good musician, but Raven suspected Ms. D hated her. Which might have had something to do with the fact that Raven went out with and later broke up with Ms. D's little brother, Greg, last year.

If it were up to her, Raven would be hanging out in her dad's basement right now, flipping open the latches of a guitar case instead of a flute case. She pulled out the main body of her flute, then the mouthpiece, and lastly, the end. She fitted all of them together, turning the pieces so the keys matched up.

Her dad had promised to teach her to play the guitar until her mom found out and put a stop to it. Ms. Valenti didn't want Raven having anything to do with rock music or "that whole scene," as she said. Being with the school band looked good on a college application. No one cared if you played guitar, and being in a rock band would never get a person anywhere.

"Look no further than your father if you want a good example," Ms. Valenti had said. "He tried that whole singer thing and we ended up broke. It's no good, Raven. That scene is no good."

Of course, if the college recruiters actually heard Raven play flute, it probably wouldn't factor into their judgment. Actually, it'd probably count against her. Last year, the band director went through every section, testing each player. The point was to score the players and give them "chair" positions. Chair number one was the best seat; it meant you were the best player in your section.

Out of five flute players, Raven was fifth chair. She hadn't put a lot of effort into being a good flutist. It was a dumb instrument. But the guitar . . . with the hard work and passion she thought she had . . . would pay off. And that was something she actually did learn from her mother.

Ms. Valenti fell in love with scrapbooking and decided she wanted to run a business centered on that art. So she started Scrappe, a scrapbooking store and café. It was voted Most Successful Business in last year's town survey and a lot of people from school hung out there on the weekends during the colder months.

There was a separate room for scrapbooking, so if you weren't into that, you could hang at the café without hearing about glue spots and acid-free markers.

Raven used to hang out there all the time, until she and Horace had their make-out session on the bus. Because Horace worked at Scrappe, she hadn't been there in weeks.

As if her thoughts had conjured him, Horace walked through the double doors of the band room. The first thing he did was look over at her and smile before climbing the steps to the third tier in the back, where the percussion section was set up.

She smiled back out of habit.

People were starting to file in the doors before the warning bell rang. Raven feigned interest in her music book, keeping her eyes on the notes as she pressed the corresponding keys on the flute.

"Ray," Horace said, sliding into the orange chair next to her.

"Oh, uh . . . hi," she said. Fumble much? Usually she was so confident and poised around guys, but Horace . . . not so much.

Horace was a geek in middle school. Everyone thought so; even she did. He used to be scrawny and short. He had braces for the longest time. Rumor had it his mother shopped for his clothes at Goodwill. In middle school, when it was all about being cool and what name brands you wore, shopping at Goodwill was social suicide.

Freshman year of high school, Horace started changing. Now, in his junior year—sans braces—he was still kind of a geek, but a cool geek. He grew a few inches, packed on some muscle, but probably still shopped at Goodwill. Except individuality counted now—at least to her—and he was very much his own person.

He shifted in his chair now, the brown material of his Western-style shirt bunching around his bicep. Beneath that he had on a black T-shirt that said PEOPLE SERVICES, across the chest. His knee stuck through a hole in his jeans and loose strings hung from the cuffs around his brown boots.

Horace was Caleb's polar opposite. He was the opposite of *every* guy Raven had gone out with.

"What's up?" he said. His husky voice slid around the chatter and instrument tuning and hit her right in the gut. Jitters took hold of her stomach.

"Nothing," she said, resting her flute on her lap, "just going over the music."

"Are you doing anything this weekend?"

The final bell rang overhead and a few people hurried in. Raven's attention flicked from Horace to the door to the band director's office window and then back to Horace. His eyes were still on her.

She smiled. Play it cool, she thought.

"Yeah, I've got a few things planned with my friends. What are you doing?"

"Some friends of mine are hanging out at Striker's after I get out of work. I thought if you weren't busy, you could hang out with us." He paused, nostrils flaring. Then, "No," he corrected, "actually I want you to hang out with me." He followed up with that hesitant smile of his.

Raven couldn't accept the invitation, even if she thought it sounded like fun. For one, she'd promised herself and her friends that she'd wait a few weeks (maybe even a few months) before going out with anyone. And two, she couldn't stand the thought of hurting Horace anymore. What if they started going out and she realized he wasn't The One either? She'd subconsciously ruin the relationship or, worse yet, drop Horace quicker than the flip of a calendar month.

She'd already gotten him punched.

"I can't." She turned a page in her music book, faking nonchalance. "But maybe another time?"

Amelia, the fourth-chair flutist, came up then and glared at Horace. "You're in my seat." Amelia took being fourth chair seriously and anyone in her seat was probably a direct violation of her flutist code or something.

"Sorry." Horace got up. "Ray," he started, turning to her, "if you change your mind, you know where to find me."

"Sure."

He shoved his hands in his pockets and hurried up the steps to the percussion section. Raven surreptitiously glanced over her shoulder, watching as he grabbed his drumsticks in hand and beat at the air to warm up his wrists. Well, maybe not so surreptitiously, since he caught her staring.

Face hot, she turned back to her music book and lifted her flute up in her hands. With the mouthpiece at her lips, she blew across the hole, pulling out a warm-up note with all the others.

She was following The Code. She was doing the right thing.

♥ ♥ ♥

The smell of crisp pages and old leather filled Alexia's nose. The history room in the library was one of her favorite places in the whole school. It felt like she was taking a step back in time. Finding the 900s in the Dewey Decimal System, Alexia slipped an American history book on the shelf. She turned back to her metal cart and saw Ben thumbing through the other books she was supposed to be putting away.

"What are you doing?" she asked.

She hadn't seen him since yesterday this hour, and when she came into the library just twenty minutes ago to find him nowhere, the disappointment had been nearly palpable. So, she'd gone straight to work, checking in returned books and filing them away, but all she thought about while pulling her metal cart around was Ben.

She hadn't crushed this hard since Owen Wilson in *Zoolander*. Not that she would call this thing . . . whatever it was . . . a crush. She looked forward to seeing him, was all. A friendly crush was more like it.

Ben pulled a book about Rome out of the stack and held it up for her. "Did you know," he cocked an eyebrow, "that in ancient Rome, the thumbs-down meant the crowd favored the gladiator in the arena?"

"No, I can't say I knew that."

Pushing the book into a random spot on the shelf, he squared himself in front of her. "If I were a Roman emperor, which I probably wouldn't be, because I'm too cool for that, and you were a gladiator, I'd give you . . . " He jabbed his thumb toward the floor. "A thumbs-down."

"So, you'd favor me?"

He crossed his arms over his chest. "Totally."

If she had a mirror right now, she'd probably see her freckles lighting up like Christmas lights. She looked away. The flattery—was that what it was?—unnerved her.

"Aren't you supposed to be in the computer lab? Assisting?"

"No, actually." He smiled. "I'm supposed to be in Mrs. Halloway's office calling my mother."

Alexia turned around, brow furrowed. "Really?"

"Really."

"Mrs. Halloway's office is out there"—she nodded to the doorway behind Ben's shoulder—"and to the right."

He wagged his finger at her. "So that's where it is. I was wondering. Well, I should go call her, before dinner is spoiled." He left the history room and headed into the librarian's office. Mrs. Halloway smiled at him and grabbed her phone. After handing it over, she left the office.

He dialed and talked to someone on the other line. Alexia knew all of this because she was peeking out the window of the history room watching him. He was so danged cute. Just watching him made Alexia smile. And talking to him usually had her laughing harder than she had in months. If she had to pick between her sacred alone time or an hour with Ben, she'd pick Ben.

When he hung up, he glanced over at the window and Alexia ducked. She went around one of the bookcases, losing herself in the books before Ben came back.

She put two more books away before he popped up behind her, making her shriek and jump, dropping the stack of books in her hands. They tumbled to the floor with a thud.

"I didn't mean to scare you," he said, then frowned as if mulling that answer over. "Well, okay, I'll be honest. I did mean to scare you, but not that bad." He bent down and scooped the books up. "Here."

She took them. "Thanks. For picking up the books. Not for scaring me." Her heart still drummed in her chest and her hands were suddenly clammy, but she had to admit it was kind of funny. It'd have been funnier if it were someone else though.

"So, what are you doing this Saturday?" He leaned his elbow on a bookshelf, sticking his fingers into his messy hair.

Was she ever doing anything on a Saturday other than laundry and watching TV? Not like she would tell him that. Of course, now that she had her friends back . . . maybe they'd want to hang out.

"Why?" she asked.

He shrugged. "Some of us go to Eagle Park on Saturday mornings to play football. I think you'd have fun."

"Me? Football?" She raised an eyebrow, incredulous. "I don't think so."

"Why? It's not like we'll tackle you. It's just for fun, and other girls come." He paused. "Sometimes."

"I don't know."

"Okay, okay. I have another idea and you have to pick between it and football."

"I *have* to pick?"

"Yes, it's the rule."

"What rule?"

"The Alexia-has-to-pick-between-two-things rule. Jeez, where have you been?"

She laughed. "Okay, what's the other option?"

"Either we play football, or . . . we go to Stixs-N-Yarn and make my brother's dog a sweater."

"Knitting?"

"Yes." He nodded incessantly. "I'm a master knitter. I'm a level three."

"There aren't levels in knitting."

He made a disgusted face. "Seriously? Well, there should be. What's the point if there aren't any levels?"

Mrs. Halloway popped her head in the doorway. "Mr. Daniels," she said in her best authoritative voice, "what are you doing?"

"I'm trying to ask Alexia out on a date, but she's rebuffing my advances."

"Smart girl," Mrs. Halloway said, winking at Alexia. "Just hurry it up then."

Grinning, Alexia said, "Okay, football, I guess. What time?"

"Nine. In the morning. At Eagle Park."

"Got it. I'll meet you there."

"So you can get out fast if the date goes sour. Nice." He made his way to the door. "Later, Alexia," he said over a shoulder.

Hugging a book to her chest, she squeaked out, "Later," and watched him leave. For the rest of the hour, Alexia couldn't think straight. All she could think about was, what if she fell on her butt in front of him while trying to play football?

That would be so embarrassing.

FOURTEEN

Rule 4: *You must forget The Ex's birthday. Forget that he was born.*

Sydney filed into the business and marketing classroom during the lunch hour, as the other student council members headed in with her. She sat down at her designated seat as junior class president.

Drew and I have been broken up for three weeks and it still seems so surreal, she thought. *Has it even hit me yet?*

It was like the Fourth of July fireworks in Eagle Park. You saw the blast of colored sparks first, but felt and heard the boom much later.

The aftershock of the breakup hadn't even touched her yet. It had to be coming soon. All of a sudden, she'd break down, probably in the middle of school if luck was still eluding her. Her dad would lock her up in a mental institution, and when she came back to school, everyone would whisper as she strolled down the halls. Getting into Harvard would be out. Actually, college in general would be out.

She'd graduate from high school—her parents would make her—but afterward, she'd adopt ten cats and move out into the woods into a kitschy cottage on a river somewhere. She'd grow tomatoes in a garden, and lettuce and potatoes. She'd hunt rabbits with a bow.

After the first year, she'd speak only cat and maybe some dog, since a stray would have attached itself to her by then and—

"Sydney?"

Sydney looked up at Will Daniels across the table from her. He was the senior class president. He always started the meetings off.

"Yes?" she said.

"Have you heard anything I just said?" Irritation furrowed his brow. He thought he was so much better than the rest of the student council members. Hell, the rest of the school really, the smug little bastard.

"Will," she said, face impassive, "I try to tune you out sometimes. You do have such a dreadful voice, a little nasal." She pinched her nose to demonstrate. "You know? It hurts my ears sometimes."

That would teach him to talk down to her.

And break up with her best friend!

Honestly, what did Kelly ever see in that guy?

Will sighed as if he expected this kind of immaturity from people beneath him. "I was saying that Mr. Thomas has brought to our attention the severe need for new marching band uniforms. We were thinking of running a fund-raiser. Might you have any suggestions?"

She hated how he talked all prim and proper as if they were in a seventeenth-century movie. Or maybe like he was a vampire. Come to think of it, he did suck the life out of people.

Tapping the end of her pen against her notebook, she ran a few things through her head. There were the usual fund-raisers: car wash, bake sale, dance. The car wash was out; it was too cold. The bake sale was a good idea, but those things never generated enough money. Dances were never well attended.

"How about an open-mike night?" she said. "With a cover charge? It's something different. And it'll give amateur artists good exposure."

A few murmurs swept through the room, people nodded at the idea.

"And a bake sale," she added. "All in one place."

"I like that idea," Lisa the treasurer said. "The cover charge will bring in a good amount and people can come just to have fun. The bake sale will be an added profit."

"Who will bake?" Will asked, doubt clearly in his voice.

"All of us." Sydney waved at the people in the room. "If everyone makes two dozen of something, it should give us enough baked goods. And I know my friends will make something, too, if I ask."

"Where would we have it?" Will asked. "Renting a place out would cost us more money than we'll make."

Sydney hadn't thought about that. She groaned inwardly when she saw the condescending quirk in Will's lips. He always seemed to get some sort of perverse pleasure out of besting her.

"Maybe someone in town would donate their space," Lisa interjected. "It's for the school's benefit, after all."

A satisfied smile spread over Sydney's face. The first smile in so many days. "Yes. I bet Raven's mom would let us use Scrappe. It's the perfect spot."

More murmurs of agreement spread through the room.

Will even looked slightly convinced. "Put it to a vote. All in favor of an open-mike night/bake sale at Scrappe raise your hands and say, 'Aye.' "

Every hand went up around the tables as people voiced their agreement.

"It's decided then," Will said, making note of it in his workbook. "Sydney, for now, you're in charge of securing Scrappe for the event. Can you let me know in a week what's going on?"

"Sure."

"Why don't you shoot for March thirty-first?"

Drew's birthday was March eighteenth.

In all the chaos between them in the last three weeks, she'd forgotten his birthday was coming up. She'd bought his gift weeks ago. A white-gold band with the words, "To the day I die," inscribed on the inside. It wasn't like a wedding band or anything, it was wider than that. The saleswoman at the jewelry store said it signified love and commitment, which she'd never doubted at the time she'd bought it.

Now it was a three-hundred-dollar purchase sitting in her desk at home, unusable. She couldn't take it back, since it was specifically inscribed for her, and the thought of giving it to another guy made her ill. She didn't want another guy. Besides, it was meant for Drew and she'd always know that, even if it was on someone else's finger.

"Sydney," Will said, plainly more annoyed than he had been the first time she'd spaced out. This probably wasn't good for her brain, thinking about Drew so much. And she didn't even want to think about how low her score was on The Breakup Code. Was there even a score?

"I heard you," she muttered. "The thirty-first. Got it."

"Aren't you going to write it down?"

"I won't forget." It'd be the first weekend after Drew's birthday and more than two months since their breakup. Thinking of all that time spent with a broken heart and without Drew made something slip in her chest. Her eyes stung, but she pulled in a calming breath.

Don't think about Drew, she thought. Like that was even possible.

♥ ♥ ♥

That Thursday after school, Sydney checked the messages on her cell phone and heard one from Drew.

"Hey," he'd said, hesitating between the greeting and the rest of the message. "I have a few things of yours at my house. Drop by after school today and you can pick them up."

She deleted the message and debated forgetting about her belongings. She'd spent so much time over at Drew's house, she was sure there'd be at least two boxes worth of stuff. Most likely books and clothes. She always stashed books around his room so she could read if he was busy with something.

But was the stuff important enough to go over there? It was going to be painful stepping into his house, knowing it'd probably be the last time she'd ever be there. It was like her second home now, after two years. How could she say good-bye to it?

Drew's message sounded like he wanted the things gone more than she needed them back. He was clearing his life of her. Her pink T-shirt hanging in the closet probably didn't help the process.

Driving out of the school parking lot, she made a left at the four-way stop instead of a right to go home. Chances were, Drew wasn't even home in the first place. Basketball practice started in thirty minutes, but he was probably going to hang out at school to make things easier when she picked up her belongings.

As she waited at a stoplight, she turned the old AM/FM stereo to the local station. A new pop song blasted through the speakers. "Ugh," she muttered, and flipped the station to classical music.

She grabbed the vanilla lip gloss Kelly had given her from the center console and spread the sparkly goop over her lips. She smacked them together and checked herself in the rear-view mirror. She looked silly. Like she was dressing up as a clown for Halloween.

Lip gloss was Kelly's thing, not Sydney's.

Sydney scrounged for a tissue, finding one in the glove compartment.

A horn blared behind her. The stoplight had already switched to green and she was holding up traffic. She stepped on the gas, hit two more green lights, and turned onto Beech Street.

She saw Drew's truck parked at the curb in front of his house.

Should I drive right past? she wondered.

Heart beating a little faster, she pulled up behind the truck and parked. As much as she wanted to avoid awkwardness or worse—more arguments—she still wanted to see him. Now that they were broken up, she hardly talked to him.

Mrs. Gooding opened the door when Sydney knocked. From the way her face softened, seeing Sydney standing there,

Mrs. Gooding obviously knew they'd broken up. "Oh, Syd," she whispered, pulling Sydney inside and into a hug. "I'm sorry." She ran a hand down Sydney's hair.

"It's all right," Sydney said. She breathed in Mrs. Gooding's perfume, a light, fruity scent. "It's not like it's your fault."

"I know, but—" She smiled. "Well, I guess I just feel bad since he's my son."

"Don't." Sydney pulled away. "I'm okay," she lied. She was actually seas away from okay, but she wasn't going to unload on Drew's mom. That'd be rude.

Mrs. Gooding nodded. "That's good to hear.

"Drew," she called, "Syd's here."

"I'm in my room," he shouted, his tone airy and casual as it would have been any other time she came over. But it wasn't any other time. Things had changed between them. Why was he acting so normal? Hadn't this breakup affected him at all? Didn't he even care?

Sydney took short steps down the carpeted hallway, pretending for a second that things were the same, until she went into his room and the box on the floor reminded her that he was kicking her out as well as breaking up with her.

They'd painted and decorated his room together. She'd picked out the taupe color for the walls. He picked the navy blue bed set. She'd whined until he bought the shadow-box shelves and hung those up. She stuffed them with CDs and a picture of the two of them at a birthday party.

She glanced at the shelves now. The picture was still there. It was just their faces, the birthday party in the background fuzzy. They were both smiling. What would he do with the picture now?

Drew sat up on his bed and set the book he'd been reading aside. His glasses dimmed the blue of his eyes. He smiled uneasily.

"I figured you'd be at practice already," she said, by way of explanation.

"I wanted to be here when you came."

"Why?"

"I don't know." He shrugged and got up. "I thought you deserved that at least, instead of my just sending you off with a box."

Drew always was polite. Sydney realized she probably would have just sent him off with a box. He'd always been the better person of the two of them.

"Thanks," she muttered, bending down to open the box. She dug inside, seeing a few T-shirts and a few books, just as she suspected. She pulled out a holey, torn, long-sleeve shirt and wrapped the material around her hands. "I'd forgotten about this." It used to be her favorite shirt last spring, hence the holes and torn cuffs.

"I was going to throw it away, but I knew you'd be pissed," he said, his tone mirthful.

"You always tried throwing it away before."

"I know, but it's your favorite."

"I appreciate you keeping it."

"No problem." He hesitated for a second, before grabbing his gym bag. "I should get going. I'll walk you out."

She picked up the box. Drew held the front door open for her.

The sun started to peek through the clouds, rays glinting off the few inches of snow. Sydney narrowed her eyes, the light nearly blinding her. Drew took the box out of her hands and slid it in the backseat of her mother's old SUV. She'd probably miss this the most, his need to take care of her, even now when they weren't together.

"So, I guess I'll see you," she said, hesitating. The void between them was growing, and she wanted to fill it with something. She stepped up on the curb and snaked her arms around his neck. A hug was safe, friendly.

Drew returned the hug, and for a second she thought maybe there was a chance they'd get back together. It was hard to even believe they were broken up, as if it were some sort of practical joke he was playing and any minute he'd laugh and say, "Gotchya!" Not that Drew was into playing practical jokes.

When she pulled away, she grabbed the stems of his glasses and slipped them off his face, folding them over the collar of his shirt. She didn't want anything between them right now.

There was something she wanted to say, no, *needed* to say, because the longer she thought about it, the more she thought this breakup had more to do with her than it did him. It was like a death, their whole relationship suddenly flashing before her eyes and, almost always, it seemed the bad parts were something having to do with her temper or stubbornness.

She was kind of a bitch.

"I'm sorry," she began, holding his hand. "I don't think I treated you right or appreciated you the way I should have."

"Syd, it's not just that—" He looked out over the street as if collecting his thoughts. "I need space and I need to have some fun. I haven't had fun lately. And neither have you. You have to admit it."

He was right, actually. She hadn't gone out and done anything fun since, well, last summer. "I know," she said.

His eyebrows shot up in surprise.

How often did she agree with him? Like never.

Letting his hand go, she kicked at the snow with her foot. "I guess that's it." She looked up, meeting his eyes. They say it only takes twenty-one days to develop a habit. She'd been with Drew, kissing him every day for, like, 730 days. That wasn't a habit anymore, it was probably an addiction.

Without thinking about it, Sydney reached up to kiss Drew on the lips. But just before she planted the kiss, he turned away.

"Sorry," she muttered, anger and embarrassment burning her cheeks. She hurried around the front of the SUV and got inside. She drove away, avoiding looking at Drew, still standing there on the sidewalk.

The aftershock had finally reached her, like the boom of the fireworks in Eagle Park.

"Damn it," she cursed. Maybe this was the first step to becoming a hermit cat-lady. God, she hoped not.

If Drew could be happy without her, then she could be happy without him. Like he said, he needed space. He wanted to have fun.

So where should she start? What would Raven do right now?

She'd burn the Drew tombstone. Sydney stepped on the gas and headed home.

FIFTEEN

Rule 7: *You are required to stay up late on a Thursday night eating popcorn as you and your girls laugh over a fifty-page list of The Ex's flaws.*

I hate Valentine's Day, Kelly thought as she parked out front of Sydney's house. The motion light on the garage clicked on, illuminating the driveway. Alexia's silver Cavalier was there, as was Raven's Sentra. Looked like Kelly was the last one to arrive. Better late than never, right?

She grabbed her fifty-page Ex's flaws list from the passenger seat and got out of the car. She zipped her white down vest up around her chin. It wasn't that cold, considering how frigid it'd been in the middle of January, but still, cold was cold to her. And any kind of cold was *bad*.

They'd all decided Valentine's Day was the perfect day to spend inside, hanging out with each other while reading their ex's flaws out loud. It wasn't like Kelly had anywhere else to be.

A twinge of sadness wedged in her chest. She should have been de-virgined by now. She should have been Will's girlfriend and they should have been together right now, eating dinner at Bershetti's.

But instead she'd barely talked to him in the last week, yet it seemed she spent every waking minute thinking about him. Wondering where he was and what he was doing. Who was he hanging out with? And whether or not he wanted Brittany as a girlfriend because she was so much skinnier and prettier than Kelly.

Will hadn't even called her once in the month since they'd broken up.

Sydney pulled the door open before Kelly rang the bell. Syd's hair was up and disheveled, as if she'd bent over, bunched her hair up, and wrapped a rubber band around it. Kelly took in a breath and her shoulders loosened. She hated to think of how much pain Sydney was going through, but Kelly couldn't help but be somewhat happy that she wasn't going through a broken heart alone. It was always better to share pain than bear it alone.

Although it'd been a month since Sydney and Drew officially broke up, Sydney was showing no signs of getting over it. It wasn't just the careless way she wore her hair now, or her neglected clothes. It was the attitude and her lack of focus, as if suddenly she didn't care. Maybe she didn't, but they knew Sydney so well. It was in her nature to care about *everything*.

Now she put a wide smile on her face. "Kelly!" She waved Kelly inside. "Finally, we've been waiting forever."

"Sorry," Kelly muttered, setting her purse on the table near the door. "Monica wouldn't leave me alone, and then my brother hid my car keys." She groaned, the irritation still fresh. Her older brother, Todd, sometimes was more of a pain in the butt than her little sister.

Kelly unbuttoned her vest and hung it on a hook beside the door. She headed into the living room with Sydney and stopped just over the threshold to look around. Black crepe-paper streamers hung around the room. Black cardstock hearts, torn in half, were taped on the walls. Spider confetti was strewn all over the coffee table. Kelly bent down and picked a piece up.

"It was all I could find." Raven shrugged as she fingered a big, silver hoop in her ear. "They should make broken-heart confetti for Valentine's Day. I bet they'd sell more of it than stupid chocolate."

"Chocolate," Kelly breathed. "You got chocolate, didn't you?"

Raven nodded. "It's for later though. After the popcorn."

Alexia turned sideways on the couch and straightened her plain green J. Crew T-shirt. "Did you bring your list?"

Kelly held up her pathetic page and nodded remorsefully. "I tried super hard." Which was totally true. She'd spent the last hour trying to think of something negative about Will, but he was just too darn perfect. Maybe that was one of his flaws.

"It's okay," Sydney said, coming up behind her. "I didn't get fifty pages either."

"I did!" Raven gloated, fanning her list in the air.

"She cheated though." Alexia narrowed her eyes at Raven. Raven stuck out her tongue. "She only put one thing on each page."

"No one ever said there were rules for the rules," Raven countered, tossing a piece of popcorn in her mouth.

"Where are your mom and dad?" Kelly asked Sydney, ignoring the argument starting in the living room.

For the first time in a few days, Kelly saw raw emotion pass across Sydney's face, but she was quick to recover her stony expression. "Dad's upstairs reading. Mom's staying overnight in Hartford."

Kelly didn't miss the air of disappointment in Sydney's voice when she talked about her mom being gone. From what she'd gathered over the last few months, Syd's mom was staying in Hartford more and more. She even had her own apartment there now and stayed a lot through the workweek.

Kelly felt sorry for her friend. She didn't know what she'd do if her mom started spending more time away from home. Mrs. Waters was like Kelly's best friend. Kelly could tell her mom practically everything.

"Should we get started?" Sydney said quickly.

Kelly sat next to Alexia. Sydney lay down on her stomach on the floor.

"Let me go first," Raven said, bringing her list in front of her. "Caleb's Flaws. Number fifty: He doesn't go over his tongue while brushing his teeth."

All the girls wrinkled their noses in disgust.

"And you used to kiss him?" Sydney asked. She bent her legs at the knees, her feet swinging back and forth. The TV behind her played a commercial for diamond jewelry. "Get your Valentine something special this holiday," a delicate female voice said over the display of glitzy diamond earrings.

Kelly waved her list around. "I only managed to get thirty-eight flaws. So, this is thirty-eight. Will doesn't eat candy."

Alexia groaned. "He is such a freak."

"How can you *not* eat candy?" Sydney asked, shaking her head in disbelief.

"Now you, Syd," Raven said.

Sydney picked at something on the floor. "Well . . . "

"Don't tell me you didn't do a list," Alexia said.

"I have a mental one." Sydney sat up, crossing her legs in front of her. "Drew always has to have a plan." She visibly swallowed, then nodded, as if satisfied with that flaw.

Raven popped a few more pieces of popcorn in her mouth. Kelly took a handful out of the pink plastic bowl and started picking at the buttery pieces. When was Raven going to bust out that chocolate?!

"All right, good enough," Raven said. "Number forty-nine for Caleb is he never puts things back where he found them."

"Drew does the same thing!" Sydney laughed. "I was constantly searching for my stuff."

"Well, that's Drew's next flaw then," Alexia said.

"Yeah." Sydney nodded thoughtfully. "I guess it is."

They continued like that for the next hour. Raven undoubtedly had the most flaws to share since her list was the longest. Kelly ran out of steam about halfway through and Sydney had a hard time listing Drew's flaws fifteen minutes after they started.

After hearing about Caleb's nasty BO and his tendency to jerk like crazy when he was falling asleep, Kelly had to wonder how Raven ever put up with him. And when Kelly asked her, Raven thought for a minute and said, "You know what, I'm not really sure."

Listing Will's flaws and laughing about them with her friends made Kelly ten times more aware of how perfect Will tried to be. Did he seriously not like candy? Or did he not eat it in front of anyone so people thought he was healthy? Did he seriously like spending ninety percent of his time doing things that would look good for colleges?

Kelly just couldn't imagine spending the rest of her life with someone who strived for such high extremes of perfection. Also, Will's habit of hoarding those little moist towelettes you get at restaurants drove her nuts.

When Kelly listed that flaw, her friends guffawed.

"He is the biggest dork," Sydney said.

And Raven said, "Does he carry them in his pockets? And get all germaphobe about touching carts and door handles?"

When Kelly thought about it, she realized, yeah, he did carry them around and sometimes wiped the handles on shopping carts, complaining about grease or something sticky.

How did she ever fall for him? It was a mystery.

With the lists finished, they all headed into the kitchen, where Raven finally broke out the chocolate. It was the expensive kind, too. The ones where you had to follow a little illustrated map on the underside of the box lid just to figure out what chocolate was what. It was a game of treasure hunting, except the reward was chocolate!

Raven hoisted herself up on the laminated countertop, her long legs hanging over the edge. Sydney threw another bag of popcorn into the microwave and punched in a few numbers.

"Get off the counter," she said, giving Raven a push. Raven rolled her eyes but slid down. Those two were always picking at each other. It drove Kelly nuts. But honestly, sometimes Sydney could be a brat.

"Thank you," Sydney said, then, "Oh, there was something I needed to talk to you about. We talked about band uniforms at the last student council meeting."

"Yeah?" Raven leaned against the counter and picked at a torn fingernail polished gothic purple.

Kelly leaned against the counter next to her and perused the chocolate box lid. Dark chocolate. Caramel-filled chocolate. Coconut chocolate. Oh, where to start?

Alexia picked a random piece out of the box and headed over to the fridge where she started alphabetizing the restaurant magnets.

"We were trying to decide on fund-raisers and I came up with an open-mike night," Sydney said. The microwave echoed with the sound of exploding corn. The smell of melted butter filled the air.

"That sounds like fun," Kelly said before biting into a piece of chocolate filled with raspberry-flavored crème. Would Will go to an open-mike night or would he deem it too frivolous? Probably if they were still sorta-together, he would have talked her out of going when really she would have wanted to go.

"There's just one thing." Sydney grinned sheepishly. "We need a place to host it, and we need it for free. You think your mom would let us do it at Scrappe?"

Raven stopped picking at her nail to look up. Her long, black lashes nearly grazed her eyebrows. "Maybe. Sounds like the kind of thing she'd say would look good on my college application."

"Well, it would. Tell her that." Sydney took out the bag of popcorn and shook it. "Let me know what she says? We're thinking about March thirty-first."

"Got it." Raven grabbed a second box of chocolates. Sydney wrapped her arm around the bowl of fresh popcorn and they all filed back into the living room.

Raven popped in her sister Jordan's *Gilmore Girls* DVD. It was the season when Jess (as in Milo Ventimiglia) was a major character in the plot.

There was just something so yummy about a slightly short bad boy. Maybe Kelly should get her own bad boy? He would be the exact opposite of Will, if she ever found one. Probably that's what she needed eventually but not now. The Code was starting to work, she thought, and dating another guy right now was definitely *not* in the rules.

Around midnight, Kelly's cell rang in her purse. It was her brother.

"What?" she said by way of greeting.

"Dude, where are you?" Todd asked.

"I'm at Sydney's. I told Mom that when I left. Why?"

"Oh," he said. "You haven't gone over there in forever."

"So? What do you want?"

"Will just called here looking for you."

Kelly's heart suddenly hammered in her ears. Will had called for her? Did he miss her? Did he finally want her as a girlfriend?

"Did he *just* call?" Will was usually in bed by ten. He only stayed up late if he was working on a major project.

"Okay, okay." Todd groaned. "He called about two hours ago, but I just remembered."

"Thanks a lot, Todd!"

"Hey, I'm not your answering service."

Anger blazed in her cheeks, but then she realized all of her friends were staring at her.

"Did Will call or something?" Sydney asked.

Kelly opened her mouth to make up an excuse, but she didn't want to lie to her friends. And she didn't want to start defending Will when they'd just had the liberating experience of reading The Ex's flaws.

"Yeah," she said. She took in a breath for courage. "But I'm not going to call him back."

"Good for you!" Alexia squeezed Kelly's shoulder. "See, The Code is working."

"Hey! Hello!" Todd said.

Kelly turned her attention back to her brother. "Sorry. Anyway, I gotta go, Todd."

"Wait. One more thing. Mom wants you home."

"It's getting late, Kelly," Mrs. Waters said in the background.

"Did you hear that?" Todd said.

Kelly rolled her eyes. "Yes. I heard her."

"See you soon!"

The phone went dead. She flipped it closed. "I gotta go," she said.

Sydney paused the DVD.

"Yeah. I'll see you guys tomorrow."

"You won't call Will back, will you?" Raven asked, raising her perfectly arched eyebrows.

"No. He called hours ago anyway. He's probably in bed by now."

"If you feel like you need to call him," Alexia said, "call me instead, okay?"

Kelly smiled. "Sure."

"Bye," Sydney and Raven said in unison.

"See ya." Kelly shut the door behind her.

"You know what?" Kelly said, as she put her coat away at home. "I really don't like you right now."

Maybe it was meant to be that Todd had forgotten Will called. With it being so late, there was no way Kelly could call over there, even if she'd been tempted to.

Todd grinned. "That's fine, as long as you like me tomorrow."

"Tomorrow is debatable. Depending on what you do then to ruin my life." She stomped down the hall to her room, thankful that at least her parents had enough sense to buy a place big enough to house their three children. Kelly envied Sydney's quiet house. It would be soooo nice to be an only child.

Though she shut her door behind her, Kelly's brother ignored the privacy sign and barged in.

"You forget how to knock?" she said, slipping out of her boots.

Flopping back on her bed, messing her comforter, he said, "Why are you in such a bad mood?"

"How many other phone calls have you forgotten to tell me about?"

"None! Jeez! Well . . ." He looked at the ceiling as if trying to remember. "I guess I have forgotten a few of Jerkwad's calls."

Jerkwad was Todd's nickname for Will. "He has a name, you know." Kelly pulled a pair of shorts out of her dresser, then a tank top.

"Yeah, I know. Jerkwad."

Did Todd know they'd broken up? He'd been pestering her to drop Will since she started hanging out with him, even going so far as to threaten Will behind her back. Of course, Will just rolled his eyes and said, "Your brother is an imbecile," when Kelly asked him about it. Which Todd was, but still, he was her brother. If Will was insulting her brother, was he insulting her?

"I'm not seeing Will anymore," Kelly muttered, slipping several silver bangles off her wrist.

Todd sat up on the bed. "Seriously?"

She sighed, finally turning to him. "Yeah."

"You . . . okay?" He furrowed his brow, clearly uncomfortable with the emotional stuff.

Was she okay? It'd already been a month since they'd sorta broken up. Some days the answer was yes, others, not so much. "I guess," she answered, pulling the rubber band out of her hair (she'd heard rubber bands damaged hair when you slept on them and Kelly needed all the hair help she could get). She slipped on a stretchy black headband to keep the hair off her face so that it wouldn't leave grease behind on her skin and make her break out.

Todd stood. "Do you want me to kick his ass?" Hands clenched into fists, he threw a few punches in the air. " 'Cause I would get so much pleasure out of breaking his nose."

She groaned. "No, I don't want you to punch him, Todd. God."

He let his hands fall. "Why not?"

"Oh, I don't know, maybe because fighting is dumb, and it wasn't like Will deliberately hurt my feelings."

"But he did hurt your feelings?"

She ignored that question, instead pushing Todd out into the hallway so she could change and get into bed.

"Who broke up with who?"

"Todd," she moaned. "Go away."

"So he broke up with you?"

With him in the hallway now, she put herself squarely in the door frame and crossed her arms over her chest. "Technically we weren't even together. We were just friends dating . . . or something. Now, good night."

She reached to shut the door, but Todd stopped her. "Seriously, sis, you're okay though?"

"I'm okay," she lied, looking him straight in the eye. She was good at lying to him. He was a guy, after all, and wasn't very in tune with emotions. He was good on the basketball court and picking on her and Monica, but that was about it.

"'Cause if you need me to kick his ass," he went on, "just say the word."

"You will not be kicking anyone's behind, Todd," their mom said, coming up the hallway. "And what have I told you about swearing in my house?"

"Sorry," he said automatically, not at all concerned with the reprimand. Their mother never punished him. Todd could get away with just about anything, something Kelly was still trying to figure out. Maybe it was his ability to pretend sincerity and remorse. Okay, so maybe he was good at *three* things.

"'Night," Mrs. Waters said, kissing Kelly, then Todd on the forehead. She went into her room, their father's snores carrying out into the hallway until their mother clicked the door shut behind her.

"Just say the word!" Todd whispered before he turned into his room.

Kelly rolled her eyes and went to bed.

SIXTEEN

Rule 12: *You must never date a friend of The Ex.*

Raven felt like she was going through DTs. How did anyone survive without a boyfriend? It wasn't even really the absence of a boyfriend so much as it was the absence of someone to hang out with. There didn't even need to be kissing or any of that. Raven just liked having someone to open doors for her. And someone to tell her how beautiful she was. And someone to hold her hand.

Would it technically be breaking the rules if she "hung out" with another boy and flirted? A boy who would open doors for her and tell her how beautiful she looked? It wasn't like she was really going to hook up with him. Or accommodate him, as Rule 8 specifically said to avoid.

Besides, if Friday nights weren't for hanging out, then what were they for? Certainly not Scrabble or homework. Or worse yet, hanging out with your mother.

There was one other option, and before Raven broke down and called a guy, she decided to check it out. She went across the hall and knocked on Jordan's door.

"Come in," Jordan called from the other side.

When Raven went in, Jordan said hi to her from her vanity mirror as she swooped her dark hair back into a jeweled barrette. There was a hint of blush on her cheeks. A swoop of mascara on her lashes. She looked like she had somewhere to go in her khaki cargo pants and oversize brown sweater.

"What's up?" she said.

Raven shrugged and sat down on the edge of Jordan's perfectly made bed. It was supposed to be one of their daily chores, but Raven never really got the habit down. Across the hall, her deep purple comforter was partially hanging on the floor.

"I'm bored," she said, hoping her little sister would catch the hint, which was: *Entertain me!*

Jordan ran a fine-tooth comb through her hair, smoothing out the bumps. Her olive skin looked perfect even sans foundation. Jordan had gotten more of their mother than their father. She looked almost one hundred percent Italian. Raven was about eighty percent her father, which made her extremely exotic-looking. Without knowing her parents, people had a hard time figuring out her heritage.

"What about your friends?" Jordan asked.

Sighing, Raven picked at a loose string on the pink bed comforter. "Sydney is studying and going to bed early because she's doing the SATs tomorrow. Alexia is having dinner with her parents, and Kelly has to babysit her little sister."

"Bummer," Jordan said absently, more involved with her hair than her sister's problems. When her hair was perfect, completely bump-free, with a few wispy strands hanging around her oval face, she sat down next to Raven. "I'd do something with you, but me and Cindy are meeting up with a bunch of people at the movie theater."

Raven grabbed the pink throw pillow with purple and green polka dots from the head of Jordan's bed. She ran her hand up and down the velvet material, watching the sway of the fabric change. "What movie is it?"

"*Underground.*"

"Oh, I want to see that one. Can I come with?"

Jordan cocked a tweezed eyebrow. "No way. You'll hit on all my friends."

Raven gave her sister a playful shove. "I would not. Besides, your friends are fourteen. Too young for me."

"You're not coming. Sorry."

Raven scrunched up her face in desperation. "Please!" If left to her own devices tonight, she wasn't sure what would happen. She was over Caleb, but the desire to hang out with someone of the opposite sex might become stronger than sheer will.

Grabbing her bag, Jordan shook her head. "We'll do something tomorrow."

"You used to love hanging out with me."

"Yeah, that was before I had a life."

"Come on, Jordan, I'm cool!"

"Not cool enough to have a life!"

Raven growled and headed back into her own room. Soon after, a car beeped out front and Jordan called out, "I'm leaving," through the house.

Since when did Jordan have more of a life than Raven?

Obviously, since now, but Raven was not going to let her little sister have more fun than her. She grabbed her cell phone and flipped through the phone book. Some of the names she'd forgotten were even in there. When she reached ZAC she stopped and tried to remember the last time she'd talked to him. He was a friend of Caleb's. She'd probably talked to him a few parties ago.

She called his number and waited.

"Yeah?"

"Hey! Zac! It's Raven."

"Raven? What's up?" Pots and pans banged in the background. A deep male voice barked out an order to "shut off the bacon."

"You busy tonight?" she asked.

"I'm working right now, but I get off at nine. Why, is there a party or something?"

"No." Raven sat down in her computer chair and propped one foot up on the edge of the cushioned seat. "I'm just bored and looking for someone to hang out with."

"Cool. Meet me here around nine? I'll call Kenny and we'll all do something."

"No," she said too quickly. "No Kenny. Just you and me. We can go to the movies or something."

"Seriously?"

She could almost hear his eyebrows rise.

"Yes, seriously. I like hanging out with you."

"Oh." He sounded surprised.

"So what do you say? You up to it?" she asked.

"Totally. I'll meet you here?"

"Sure. I'll see you at nine."

Hanging up the phone, she smiled another pleased smile. Zac was a cool guy. She'd always thought he was the cutest one of Caleb's friends. Maybe they'd have fun tonight. It'd been so long since she'd hung out with a guy, she was really looking forward to it.

Well, okay, it'd only been a month since Caleb broke up with her, but that was like nine months in dog years. Or would it be ten? She was never very good with numbers.

♥ ♥ ♥

Closet light blazing, Raven flipped through her clothes. She had a few special outfits for nights like tonight, i.e., Boy Nights. There were her hot jeans that she thought hugged her butt perfectly and looked awesome with her black stretchy Soweto shirt.

Deciding on that outfit, she pulled the two items from the closet and got dressed. The weather had been mild today, but temps were still only low forties. Which jacket would look good with the outfit?

Back in the closet, she searched for the military-style jacket she'd bought at Two-One, a vintage store downtown. The jacket had dull gold snaps and a high collar. The faded army green would go perfectly with the black long-sleeved shirt.

She laid the jacket out on the bed and went down the hall to the bathroom she and Jordan shared. Looking in the mirror, she tried to decide what to do with her hair. Wanting it down but messy, she grabbed the tub of expensive hair product she'd bought online at Sephora and ran some of it through her hair. She bent over and scrunched the tresses, then flipped her head back. Now she had a messy, wavy look going.

Perfect.

With one swoop of mascara and a little bit of dark brown eyeliner, she was ready to go. Back in her room, she slipped into the jacket, sliding her cell phone in the pocket.

"Mom, I'm going out!" she called from the hallway.

"Where?" Ms. Valenti called from her workroom. She was probably piecing together another intricate scrapbook design for a class at Scrappe.

"The movies."

"Which movie?"

Raven ducked her head in the workroom. Her mother was hunched over a long white table, paper and glue guns and markers spread out in disarray.

What was a safe answer? Anything rated R was out. Romance or family movies were usually on her mother's OK list.

"Uh . . . *Summer Camp.*" Lots of PG action in that movie. Instead, she and Zac would probably skip the movie altogether, or see *Underground*, the one Jordan was going to.

"Okay," Ms. Valenti said, whipping out a black marker. She turned in her seat. "Be home by midnight, okay?"

"I will." Raven said good-bye and left.

♥ ♥ ♥

"Hey, Ray," Zac said, running a hand through his unruly blond hair. Zac was a good-looking guy. He had a model's face: strong jawline, prominent nose bridge, and deep green eyes. Raven had always been attracted to him.

Gorsh, the small restaurant where he worked, was packed. Conversation hung in the air, mixing with the crisp sound of fifties jazz playing from the jukebox.

Zac wove his arm around Raven's shoulders and gave her a friendly hug. He smelled like French fries and cologne. Suddenly, her stomach was growling.

"So what do you want to do?" he asked.

Shrugging, she ran the options through her head. "Well, I'm kind of hungry."

"You want to sit? We can get something to eat."

"Really? I figured you'd want to leave as soon as possible, since you work here."

He waved the argument away. "I love this place. Besides, the food would be free." He led her to a booth. "Sit. Can I get you anything to drink?"

"Coke?"

"Coming right up."

She slipped out of her jacket and tucked her hands in her lap. The restaurant had an inviting temperature, but her hands were still cold. She rubbed them together and heat spread through her fingers.

Zac came back with two Cokes and a menu. "Here you go."

"What about you?"

"I don't need a menu. I have it memorized." He smiled, ripping the wrapper off his straw.

Flipping the menu open, she scanned the food. Burgers, French fries, spaghetti. She'd never eaten at Gorsh. "What do you recommend?"

"The chicken wrap. Melted cheese, lettuce, bacon. It's amazing."

"I'll have that, with French fries."

"Good choice. I'll go put our order in the kitchen."

As he wove through the tables toward the swinging kitchen door, Raven watched him. His jeans—a pair of baggy Abercrombie's—barely hugged his butt. And his shoulders looked broad in his vintage sporty T-shirt.

She started thinking about him in boyfriend terms. Would he open doors for her? Would he buy her gifts? Would he respect her? Would he try to push her into having sex? He didn't seem like that kind of guy and all the relationships in his past—there were only two if Raven remembered right—had been serious, long-term relationships.

It felt good to be out with a guy, even if it was just a friendly dinner. There was something about hanging with a guy that was satisfying. Girlfriends couldn't elicit butterflies with simple conversation or a smile. And butterflies to Raven were like an adrenaline rush to a risk taker. Raven just couldn't get enough of that feeling.

Zac came out of the kitchen and she smiled at him again. His mouth quirked into a grin, too, but it abruptly slipped away when he looked toward the front door. Raven followed his gaze.

Caleb.

Damn.

Caleb walked over to Zac and they did that guy handshake of theirs. Caleb said something about a party and Zac shook his head.

Raven heard Caleb say, "Why? You got something better to do?"

And Zac said, "Yeah," and gave an awkward nod toward Raven in the booth along the wall.

Raven wished she could disappear into the booth. Suddenly, hanging out with Zac didn't seem so innocent. Caleb didn't rule her life and she wasn't going to do anything with Zac, but one of Alexia's stupid rules ran through Raven's head.

Do not date an Ex's friend.

Raven was so busted.

Caleb looked over and anger, then maybe jealousy, flashed across his face. His jaw clenched. "Are you serious, man?" Raven heard that clearly because Caleb raised his voice an octave and a few people turned to look at him.

The memory of their breakup flashed in her mind. Déjà vu. He was freaking out in a public setting because of his temper and more importantly, because of her.

Double damn.

Raven grabbed her jacket and slid out of the booth, the red vinyl making that obnoxious smudging noise. She stalked up to Caleb. "We were just hanging out," she explained. Not that she owed him that much. She didn't owe him anything actually.

"Yeah, but with my friend?" he challenged.

"Shhh." She scowled. "You don't have to tell the whole restaurant our business."

"What, that you're a serial dater?"

Zac stepped up. "We were just hanging out, like she said. We're allowed to be friends, aren't we?"

Caleb shook his head, jaw tensing more. "Whatever." He swiveled on his feet and left.

A breath of relief whizzed past Raven's dry lips. Tonight had not gone as planned. Whatever happened to just having fun? Guys were so complicated.

"I'm gonna go." She put her coat on. "Thanks for what was supposed to be a fun night, Zac. We'll hang out some other night."

"We can still hang out tonight," he said, sounding hurt that she'd leave so soon.

"I know, but I just don't feel like it now."

She should have figured this was a mistake as soon as she considered going out with a guy. That's what The Breakup Code was for: Follow the rules, avoid mistakes.

On tiptoes, she planted a kiss on Zac's warm cheek. "Call me sometime," she said and left.

In the car, she cranked the music up as she headed home. Early. Lame.

If there was anything good about tonight, it was that Caleb saw her out with Zac, instead of Horace. That probably would have been ten times worse, and Raven wasn't sure she could stand to hear Caleb harass Horace again. If he did, *she* might just punch *him* in the face.

SEVENTEEN

Rule 9: *Don't allow The Ex to talk to you for longer than two minutes during the initial three-month cooling-off period. You must not be his friend.*

Usually, Kelly slept in on weekends. There was nothing like waking up, looking over at the alarm clock to see a bright red 8:00 A.M. on the screen, then snuggling back beneath the blanket when she remembered it was Saturday: the warm blanket covering every inch of skin; the pillow welcoming her back down; closing her eyes.

It was like chocolate-chip cookie-dough ice cream that was calorie-free. Perfect. Blissful.

Until someone dove on top of the bed and started jumping and yelling.

"Wake up! You going to sleep all day?"

"Quit!" she muttered. "Mom!"

"You're wasting the day," Todd said.

Another voice laughed; someone who was not her brother. She pulled the covers back, coherence creeping in now. Drew sat in her computer chair, twirling in a half circle.

This wasn't the first time she woke up to find Drew in her house, though usually not in her room.

"What do you want?" she said, her voice hoarse with sleep.

"We don't want you to waste your life sleeping," Todd said, pinching her cheek.

She swatted at his hand but she was too slow and too tired. "I'd rather sleep."

"We'll make you breakfast," Todd sang.

Thinking about it, she rubbed the haze from her eyes. "What will you make?"

Todd glanced over at Drew. "What are you going to make?"

"Me?" Drew raised a brow. "Like I can cook."

"Seriously, why do you care if I sleep?"

Drew stopped twirling in the computer chair. "He wants you to play football with us today."

Now it was her turn to raise her brow. "Football?"

"We're short a player," Todd said.

"Todd, I don't even know how to play football!"

"Well," Drew said, "neither does Todd. So no big deal."

Todd threw something at Drew, which Drew caught. Kelly's face went fire hot when she realized what it was. Her Victoria's Secret bra! She jumped out of bed and snatched it from Drew's hands, his face blank as he stared at it. She shoved it in the hamper, out of sight.

"Good, you're up," Todd said. "Let's make breakfast and hit the field!" He wove his arm around her shoulders and shoved her out the bedroom door.

"I hate you," she muttered under her breath.

Todd put her in a headlock and ran his knuckles through her hair. "Well, I love you!"

"Mom!"

Their mother poked her head out down the hall. "Todd, let your sister go."

Todd laughed, lightening his grip. "Fine."

They headed into the kitchen. Their dad was there finishing up a cup of coffee. He set the empty cup in the sink and turned to them. "Todd, what did I tell you about annoying your sisters?

Todd rolled his eyes. "Yeah, I get it."

Mr. Waters gave Kelly a kiss on the forehead.

"Thanks, Dad," she whispered. He winked and disappeared into the living room.

Kelly sat at the table in the corner of the kitchen. "Now, what are you making me?"

Todd opened various cupboards, then the refrigerator. "If I make you breakfast, you'll play football?"

She groaned. "Do I have to do anything?" She did need the exercise. Last night when she put her jeans on, she'd had an awful time trying to get them buttoned *and* zipped. Since the breakup, she'd been eating more than she probably should have.

"Just look tough," he said.

"Fine." She sighed. "Cheese omelet."

"Drew, grab a bowl and a spoon," Todd instructed as he disappeared into the pantry.

Drew went to the cupboard and pulled a red plastic bowl out, then slid the silverware drawer open. He sat down across from Kelly at the table. "I don't know what he's doing," he said apologetically, then slid the bowl in front of her.

Todd came out with a box of Cookie Crisps in his hand. He grabbed the milk on the way to the table. He filled her bowl with cereal, then drowned it in milk. He gestured to it with a flourish of his hand. "Your cheese omelet, milady."

"This? This is my cheese omelet?"

"As close as I can get." He gave her a rough pat on the back. "Eat up. We have armies to conquer. I'm going to suit up." He left the kitchen.

Kelly took a bite of Cookie Crisp thinking probably the cereal had less calories than the omelet, anyway, so she shouldn't complain. "How can you voluntarily spend time with him?" she said to Drew.

He shrugged. "He's a moron, so I look cool standing next to him."

Kelly laughed, forgetting her mouth full of food. She covered it quickly with her hand. After swallowing she said, "That's a good one."

He smiled, clearly flattered and maybe a little surprised with his quick wit. "Well, thanks."

For a minute there, she'd almost forgotten he'd broken Sydney's heart. Was it wrong to talk to him? Did that make her a traitor? Yeah, but how could she *not* talk to him? He was over all the time.

Still, she couldn't help but feel a little pinch of guilt sitting here with him right now when Sydney was probably crying at home by herself. As strong as her happy front was, they all knew she was hurting more than she was showing.

Was Drew hurting, too?

Kelly watched him inconspicuously. His neon blue eyes were staring out the window at the backyard. He propped his chin in his hand. He looked tired.

"Ready?" Todd walked in, zipped up his fleece, and then rubbed his hands together anxiously. "You're not done with your omelet yet?"

She scowled. "Very funny."

♥ ♥ ♥

Alexia was not a football player. She did not do sports, period, but here she was, on a football field at nine on a Saturday morning. Just what was she thinking when she agreed to come to this thing?

Answer: She hadn't been thinking.

No, Ben Daniels had the ability to stop her synapses from firing, which was why she was standing on a football field in the freezing cold. Well, five degrees above freezing, if you wanted to be technical.

As soon as she noticed Will Daniels's black BMW pull into the park, her brain did that funny stop-start thing again and the cold air was forgotten. She could see Ben sitting in the passenger seat through the windshield.

They parked right next to Drew's truck as Kelly and Drew and Todd piled out.

Alexia ran up to the fence and waited for Ben as he walked over, his breath puffing out in front of him. He was actually wearing a coat for once, a pair of black track pants, and a worn gray sweatshirt. There were holes in the kangaroo pocket, tears in the cuffs. His hair stuck out at odd angles as if he'd just rolled out of bed and didn't bother with a comb.

"Hey," he said, unlatching the gate on the fence. "You came."

She smiled. "You sound surprised."

"I am." He paused, glancing to the right. "Hey, give me a second? I have to go tell Tanner how dumb he looks in blue."

Brett Tanner strolled up the field with a few other guys.

"All right. I'll wait here."

"Cool. Just two seconds." He walked off.

Feeling self-conscious standing by herself on a football field, Alexia went through the still-open gate hoping to catch Kelly. Was she going to play today? Alexia hoped so, since, by the looks of it, she was the only other girl there.

Following the sidewalk, Alexia headed down to the parking lot and noticed Kelly talking to Will. Kelly frowned, then shook her head. She crossed her arms over her chest. Even from this distance, Alexia could see Kelly's lower lip shivering from the chill air.

Thankfully, the snow had melted yesterday; the ground was still a bit damp from it. Probably it'd snow again soon, but at least the worst of the winter seemed to be over. March was right around the corner, and Alexia always thought of it as the signal spring was soon to follow.

Before reaching the cars, Alexia glanced at her watch. Kelly had to have been talking to Will for more than two minutes. She walked over. "Will, you wouldn't mind if I stole Kelly, would you?"

Will shook his head. "I'll call you later," he said to Kelly. Kelly didn't say anything. When Will drove off, Alexia turned to her friend. "You just broke rule nine."

Kelly looked apologetic. "It's hard to get away from him when he starts talking."

"Well, you have to try harder, otherwise The Code won't work. What did he want anyway?"

"To ask me if I've seen his pen."

Alexia suppressed a laugh. "A . . . pen?"

"Yes." Kelly rolled her eyes. "I know. It's so lame. But it's his favorite pen and I guess it was expensive. He hasn't seen it in a few weeks and thought maybe he'd left it at my house or something."

"You broke a rule to talk to The Ex because of a pen?"

"Well, technically I've already broken that rule, since I had to talk to him at the shelter, but . . . "

"Kelly!"

She shrugged. "What?"

Alexia sighed. "You should be docked like a bazillion points for that."

"I didn't know we were keeping points!"

"Well, if we were, you'd be in last place."

They both burst out laughing.

"I never was good at competitions," Kelly mused. "So are we both playing football?"

Alexia sighed. "I guess."

"I don't get geometry," Kelly said.

Alexia nodded at all the right intervals. She was trying to focus on what Kelly was saying, but it was hard to listen to her and watch Ben at the same time. He was a class clown in school, but here, on the football field, he was all business and it was kind of attractive, the way he commanded the game and poked fun at the other team when they fumbled.

Someone threw the ball to him. He scooped it out of the air effortlessly and started running toward her. Was she supposed to be doing something? Defending the goal? The rules were still kind of fuzzy. She put her hands up, since that seemed like a logical thing to do.

And then . . .

Wham!

Something barreled into her and she went down, her foot catching in a depression in the ground. Pain started in her ankle and shot up her leg. She winced, rolling over, trying to bite her lip so she didn't scream and cry like a little baby. The first five seconds were the most brutal, but the longer she bit her lip, the more the pain in her ankle subsided until it was a dull, throbbing ache. Her whole back was sopping and muddy from the wet grass. She sat up.

"Alexia!" Kelly shouted.

Feet pounded on the ground as everyone ran over to her.

"I'm okay," she managed to squeak out. At least she was hoping she was okay.

"Can you get up?" Ben asked.

She nodded, tears stinging her eyes. He wrapped his arm around her waist and hoisted her up. She put weight on that foot and the pressure produced a soft throb in her ankle, but she was otherwise okay.

"Tanner," Ben said, "what in the hell were you doing?"

Brett Tanner stood off to the side, hands on his hips. "I didn't see her," he said. "Sorry."

He must have been the one who slammed into Alexia. She nodded. "It's okay."

"I'll take you to the hospital," Ben said. "Where are your keys?"

"No." Alexia shook her head. "I'm fine. Look, I can move it." She wiggled her foot. "It's not broken or anything. Probably just some ice would make it feel better."

Ben pursed his lips and seemed to think this over, then, "All right. I'll drive you home."

She pulled her car keys out of her pocket and handed them over. He wove an arm around her waist and let her lean into him. He smelled like cool winter air and some sort of musky sweet cologne.

"Do you need me for anything?" Kelly said, following them as Alexia hobbled off the field with Ben's help.

"No. I'll be okay."

"Call me later then, when you feel up to it."

Ben led Alexia to her car. He held the passenger door for her and helped her settle into the seat. He went around to the driver's side and started the car up.

"I'm going to hang out for a while to make sure you're okay. Looks like you're stuck with me for the next couple of hours," he said, grinning.

Alexia felt herself smile despite the stiffness of her ankle. Being stuck with him didn't sound all that bad.

♥ ♥ ♥

"Better?" Ben said.

Alexia leaned back into the pillow he'd just fluffed for her. "That's fine." The Advil he'd given her as soon as they got to her house had kicked in. She felt fine unless she moved her ankle. It'd probably be sore for a few days, but thank God it wasn't broken.

Ben searched around her living room for all the remotes. He grabbed the surround sound, the TV, the digital cable, and the stereo remotes and put them all on the coffee table within arm's reach.

"Anything to drink? Or eat?"

"Water?" she said, feeling a little guilty that he was waiting on her.

"Water. Got it."

He was gone for a good ten minutes. When he came back, he had a bowl of fruit and a glass of ice-filled water, the cubes clinking against the cup's edge. "Fruit is good for you. Especially when you're in need of healing."

She laughed. "Can't I just take a vitamin?"

"Not the same thing. Vitamins don't have the natural antioxidants that fresh fruit does."

"Oh." She sipped from the water as she eyed the grapes. She wasn't much for fruit, but if Ben said it was good for her, probably it was. He was like a walking book of facts. She popped a grape in her mouth. They were fresh, crisp. "Thanks."

"No problem. So when are your parents coming home?"

"They said they'd be back by nine." They'd left for the day to visit her brother in Hartford.

"I'll stay until they get back."

"No. You don't have to do that."

"It's not like I have anywhere else to be." He settled into the chair that was angled off the end of the couch. "And what if you run out of fruit or something? Are you going to make more appear with your brain waves?"

She laughed, feeling the giggles of exhaustion creeping in. She just needed to sleep. "Well, thanks for staying."

"You're welcome."

Propping herself up with an elbow, she took a long drink of water. Her throat was dry from playing outside. As she pulled the glass away, she spilled, water dribbling down the front of her.

"Crap." What was her problem today? Was she losing all of her fine motor skills?

"I got it." Ben jumped up and ran to the kitchen. He came back with several hand towels. He crouched by the side of the couch and wiped the water up.

"Thanks." She lay her head back down, and she realized that she was now only inches from Ben's face.

"Alexia?" he said, his voice going soft, his fruity breath fanning across her face. His unruly brown hair had been matted down since earlier that morning and several strands hung in his line of sight.

"Yeah?" she said.

"Can I kiss you?"

Now she was too hot. And parched again. "Are you serious?"

"Yes."

"I . . . uh . . . " Words were suddenly failing her. His breath smelled like grapes, but what if hers smelled like feet? She'd always imagined her first kiss with a boy would be somewhat planned out so she'd have time to brush her teeth or pop in a mint. Ben was ruining the plan! She almost asked him to wait a while, at least five minutes so she could hobble to the bathroom to scrub her teeth (twice, maybe even three times).

And what if she did it wrong? The kissing. Not the teeth brushing. What if she used her tongue when he just wanted to smooch? How were you supposed to know these things?

"I'll count to five," he said, sitting on his knees. "So it's not so awkward."

Was this protocol? To talk about a kiss before it happened? She had no idea because she had never been kissed!

"One . . ."

She got that weak feeling in her stomach.

"Two . . ."

And then he kissed her. A breath sputtered down her throat from the surprise. He guided her gently as if sensing her unease. Her mind went blank and she threaded her fingers through his hair, pulling him closer.

I'm kissing a boy, she thought absently. And it is perfect.

EIGHTEEN

Rule 2: *You must not call The Ex's answering machine or voice mail just to hear his voice.*

"Please, work the night shift for me, Raven," Ms. Valenti said. "I can't get hold of anyone else and I have to work on this design tonight." She nodded at the desk piled high with paper and old photos of the family.

"Mom," Raven began, running through the list of possible excuses. She had homework? A huge essay due? She was ill?

"I don't have anyone else, honey, and it's just one night. You know I wouldn't ask you unless I really needed the help."

She was right. She didn't ever ask Raven to work at Scrappe, and seeing the look on her mother's face—brow furrowed with worry—Raven was having a hard time saying no.

She sighed. "How about we make a deal?"

"A reasonable one?"

Raven nodded. "I think so."

"Well, try me."

Raven explained how the student council was going to hold an open-mike night/bake-sale fund-raiser for band uniforms. Then she slipped in the fact that they needed a place to hold it. For free.

Ms. Valenti's frown deepened and she rubbed the bridge of her nose. "It's a lot of work, holding a party."

"I know, but you wouldn't really have to do anything."

"Let me check the calendar. Which night were they thinking?"

"The thirty-first of March."

Ms. Valenti flipped through her planner. "Well, I don't have anything scheduled for that night, so I'll say yes, if you please cover tonight's shift."

Sydney would be happy to hear the student council had a place to hold their fund-raiser for the stupid band uniforms, but Raven wasn't so happy she had to work tonight. What if Horace had tonight's shift, too? Her stomach knotted, thinking about it, for good reasons and bad. She always looked forward to seeing him, but when she did, there was always an uncomfortable tension, though mostly that was on her part. Horace never seemed uncomfortable anywhere, even in school. He was like a chameleon, moving seamlessly through the cliques. Everyone liked him. Well, except Caleb.

"I guess I better go get ready," Raven said. "I have to be there when?"

"Four."

She looked at the clock on her mother's white walls. She only had an hour. Better hustle.

♥ ♥ ♥

"You want me to come over?" Sydney asked through the phone, crossing her legs beneath her as she sat at the kitchen table.

"No, I'm fine," Alexia said. "I've got plenty of Advil, and I think I'm going to go to sleep soon anyway."

"Okay." Sydney tried sounding upbeat, but truthfully she was dying to get out of the house. It was so quiet she could hear the ticking of the fish clock behind her. The one her father just had to have when they went on vacation to Canada five years ago. The ticking was the fish's tail swinging back and forth.

That trip seemed so long ago now. It was before her mother became so immersed in her work that she forgot she had a house and a family inside of it.

Sydney was waiting to hear the D-word any day now. There was no doubt in her mind that her parents loved each other, but they didn't spend time together anymore.

Ms. Valenti and Mr. Andrews (they always had different last names because Ms. Valenti was *crazy* independent) had divorced several years ago, and Sydney had never seen Raven as depressed as she had been during the divorce.

It frightened Sydney to imagine herself going through the same pain. Of course, Mr. Andrews had been having an affair, which probably made that divorce worse.

"I better go," Alexia said, bringing Sydney out of her reverie.

"If you need anything, just call." God, let her need something, like some company! Sydney was going to go insane soon if she didn't get out of the house.

They said good-bye and Sydney hung up. She propped her elbow on the table and set her chin in her hand. Her homework was done, there was nothing on TV, her dad was upstairs reading.

It was Saturday night and she had *nothing* to do!

Eyeing the phone, an itch in her fingers, she picked it up and flipped through the old numbers on the caller ID. The oldest call was from February fifth. Drew's number wasn't even on there. Probably it'd been at least six weeks since he last called.

Sydney hit the ON button and dialed his number. She had no idea what she was doing. If he answered, she'd make up an excuse on the spot. Or at least she'd try.

But more than anything, she just wanted to hear his voice.

After three rings, voice mail picked up and Sydney closed her eyes, listening.

"This is Drew. Leave it after the beep." *Beep.*

She hit the OFF button, his voice echoing in her head.

This is Drew. This is Drew.

Now he was going to see her name on his caller ID and he'd realize what a pathetic ex-girlfriend she was. Why didn't she think to dial *67?

She dropped her face in her hands. Everything seemed to be going wrong. All she felt like doing was hiding away in her bedroom with a box of Cheez-Its and twenty-four hours worth of Lifetime movies. She and her mom used to watch them on Sundays in the middle of winter.

I wish my mom were here right now, she thought.

When the fish clock behind her made a splashing sound effect on the hour, Sydney sat up and rubbed her eyes. She tried hardening her emotions, pushing them away, throwing them out over the proverbial dating lake like skipping stones.

Maybe Drew was right. Maybe they did need space. Time to be their own selves, not one-half of a whole—time to have fun. She reached behind her to the small phone table and grabbed the phone book. She stopped on the Ts, found the number she was looking for, and dialed.

When someone picked up the other end, Sydney took in a deep breath, a new breath, for the new her. "Hey, Craig," she said. "It's Sydney. Where's the party at tonight?"

♥ ♥ ♥

The first noticeable smell in Scrappe was ground coffee beans and beneath that, chocolate and vanilla and tea and glue. The scrapbooking area was in a separate room from the coffee shop and was big enough to house two dozen worktables. There was an entire wall of just paper and several racks of stickers and other accessories.

Saturday nights were mostly coffee connoisseurs. The scrapbookers liked coming in the morning, especially during the week when their kids were at school.

Raven headed toward the back room, sending an inconspicuous look off to her right where the coffee bar was. All she had to see was the reddish-blond hair above the espresso machine to know Horace was working tonight. A giddy feeling flipped her stomach and a smile touched her lips as she shut the back room door behind her.

The shift she was covering was five hours. The thought of spending that much time with Horace . . . no, she wasn't going to go boy-crazy now. She'd vowed to leave Horace alone. She was like a wrecking ball with the opposite sex.

Leaving her bag and coat in her mother's office, Raven went into the coffee shop and made her way to the counter. When she came up, Horace had his back to her, waiting on someone.

He was wearing a pair of destroyed jeans, faded on the legs. They were loose-fitting but oh-so-perfect, especially with the navy blue Henley. His leather boots scuffed the floor as he moved between the espresso machine and small refrigerator.

"Hey," she said, stepping behind the counter.

He whirled around. "Ray." A crooked smile spread across his face. "What are you doing here?" He went back to the drink he was making, pouring cold milk in an iced coffee.

"My mom asked me to cover a shift." She leaned against the counter. "What time do you get out?"

"I work till close." He stirred the drink, popped a top on, and handed it over to the woman who was waiting. "Thanks," he said, and she sauntered off to a table, sipping from the cup.

"Looks like we're working together then," Raven said.

"Yeah." He pushed up on the leather cord he had wound around his wrist, then the sleeves of his shirt. "Is that cool?"

She looked over at him. He was watching her intently.

"Yeah. I mean, why wouldn't it be?"

He tipped his head to the side, putting his hands on the edge of the counter behind him. "Come on, Ray. There's something weird between us and you know it." It was a statement, not an accusation, which made her feel like crap because she was pretty sure she was responsible for the weirdness.

"I . . . uh . . . " She could feel her face grow warm beneath his gaze. What was she supposed to say to that?

He walked over to her, close enough that she could smell him. He smelled like winter, like cold wind and evergreens. "Listen, I don't need an explanation. I just want to be sure we can be friends."

Her heartbeat was coming faster now, her fingers clammy. "I'd like that," she managed to say. "Friends."

"Good." He tipped his head in agreement.

"Excuse me." A woman waved from the other side of the counter. Raven recognized her skunky blond highlights. She was a regular—Mary or Meredith or something. She was a legal secretary for the Daniels, but she acted like she was the top lawyer in Birch Falls. She expected everyone to bend over backward for her. If Raven remembered correctly, she always ordered a small latte with a half shot of crème de menthe, half shot of espresso, with skim milk but whole-milk foam. That was one of the most complicated drinks Raven had ever concocted. And seriously, did she *have* to get whole-milk foam? What was the difference?

"I'd like to order now," Mary/Meredith said as she flipped through something on her cell phone.

"I got it," Raven said to Horace.

"Okay. I'll be in the back if you need me. I have to move some stuff around for your mom."

She nodded as he slipped past her. She watched him cross the shop.

"Excuse me," Mary/Meredith said again. "I'm kind of in a hurry."

Of course she was. She probably had some papers to file or something. Raven groaned internally. "Sorry," she said, projecting cheerfulness. "What can I get for you?"

♥ ♥ ♥

The night had gone well, Raven thought. The awkwardness between her and Horace had seemed to settle down after he confronted her. She felt ten times better around him.

She pushed the ON button for the espresso machine, running boiling hot water through the ports to clean out any leftover grounds. When the water ran clear, she got out the scrub brush and started scrubbing.

Horace went to the front door and locked it, then turned off the neon OPEN sign hanging in the window. "You're getting the machine?"

"Yeah."

"I'll do the coffee thermoses then." He grabbed two of them off the counter and took them in back.

Outside, the sun had set a few hours ago and the night was dark from the absent moon. It wasn't even ten o'clock yet. It'd take them probably twenty minutes to close up and then . . . she'd have nothing to do for the rest of the night. She wondered what her friends were up to.

After everything was clean behind the counter, Raven put all the dirty dishes in a tub and took them into the back room where the big utility sink was. Horace was just finishing with the thermoses.

"I'll rinse if you want. I'm done here," he said, moving the thermoses out of the way.

"Yeah, okay."

Raven filled the sink with hot soapy water and started washing as Horace hiked up his sleeves.

"You think you'll work again anytime soon?" he asked, turning on the faucet to start rinsing.

She shrugged. "If my mom needs help, maybe."

"I liked working with you." He turned a measuring cup beneath the stream of water, the suds cascading down the drain. "Really. I like hanging out with you, Ray."

"I like hanging out with you, too."

"We can do it more often. As friends. You don't have to avoid me because of . . . everything."

"I wasn't avoiding you—"

"You were avoiding me," he argued, but with a smile.

She didn't say anything because 1) she didn't know what to say, and 2) he was right.

"You know," he said, "I keep thinking, I never should have kissed you on the bus or at that party. We'd still be—"

"Stop."

He glanced over. "What?"

"It's not your fault. Don't even think that."

"Then what is it?"

She dropped the sponge in the soapy water and dried her hands off. Could she put into words what her problem was? And if she could, would it even make sense to Horace? Forget The Code. This wasn't so much about following the rules as it was saving Horace some trouble. A relationship with her was an atom bomb waiting to explode. Didn't he see that? It was no secret around school that she *was* a serial dater, just like Caleb had accused last night.

Maybe Horace had a penchant for pain.

She decided he deserved honesty if nothing else. "I don't want to hurt you."

He grunted. "Maybe I'd rather risk being hurt."

She shook her head. "You say that now—"

"Ray."

"What?"

"You're being too hard on yourself."

"I have a problem with relationships, Horace. You deserve someone better than me."

"There is no one better than you."

A lump formed in her throat. No one had ever said anything like that to her. Not a single one of the boys she'd gone out with in the past. And how many had there been? Twenty? Jordan held the official count.

Raven flicked her eyes to him. "Thanks . . . for saying that. It means a lot."

"I meant it."

She smiled. "I know you did." But even if he thought it was true, it didn't mean it was.

NINETEEN

Rule 24: *You must never ask or beg The Ex to date you again, nor should he ever see you cry about the breakup.*

Sydney pressed into the SUV's brake knowing the unnamed dirt road she was looking for was somewhere close. There, just thirty feet ahead, was a barely noticeable break in the trees. She turned onto the two-track and cursed beneath her breath when a few branches scraped against the window.

What in the hell was she doing coming out here?

It had seemed like a good idea an hour ago when she called Craig Thierot, but now, with the darkness making the road and the woods uninviting, she was seriously considering turning around and going home.

That was the safe option, but Sydney was tired of safe, if it even existed anymore. She'd thought her relationship with Drew was safe. She never worried about losing him and now look.

No, she decided, safe didn't exist. She kept going deeper into the woods and finally, just through the trees, she could see light. She'd reached her destination: Turner Place. Or the abandoned barn on Matt Turner's grandfather's forty acres. His grandfather never came out here and Matt threw parties all the time. At least, that's what she'd heard.

Finding an open slot among the two dozen or so cars, she parked and got out, her heart thumping against her rib cage.

I'm not intimidated by these people, she said over and over in her head like a mantra, but the flight instinct was rearing in her gut and her fingers were suddenly clammy despite the coolness of the air.

The small door on the barn burst open just as she walked up. Two people moved past her, bringing with them the sound of pop music and the smell of beer. She went inside, sliding along the wall at first as she watched.

The air was warm with body heat and the fire burning in the brick pit in the middle of the barn. Cigarette smoke rose to the rafters, slipping out through the cracks in the roof.

Scanning the many faces in the barn, she hoped she'd see someone she knew and didn't just recognize. Every face was familiar, but most of these people she'd never bothered talking to.

In the far corner she saw Craig Thierot talking to Lisa, the student council treasurer. Thank God for a familiar face. Sydney made her way through the crowd.

"Sydney!" Craig shouted when she neared. His cherubic face was red, probably from dancing. Several springy blond curls hung over his forehead. He had on a plain white T-shirt, but over that, he wore a tie shaped like a pineapple. "I didn't think you'd come."

"I almost didn't," she said, glancing around nervously. "This isn't usually my scene."

"But it should be. There is much fun to be had." Craig waggled his eyebrows at her. "Let me get you a drink."

Did he mean drink like water or drink like alcohol? She decided not to question and said, "All right." He disappeared into a separate room.

"So," Lisa said, "it's cool that you're here. I've been dying to talk to someone that doesn't have air for brains." Big gold hoops swung from her ears. Her layered auburn hair was pulled back in a ponytail.

Sydney laughed, checking out the other girls who were hanging around. "You mean like Melody?" She nodded toward a blonde girl near the fire pit who was wearing a cleavage-revealing top and a miniskirt.

Lisa rolled her eyes. "Oh, yeah. You should have heard her a half hour ago. She was trying to tell me the water she drinks seriously makes her smarter."

"What?" Sydney frowned.

"Yeah. They're called BrainLytes and she swears they're infused with some sort of herb that produces more brain cells."

"Oh, my God. How did she ever make it to the tenth grade?"

Lisa shook her head. "You got me."

Craig walked up, two drinks in his hands. "Here." He thrust the cups toward them. "Squirms for the ladies."

Lisa took the drink and started sipping from the pink straw sticking out of the cup.

"Squirms?" Sydney grabbed the other cup.

"Squirt and rum," Lisa explained. "It's one of Craig's many concoctions."

"The best one," Craig said. "Try it."

Sydney sniffed it first but could smell only the citrus of the Squirt. Then she took a drink and it warmed her throat as it went down. "There's alcohol in here?"

Craig nodded. "That's the beauty of it. You can't really taste the alcohol when it's mixed with Squirt. It gets you drunk faster."

"I'm driving tonight," Sydney said, her old self chattering in her ear like an annoying horsefly. She mentally swatted it away.

"I'm DD," Craig replied. "No worries. I'll get you home safe and sound." Someone called his name out in the crowd. He turned and waved. "Duty calls. Drink up, ladies. Enjoy!"

Sydney turned to Lisa after Craig had walked off. "Are you getting drunk?"

"You bet your ass." Lisa slurped more Squirm through her straw. "That's what I came here for."

"I've never been drunk before," Sydney heard herself confess. It'd never seemed important before, but now she felt kind of lame.

"There's a first time for everything." Lisa smiled. "And trust me, it probably won't be your last."

Had Drew been coming to these parties to get drunk? Was that what he'd wanted her to do? To live a little, to act like these people? Now that she was here, it didn't seem so bad. Maybe she'd been overreacting. It was true, what Drew said. It was time they tried new things, had a little bit of fun. She didn't want to look back on this time of her life and realize she wasted it sitting at home studying.

"Bottoms up!" Lisa yelled, chugging her drink as she held her straw aside.

Sydney ditched the straw and tipped her cup to her lips. When she could see the bottom, she looked over at Lisa.

"Refill!" Lisa said, grabbing hold of Sydney's hand and tugging her toward the drink room.

♥ ♥ ♥

Sydney stumbled and her drink sloshed over the rim of her cup, down her arm. She laughed as Craig steadied her.

"Sit down," he instructed, pulling up a rickety bar stool behind her. She sat, the ripped vinyl poking her in the butt through her jeans. "I think you had too much to drink, Chutney." He took the cup from her hands and emptied it out on the cement floor.

Somehow, in the last two hours, she'd been given the nickname Chutney. Craig said, "Because you're full of sugar and spice and a little bit of vinegar!" She'd tried telling him chutney had fruit in it, too, but he said, "So what," and shrugged. And when she raced Brad Baker in Shot Put—as in slugging back shots of whiskey—the crowd had hollered, "Chut! Chut! Chut!" as they egged her on. She'd won, too.

Now though, the world was tipping back and forth like a seesaw and even sitting was becoming difficult. She put her head against Craig's side and felt his ribs poking her in the face.

"Drew's going to be totally pissed if he shows up," Craig mused.

"Drew," she muttered, trying to remember why he would be pissed. Then she laughed, tears streaming out the corner of her eyes. "We broke up, you know."

"Yup. I know."

"He won't care."

"Oh, I bet he will."

And even through the alcohol haze she hoped that he *would* care, because if he cared that meant he still loved her. "Call him."

"Hell, no!"

"Come on, Craigy. Call him."

"No freakin' way am I calling him with you slurring in the background."

The music cut out as someone changed CDs. A few seconds later, an R&B song pounded out of hidden speakers.

"Wooo!" Sydney yelled. "I like this song!" She stood and started dancing. Lisa came up then and grabbed her hand. They swung around together until Sydney lost her balance and tumbled into an old beanbag chair, laughter straining her stomach muscles.

"Sydney?"

She opened her eyes at the same time she heard Craig say, "Oh, shit," somewhere off in the distance.

"Drew?" she said, then stood and lunged at him. "Drew! Where've you been?" He was wearing that army green jacket with the high collar she loved so much. His broad shoulders looked really good in it.

"Are you drunk?"

The feel of his hands around her waist, his blue eyes on her face . . . wow, she'd missed that and it'd only been . . . how long? Too long obviously. How could she ever live her life without him as her boyfriend?

"We're broken up," she said, leaning into his chest. She wrapped her arms around him and hooked her hands together. "I'm not letting go."

"Sydney." His voice reverberated through his chest.

"Dude, I'm sorry." That was Craig. "I didn't think she'd get so drunk. Serious. It was like she was bent on destruction tonight."

"I'll take her home," Drew said.

She pulled away and stumbled into Craig. "I don't want to go home. It's boring there. And quiet. No one talks to me at home." Tears blurred her vision. "Make me a Squirm, Craig." She sniffed and wiped her eyes.

"What the man says goes." Craig put his hands up, backing away.

"Fine." She went into the drink room and grabbed a new cup.

"You don't need to drink more." Drew took the cup away.

"Give it back."

"You don't need any more, Sydney. Listen to me."

"Damn it, Drew! I'm having fun! It's what you wanted, wasn't it?"

He chucked the cup in a trash can. "This isn't what I meant."

The room careened more, but her senses were coming back and now she was crying. "I don't want to go home, Drew. I can't stand it there."

He grabbed her face in his hands and for a second she thought he was going to kiss her, but no, he was just steadying her so he could look her in the eye. "I'll stay with you until you fall asleep."

"You will?"

He wiped the tears from her cheeks. "If you leave now and let me drive you home. Yes."

"But you don't love me anymore."

"Yes, I do."

"Then why did you break up with me?"

He sighed. "Not here, Sydney." He put his hand on the small of her back and led her out of the drink room and through the barn. Drew grabbed her coat from somewhere and put it around her.

Lisa waved good-bye, and Sydney nodded before slipping into the cold. Drew walked her to his truck and helped her inside, even buckling her in. The inside of the truck was warm and cozy and dark and before she knew it, she was sleeping.

♥ ♥ ♥

"Sydney. Wake up."

She opened her eyes and looked over at Drew. Had the breakup been a nightmare?

No, the pounding in her head, the dryness of her mouth, the rolling of her stomach reminded her that it was very real, as was the night of drinking.

Now, sitting in Drew's truck in the alley behind her house, the pain doubled with the toxicity of the alcohol and she jumped out of the truck and heaved everything in her stomach on the ground.

Drew was suddenly there, his hand warm on her shoulder. When she was finished, he wove his arm around her waist. Leaning into the crook of his arm, she shuffled forward, her feet like lead weights beneath her.

"Shhh," Drew whispered as they went inside, locking the door behind him.

"My dad won't wake up," she heard herself say, maybe too loudly. Or maybe Drew hadn't heard her at all.

They crossed the kitchen to the hallway and then they were in her room safely, her dad still sleeping upstairs, oblivious as he always was, and her mother a good hour away in her other life, trusting that her daughter would be the same, even without her around. But Sydney wasn't the same now. Nothing was the same. She hated change.

"Bathroom," she said and went into her private bathroom, shutting the door behind her. She brushed her teeth, eyes barely able to stay open. Worry made her hurry through the ritual, fearing that when she went out, she'd find Drew gone.

She rinsed and pulled the door open. He was still there, leaning against the headboard of her bed. She peeled her shoes off, nearly toppling over as she did. Then she took her pants off, slipping into a pair of shorts. She curled beneath the blanket against Drew.

"You're okay?" he asked.

She was silent for a long time, wondering what the right answer to that question was. If she said she was okay, would he leave? Did he mean "okay" as in was she going to vomit again, or okay as in was she mentally okay?

"I've been better," she muttered. "How long will you stay?"

His fingers stroked her hair, pushing it across her forehead, behind her ear. She shivered. It was little things like this that she missed the most.

"Until you fall asleep," he said.

"Stay until morning. I miss you." She snuggled farther beneath the blanket, hooking her leg around his. "I can't stand this. Not being with you."

The thumping of his heart filled the silence that stretched out. She could hear it through his chest as she lay there waiting, waiting for anything. She sat up. "Drew?"

"Go to sleep, Sydney."

The pounding in her head, the heaviness in her eyes said that yes, sleeping sounded good. She cuddled up next to him again. If this was the last time she did, she wanted to remember it this way. She didn't want it ruined with an argument.

"I love you," she whispered.

"You know I love you, too."

She repeated the words over and over in her head as she fell asleep.

TWENTY

Rule 14: *The Ex's name can't be mentioned unless the person who broke up with him brings up the name.*
Rule 19: *If you see your girl's Ex, you must never mention it to her.*

On Sunday, all three girls converged at Alexia's house. It was snowing again, light, sparse flakes, but the wind was blowing harshly and no one felt like doing anything other than hanging out.

The teakettle on the stove whistled as Alexia set out three mugs.

"I got it," Sydney said. "You sit down."

Alexia hobbled over to the kitchen table. Her ankle felt much better today. It wasn't swollen or bruised, just a bit sore. She could have gotten the tea herself, but there was no use arguing with Sydney.

Sydney poured the hot water into the waiting mugs. "What kind do you guys want?" she asked over a shoulder.

"Green tea for me," Alexia said.

"What's that kind I had last time?" Kelly frowned, raking her bottom lip with her teeth. "Was it orange-something?"

"Wild sweet orange," Alexia supplemented. "Check the cupboard, Syd. The one by the fridge."

Sydney went to the cupboard and found the wild sweet orange. With the bags in the mugs, she carried the cups over to the table. "Anything for you, Ray?"

"Nah." Raven twirled the saltshaker between her hands. "I'll just get some water later if I get thirsty."

"Is everything okay?" Alexia asked, dipping her tea bag in and out of the hot water.

Raven shoved the saltshaker aside. "Everything's fine." She looked up then and smiled.

Alexia would bet that everything was *not* okay. Raven didn't smile like that unless 1) she hated you but didn't want to tell you to your face or 2) she was feeling like crap but didn't want to sound like a whiner, so she tried to pretend everything was fine. It frustrated Alexia that Raven couldn't come right out and say she was upset about something. Why couldn't she be honest with her friends?

Alexia was tired of coaxing Raven into talking, so she just let it go. She grabbed her notebook. "You guys ready?"

"Yeah," Kelly answered, then blew across her tea, steam whirling away.

"So what, exactly, are we doing?" Raven asked, setting her hands in her lap.

Alexia said, "We're going over The Breakup Code again, to see if it needs any improvements."

"I think it's working fine," Raven said.

"Yeah, but you went out with a guy Friday night," Alexia countered. "Which is against the rules."

"I didn't go out with him." She narrowed her eyes. "I was *hanging* out with him."

"You went out with someone?" Sydney asked. "Who?"

Raven pursed her lips, so Alexia answered for her. "Zac."

"Oh, he's cute," Kelly mused. "He's like one of those cute Greek gods."

"Whether you were hanging out, making out, or hooking up," Alexia said, "it doesn't matter. You still broke a rule. So I got to thinking last night and wrote this up."

"Did you consider that you might have been delirious from the pain meds?" Raven said, taking the piece of paper.

"Very funny."

Raven read aloud. "'Additional rules. *Number twenty-six: You cannot kiss any boys for at least three months after the breakup.*

"'*Number twenty-seven: You must not allow yourself to develop any new crushes for at least three months after the breakup.*'" She set the paper down and looked at Alexia across the table. "Rule number twenty-eight: Join a nunnery because you aren't going to have a life after this."

"Raven." Alexia gave her a blank stare. Something was definitely going on with her. She wasn't usually this snarky.

Raven sighed, running her fingers through her hair. "Sorry. I'm just . . . tired today."

"Did something happen to you last night?" Sydney asked, her mug of tea clutched between her hands.

Raven shook her head, avoiding eye contact.

"I like these rules," Kelly said. "I mean, they make sense."

"I don't think I'm going to have a hard time with number twenty-seven," Sydney said. "I probably won't be developing any new crushes for at least a year."

"How are you doing, anyway?" Alexia asked tentatively. "You okay?"

Sydney shrugged, sipping from her tea before answering. "I'm fine. I mean, I miss Drew . . . but I'm fine."

"I heard you got a little wild last night," Kelly said, eyeing Sydney across the table.

"Who did you hear that from?"

Kelly looked chagrined. "Uh . . . well, from Drew."

"When did you talk to him?"

"Today. At my house. He came over to see Todd."

Sydney looked away. "Oh."

"You totally just broke a rule," Raven said, curling the corner of the paper Alexia had handed out. "Number . . . whatever it is . . . you're not supposed to mention The Ex."

"Actually numbers fourteen and nineteen," Alexia said. "You're not supposed to mention the name of your friend's Ex or mention seeing him."

"She asked me, though!" Kelly said. "Was I supposed to lie?"

Raven and Alexia looked at each other.

"Well . . ." Alexia said.

Raven shrugged.

"I vote for an amendment," Kelly said.

Alexia pulled her Breakup Code journal from her bag and flipped it open. "We probably should. Lying is wrong. How about, *'Rule twenty-eight: Do not lie to your girl about The Ex even if it breaks a rule.'*?"

"That sounds good," Sydney said.

"Perfect." Kelly nodded.

"Now I have to mess up my journal," Raven mused as she wrote the new rules on a piece of paper. "And I had it looking so good."

"What is wrong with you today?" Sydney asked.

Raven grimaced. "I'm just tired. I already told you that."

"Being tired makes you goofy, not mean."

Which was true, Alexia thought but wasn't about to say out loud.

Sighing, Raven tilted her head back with obvious mental exhaustion. "I'm just . . . confused . . . about some stuff."

"Like what?" Sydney coaxed.

Raven shook her head. "I don't want to talk about it. Yet."

"It's a guy, isn't it?" Alexia raised a brow knowingly. She knew that crazed look Raven got when she was thinking about a guy she liked, except this time, it seemed like she was afraid of acknowledging the crush out loud or even to herself. Maybe that's why she was in such a bad mood.

Instead of answering the question, Raven stood up and shoved the chair back. It groaned over the tile floor. "I have to go to the bathroom." She didn't wait for a reaction or response, just bolted out of the room.

"Should we go after her?" Kelly said. "Maybe we shouldn't have confronted her with the topic of boys."

Sydney shook her head. "We should let her cool off."

"It's obviously a boy," Alexia groaned. "But you guys don't think she's back with Caleb, do you?"

"Better not be," Sydney retorted. "Caleb is a bonehead and Raven knows that now that they aren't together. It has to be someone else."

Alexis capped her pen and slid it into the spiral of her notebook. "Maybe the new rule about not developing any new crushes put her in a bad mood."

"Except she was snarky before you even mentioned the new rule," Kelly pointed out.

"True." Sydney nodded, taking her mug in hand. "I think she's fighting this crush because of The Code and that's what's putting her in a bad mood."

"If that's the case, it might actually be good for her," Alexia said.

♥ ♥ ♥

More rules to follow? Raven grunted, grabbing a Kleenex and blowing her nose. She'd been doing so well with the rules until Horace had to make things more complicated. She was pretty sure she'd broken rule twenty-seven before it was even invented.

There was no more denying it, she was crushing on Horace and crushing hard. That's not to say she was going to act on it.

No.

No.

No.

She couldn't. She wouldn't.

Horace was the best guy friend a girl could ever ask for. Screwing that up would be beyond horrible. It'd be a tragedy, because she'd never get him back if—no, *when*—they broke up. As forgiving as he was, there was no way he'd survive the Raven Wreaker and come out with a smile on his face.

Which was the whole reason for her bad mood. She couldn't have the one guy she wanted. Probably the crush was worse for that reason. It was natural to want something you couldn't have, and that turned her into a mega bitch. She hadn't meant to let the bad mood spill over onto her friends. It just came out, but she knew they'd understand as long as she removed herself right now, before her foul mood got the best of her.

Leaving the bathroom, she went back to the kitchen. Her arrival shushed the room. They'd been talking about her. Her face flamed with embarrassment. She should explain, that's what friends were for, but she didn't feel like talking about it right now. About Horace. She didn't want to talk about anything. Maybe she'd go home and hang the blinds up on her windows since her dad hadn't made a visit to their house in ages. Hanging blinds was a great distraction, wasn't it?

"Hey," she said, shifting her eyes down for a second. "I'm sorry about the bad mood, you guys. I'm just gonna jet before I ruin your day."

"Ray," Alexia said, "you don't have to leave."

"Yeah." Kelly nodded. "Stay."

She shook her head, grabbing her bag from the table. "I need some silence. You know?"

Kelly stood and gave her a hug. "If you need us, call, okay?"

"I will. Thanks."

Kelly shrugged. "What are friends for?"

TWENTY-ONE

Rule 21: *You must always look beyond extraordinary in the company of The Ex.*

The next weekend, Kelly got a call from Morris at the animal shelter asking her to come in an hour early. She'd agreed, but the loss of an hour was throwing her completely off schedule.

"Where are my crappy clothes?" she yelled up the basement stairs.

"You have *special* crappy clothes?" Todd appeared at the top of the steps. "I thought all of your clothes were crappy clothes."

"Ha-ha," she muttered as she picked through three laundry baskets full of clean clothes. Her mother always had the laundry done. But this week, she'd been busy putting together a baby shower for one of her friends, so the laundry was behind. Kelly had only thirty minutes before her shift started. That wasn't enough time to wash and dry her crappy clothes. Well, crappy as in she only wore them to the shelter, but they were still okay clothes. Just a pair of old jeans and an old Abercrombie & Fitch T-shirt. Crappy, but still fashionable.

"Whatchya doin'?" Monica asked as she made her way down the basement steps. She was still in her pajamas, a pair of shorts and a tank top that said BRAT across the front in gold glitter. Her sandy-blond hair was in a tight French braid.

"Looking for my clothes."

Monica went to the overflowing dirty clothes hamper. "These ones?" she said, holding up a pair of jeans that had dog hair all over them.

"Yes." Kelly sighed, plopping her butt on the floor. She'd already looked in the hamper. How did she miss them? Monica brought the jeans over. "Thanks." Kelly held them up in front of her. There was a mixture of golden dog hair and black cat hair, dirty paw prints, something crusty on the knee (probably dog food) that had dried like a rock. She couldn't wear those, no matter how dirty her job was.

She ran upstairs and rummaged through the bottom of her closet. Finding nothing but a pair of holey boxers, she went to her dresser next and opened the pants drawer. She pulled out a pair of drawstring khakis that she wore last in sixth grade, when she was as big as a house.

Glancing at her clock, she realized she didn't have time to screw around anymore. She got into the pants and tied the drawstring tight around her waist. For a shirt she wore the black one her mother had bought at Goodwill. It was an 'N Sync shirt. Her mother was so out of touch with the present-day. She'd thought Kelly would love the shirt since she used to love the band. Yeah, like in elementary school.

But, today the shirt would suffice. She didn't have anyone to impress anyway. She'd switched days, so she and Will didn't work together. Today was going to be a quiet, relaxing Sunday at the animal shelter.

♥ ♥ ♥

The baying of puppies, twenty-three of them to be exact, was starting to give Kelly a headache. So much for a quiet, relaxing afternoon at the animal shelter. After several weeks' worth of work, animal control busted an older couple for running a puppy mill.

The twenty-three puppies were now safe in the holding room, but there was still a ton of work to be done. The vet was giving each animal a checkup. They all had to be cleaned and fed. On top of that, Kelly still had all the other dogs to attend to.

"I'll go call someone in," Morris said, heading off to the front desk.

Kelly barely noticed him leave. There was a black Lab mix running around her legs, nipping at her heels. She scooped him up and scratched behind his ears, trying to settle him down. It worked. He was so settled he peed on her.

"Oh!" She put him on the floor, but by that time he had already done his business. Of course. His siblings were running in circles now, chasing after each other. Using some paper towels, she cleaned up as best she could since she didn't have another shirt with her. And why not? It wasn't the first time she'd been peed on. She kept meaning to throw an extra set of clothes in her car for this very reason. As soon as she got home, she was putting together an emergency animal shelter outfit and throwing it in the trunk of her car.

"Dr. Burne?" Kelly said. "Are you done with the black Labs?"

"Yes." He pushed the sleeves of his plaid shirt up before grabbing another puppy. "You can get them settled in the kennel."

Thank God.

The timid, all-black female was easy to catch. She'd hardly moved since arriving. The other female, who had a white spot on her toe, was more rambunctious than her sister, but with a little luck, Kelly was able to grab her next and get her in the kennel.

The two remaining boys were probably going to be trouble. Right now they were running the perimeter of the holding room, barking at the other dogs and getting everyone riled up. Their long nails clicked along the concrete floor.

Just as she dove to corner one of the puppies, Will walked in looking extremely good in a pair of worn jeans and a long-sleeved brown shirt. "Hi," he said, giving her a crooked smile. "You look like you've been struggling. Let me get them."

She stood, smoothing the front of her pee-stained shirt. Hair hung in her eyes as she watched him. With slow steps, he came up on one of the puppies, then lunged at it, scooping the puppy up in his arms.

"Easy," he said to Kelly. "You just have to be patient."

Grumbling, she let *him* deal with the puppies while she moved on to the adult dogs. A husky mix barked as she neared, accidentally tipping over both his food and water bowl in his eagerness to get her attention.

"I'm coming," she said, unlatching the door. The husky lunged at her, dirty paw prints now running up the shirt.

"Down," she scolded, pushing the top of his head. The husky obeyed but whined.

Today was just swirling right down the drain, getting worse and worse by the minute.

"So, how have you been?" Will asked, coming up behind her.

"I've been fine."

Will grabbed the broom and started sweeping out the inside of the kennel. "I haven't talked to you in a while."

"Yeah."

"Have I done something wrong?"

She glanced over at him as he leaned on the broom handle, watching. Why today, of all days, did she have to be so unkempt? Dog pee, paw prints, an 'N Sync T-shirt?

"No," she answered. "You haven't done anything wrong."

"Good." He smiled, flashing that smile she knew he used to get the upper hand in a situation. It usually worked, too. "Come out with us tonight. We're going to Emerson's for dinner."

"Who's 'we'?"

"My brother. Jessie and Dan. April." He shrugged. "It's nothing formal."

She was so stressed after a crappy day that all she wanted to do was hang out with friends and relax. And Emerson's had the best chicken sandwich in all of Birch Falls.

If she treated the outing like they were friends, it wouldn't be such a big deal. Would she be breaking The Code? It wasn't like she was jumping back on the Will bandwagon. Hanging out with some different people sounded like fun and that's what one of the rules suggested: Do group activities with friends—both girl and guy friends. Was that rule four or five? It was so hard keeping them all straight. She'd yet to make her journal for The Code, which, now that she thought about it, might be the reason why she didn't know The Code by memory.

Maybe it was time to make her Breakup Code journal? She also had Spanish homework to do tonight. As soon as she got home, she'd do both tasks.

"All right," she said. "I'll go."

Will smiled again. "Great. Meet us at Emerson's around six."

♥ ♥ ♥

Ding.

Raven looked up from the issue of *Blender* in her hands to her computer screen. A new email blinked, waiting for her attention. She laid the magazine down and scooted into her computer chair.

She was expecting Sydney or Alexia. Instead she read the screen name, Ace23, and her heart tripped in her chest.

Ace23 was Horace.

She knew that because she'd found his profile on MySpace, which listed his Instant Messenger user name and other things. His love of music and his amateur band that didn't have a name yet. And that his favorite movie was *Lost in Translation* and his favorite TV show was *American Idol* and . . .

Hmmm . . . maybe she was crossing over the line from curiosity to stalkerosity.

Hey, she typed back.
Ace23: *hey how r u?*
Ray: *fine. how did u find my user name?*

Ace23: *i asked ben, who asked alexia, who gave it to me. i went to alot of trouble to find ur user name.* ☺

Ray: *ben as in daniels?*

Ace23: *yeah*

Why would Ben ask Alexia? They weren't even friends, were they? She'd have to ask Alexia later.

Ray: *so what's up?*

Ace23: *i need to ask u a huge favor.*

The fact that he needed her for something made her grin unexpectedly. The only time Caleb needed her for something was when he wanted to make out.

Oh, great, she just thought about her past with Caleb, which was against Rule 10. She grabbed hold of the four-leaf-clover rubber band and let it snap. "Ewwou." She rubbed beneath it quickly, trying to stop the stinging sensation. Was Alexia getting off on torturing them?

Ray: *what's the favor?*

Ace23: *i can't tell u yet.*

Ray: *y not?*

Ace23: *i'm afraid if i tell u right now u'll say no.*

Ray: *okay, that doesn't sound good. u want me to join ur cult or something?*

Ace23: *ha-ha. no.*

Ray: *give me a clue and maybe I'll say yes.*

Actually, she was already leaning toward saying yes, but it was fun to tease him. Besides, a clue couldn't hurt.

Ace23: *it has 2 do w/ music.*

Ray: *u want 2 start a folk band and u need me 2 play the banjo?*

Ace23: *close.*

Ray: *all right, i'm curious. what do u want me 2 do?*

Ace23: *i knew i could count on u. be at my house at 6?*

Ray: *sure, as long as there's no ritual involved.*

Ace23: *promise, no rituals, and ray?*

Ray: *yeah?*

Ace23: *thanks*

Ray: *ur welcome.* ☺

She signed off. The grin grew wider and then she couldn't turn it off. How cool was it that Horace IMed her for a favor? Not that she was going to allow herself to get overly excited. Well, a little excited. It was cool that he thought of her, whatever the favor was.

The clock said 4:09 P.M. She hurried into the bathroom to check her reflection. Angling her head, she checked her hair. It was iffy. She hadn't showered yet today. Best get in.

TWENTY-TWO

Rule 8: *Take three months and only do the things you like to do. You are not to accommodate any male for any reason.*
Rule 12: *You must never date a friend of The Ex.*

The first thing Kelly noticed when she walked into Emerson's Pub was not the smell of fried food or the sound of jazz blasting from the neon-lit jukebox. What she noticed first was Brittany. And then Mr. Daniels's deep baritone voice asking the waitress to take back his scotch because he'd asked for it on the rocks and his was rockless.

Both of these observations had Kelly inwardly groaning.

Brittany, obviously, wasn't her favorite person and Mr. Daniels was hard to deal with. Sitting next to him was Mrs. Daniels. Three square tables had been pulled together to accommodate the large group of people. There was enough room to seat a good ten people, but Brittany's chair was so close to Will's, Kelly was sure they were breathing the same air.

Kelly inhaled deeply and went over. "Hey," she said, taking the seat next to Ben. It was the safe seat. Ben made her feel comfortable because he was nice and always had something to say. That meant she didn't have to pretend to be chatty or sit in silence while Mr. and Mrs. Daniels ignored her, focusing instead on how wonderful Brittany was.

"Hey, Kelly!" Ben said.

"Kelly," Will greeted her, pulling a few inches away from Brittany, which made her furrow her eyebrows.

"Hi," Kelly said again.

"So nice of you to join us, Kelly," Mr. Daniels said. "Albeit late." He smoothed a hand over his neatly trimmed beard. Although it was a casual Sunday dinner, he was dressed as if he was about to enter the courtroom, in an expensive black suit and red silk tie.

Mrs. Daniels was in a matching pantsuit, her hair freshly highlighted and styled. She rubbed her ruby red lips together as she checked her watch.

"Sorry," Kelly said. She could have told them that Will said six o'clock and that her watch said 5:54 P.M. but the Daniels weren't about to accept any excuses. Kelly often wondered how Ben survived his family. He was so laid back and carefree, as if he'd been raised by a wildly laissez-faire family.

Kelly swallowed, trying to stifle her embarrassment, and looked around at the other faces at the table. She knew April and Dan and Jessie, but the last guy, the one with the green polo on, golden hair hanging in his face, he was unfamiliar.

"Hi," he said, thrusting his hand across the table. "I'm Breckin."

Breckin? What kind of a name was that? Probably his last name was something like Jagger or Carswell.

"Breckin." She smiled, shaking his hand. His skin was soft, softer than hers even, and she was a girl. "Breckin what?"

"Waverly," he said, pride affecting his tone.

That name sounded familiar.

"It's nice to meet you," she said, pulling her hand back and tucking it in her lap.

"Breckin's in the Birch Falls Historical Society with me," Will explained.

Mr. Daniels cleared his throat. "Breckin goes to Waverly. A fine school. I tried to get Will to go but to no avail."

Right, that's where Kelly knew the name. Waverly was the private school forty miles north of Birch Falls. It was super expensive to attend and hard to get into. Obviously, Breckin Waverly was an automatic admission, since his family founded the place.

"He's a real piece, huh," Ben whispered in her ear and she burst out laughing. The whole table went silent and everyone stared at her.

"Sorry." She stifled the laugh, giving Ben a look.

"What?" A crooked grin spread across his face.

"I think its about time for us to go," Mrs. Daniels said. "Come on, honey. Let's allow the kids some time to hang out without parents watching over them."

Mr. Daniels handed Will a credit card. "Treat all your friends tonight." He stood up and buttoned his suit jacket. "Your mom and I are going back to the office to get some work done. Don't stay out too late tonight, boys." His eyes lingered a bit too long on Ben, as if the message were really for him.

Everyone said good-bye to Mr. and Mrs. Daniels as they headed out. Kelly was secretly thankful they were leaving. Will's parents scared the crap out of her. They were intimidating, had high standards, and they obviously didn't care much for Kelly. What had they thought of Brittany? They hadn't said much to her, and Kelly wondered if their ignoring her was a good or bad sign. At least Brittany hadn't been chastised for being late.

The waiter came up and passed out menus. Most everyone at the table, except for Breckin, knew what they wanted since they had the menu practically memorized. Kelly usually got the chicken sandwich, since it was low cal and oh-so-delish.

When the waiter came back she ordered the usual with a Diet Coke while Will and Breckin grilled the waiter on what kind of mayo was used, full fat or light? Were the hamburger buns white flour or wheat?

"It's bread, dude," Ben said, chomping on a piece of ice from his water.

"Benjamin," Will said, frowning. "It's not just bread."

"Whole wheat is better for you," Breckin said.

Kelly had to agree with that. She was always health-conscious, but still, the way they were quizzing the waiter on every little detail about the meals was getting a bit tedious.

The waiter shifted around nervously, answering all the questions, but Kelly could tell he was getting annoyed. She didn't blame him. Finally, Will settled on the chicken sandwich, and Breckin the Cobb salad.

While they waited for their food, Breckin and Will discussed important things—college application essays and the state of historical sites.

"This is painfully boring," Ben whispered.

"I agree."

"You aren't seriously still seeing my brother, are you?" he asked, hiding behind his glass of water. "I mean, it's cool if you are, but, wow, totally *uncool* if you are."

"That doesn't make any sense."

"Neither does dating my brother."

"Ohhh." She scrunched up her face. "I walked right into that one."

"That you did."

"Well . . . we're not really seeing each other."

"He's practically in love with you."

Kelly frowned. "No, he's not. He's constantly with Brittany. He blew me off that night after the art show . . ."

"He uses Brittany for show. You're for real, he just won't admit to it."

Flicking her eyes down the table, she caught Will watching her. He smiled then looked away. Brittany noticed the exchange and scowled at Kelly.

"Why did you just tell me all that if you don't think I should go out with him?"

"Because you have a right to know and make your own decision about it." He cocked an eyebrow before sipping from his water and setting it down. "But it's worth repeating . . . it would be uncool if you were still with him."

"I don't know what's going on," she admitted.

The food came, and Kelly ate in silence while conversation buzzed around her at the table.

What was that saying, exactly, if Will's own brother thought he was undateable? It was saying a lot. Coming here now, it hadn't been about Will. She didn't want to get back with him, but now, knowing that maybe he did care for her?

No . . . it didn't change anything. There were no butterflies, no giddiness. She was over Will. Somehow, some way, her feelings for him had lessened in the two months since the breakup.

Apparently, The Breakup Code was working.

Finished with her sandwich, Kelly excused herself and went to the bathroom. On her way out, she noticed a familiar face in a booth along the wall.

Drew.

She caught his eye and waved, expecting nothing more than a wave in return, but Drew slid from the booth, leaving his dad alone at the table, talking on his cell.

"What are you doing here?" he asked.

"Here with some friends." She nodded at their table near the front door.

"Did you just get here?"

"No. Actually, I'm just leaving." Thank God.

Drew shoved his hands in the pockets of his jeans, shoulders lifting uncomfortably. "Would you . . . uh, mind if I left with you?"

Kelly frowned. "What about your dad?"

"He hardly knows I'm here. He's been on his phone the whole time."

Kelly couldn't help but detect a note of anger and maybe disappointment. "Yeah, sure. Let me go say good-bye."

They headed over to the table. Ben gave Drew a guy handshake and they started talking about sports or something.

"I'm leaving," she told Will, then turned to Breckin. "It was nice meeting you, by the way."

Breckin flashed his expensive smile and stood. "Would you mind if I called you sometime?"

The rest of the table went silent watching her, including Ben, which was almost unheard of. He was hardly ever silent.

"Um . . ." Her face felt hot, but her fingers were ice-cold. Nice of him to put her on the spot. "Actually," she took in a breath and looked straight at Will as she said, "I'm happier being single right now."

Will's expression went still.

"But thanks."

She grabbed Drew by the arm and said, "Let's go."

♥ ♥ ♥

Horace's house was on the outside of the Birch Falls city limits, where the houses were far apart and the backyards were as big as fields. His was a two-story farmhouse with a wraparound screen porch. It reminded Raven of one of those storybook houses, with the yellow siding, white shutters, and a cobblestone walk.

As she pulled in the driveway, she noticed several cars parked near the garage farther back from the house. Either Horace was throwing a party or his family owned a lot of cars.

She got out as the side door to the garage opened.

"Hey," Horace said, meeting her in the driveway. "We're in the garage."

"We?" She raised her brow.

"Just wait and see." He held the door open for her and she went inside. Heat blasted from a vent just overhead. The first thing she noticed was the drum set, the amps, and the guitar. Then she recognized Hobb and Dean, two guys in the high school band. They were sitting on a torn orange couch along the wall, Hobb strumming on the strings of a bass guitar, and Dean tapping drumsticks on a tin can.

"Ray," Horace said. "You know Hobb and Dean."

"Hey," they both said.

"Hi." She waved, then turned to Horace with a look of "What the hell is going on?"

"We've been playing together for about a year now," he explained, "but our vocalist jumped ship and we need a replacement."

Three sets of eyes watched her.

"Okay," she said, crossing her arms uncomfortably over her chest. "What does that have to do with me?"

"We want to play at the open-mike night you were talking about," Horace said. "But we don't have a vocalist."

They wanted her to sing? Were they crazy?! "I don't sing. I play the flute."

"I've heard you sing, Ray," Horace argued. "I know you're good."

"When have you heard me sing?" She only sang at home, in her bedroom or the shower. Sometimes she'd start singing along with her iPod, but she was mindful when the headphones were on at school.

Horace swallowed, eyes sliding from her to the floor. "That night on the bus. After the band competition."

Oh. *That* night.

She'd been listening to her iPod before Horace moved seats and tapped her on the shoulder. She remembered singing, but she'd thought she was only mumbling and the rest of the bus had been alive with conversation. She didn't think anyone had heard her.

"I just sing for fun," she argued.

"Come on," Hobb said, chewing on a piece of his long brown hair. "Having a chick sing our songs would be way cool."

"Hobb," Horace said, shaking his head.

"What?"

"We need someone," Dean added, standing. "We're desperate."

She shifted her weight around. "Do I need to remind you guys that I don't sing?"

"Just try it," Horace said. "We can do a cover song. Pick something."

No way was she singing in front of all three of them! She didn't even know how to sing. She'd probably make a fool of herself, and then Horace would think she was a huge dork.

"I can't. Besides, I don't know the words to any songs. I can only sing along if I sing to my iPod."

"That's fine. Go get your iPod," Horace said.

It was sitting in her car. She could say she didn't have it, but something told her Horace would know she was lying. When did she ever *not* have her iPod?

"And then what?" she asked.

"You sing to the iPod and we'll play along."

"But what if you don't know any of my songs?"

"You have Greengers on there? You were singing it on the bus that night."

"Yeah."

" 'Save Me Yesterday'?"

"Save Me Yesterday" was one of her favorite songs. The band, Greengers, was an up-and-coming alternative band.

They weren't quite Three Days Grace yet, but their popularity was growing. She'd heard of them two years ago when they started making the scene in Boston.

"Yeah. I have it."

"We can do that song," Hobb said, unfolding his long legs from the couch. "Let's do it."

Raven hesitated as the boys set up the equipment. Horace just stood there, staring at her. Singing to her iPod was easy, singing here, in front of them, that was the hard part. And it was just a high school open-mike night. Why was it so important that they play?

Maybe it was important to them, to Horace, because it was their passion and it didn't matter where they played—open-mike night or a serious gig—just so long as they got to play and people heard their music.

Music was a big influence on Raven's life; she could appreciate the passion.

"Please, Ray?" Horace said, the plea pinching the corners of his eyes.

Despite the embarrassment already heating her face, she nodded and went out to her car to grab her iPod. She wanted to make Horace happy. For some reason, pleasing him pleased her and she tended to believe the things he said, even if they were compliments that didn't involve her boobs or her talent for making out.

Inside, she put the headphones on and turned to the guys. Hobb had the bass guitar hanging from a strap. Dean was behind the drums and Horace was on the guitar.

"I didn't know you played," she said, nodding. Horace was in the percussion section in the school band. It seemed natural that he would play the drums.

He shrugged, pulling a pick from the strings. "I've played the guitar longer than the drums. It's just the school band doesn't allow guitars in."

"Why is that, anyway? It seems so unfair."

"I don't know, but it sucks." He started strumming a few practice notes on the guitar as she flipped through her playlist on her iPod and got the song ready.

"We'll start off," Horace said. "Jump in when you're ready."

"Okay."

Horace positioned his fingers over the arm of the guitar and started strumming with the pick in the other hand, notes sounding through the amp behind him. She couldn't help but watch him, his fingers moving effortlessly through the chords, sliding up and down the neck of the guitar.

He looked up then, caught her staring, and he smiled. "Go ahead," he mouthed as Dean started in on the cymbal—*tick, tick, tick*—and Hobb on the bass—*dum, dum, dadum.*

Her foot started tapping on the cement floor. She pressed PLAY on the iPod and the live music mingled with the recorded. She closed her eyes, taking the mike and the stand in her hands.

Don't think.

Just jump in.

She took in a breath, quieted the voice that told her this was crazy, and she sang.

When the song was over, her heart hammered in her chest.

"Wow," she whispered. She'd never felt anything like that, the music not just sounding in her ears, but vibrating through the floor, bouncing off the walls, pouring out of her.

"That was wicked!" Hobb said. Dean nodded in agreement.

"Ray, that was awesome," Horace said.

She felt like she was glowing. "It *felt* awesome."

"So join Hobb and the Heartbreakers!" Hobb said.

Dean shook his head. "That is not our name."

"Will you sing with us?" Horace asked, ignoring the argument starting behind him.

Her mother would kill her if she joined them. A rock band to Ms. Valenti was synonymous with joining the circus. But right now, Raven didn't care what her mom would think. She just wanted to make music.

She smiled. "I'm in."

TWENTY-THREE

Rule 27: *You must not allow yourself to develop any new crushes for at least three months after the breakup.*

After school the next day, Kelly came straight home and dropped her homework in her bedroom. She'd do it later. She went into the den and signed on the Internet, going to Yahoo mail.

She typed in her email password and hit ENTER.

You have 1 new message.

Was it from Will?

It doesn't matter, she thought. I'm not going to answer it even if it is. I'm so over him.

She clicked on her inbox. It was from Drew. The subject of the email said, "I need your help."

Kel,

I need your help. Kenny is flaking on poker tonight and I need another player asap. I already told your brother you were doing it. Please tell me you can fill in.

—D

Hanging out with Drew sounded like fun, but playing poker with her brother did not. She hit the REPLY button.

Hey, Drew! I don't know about . . .

"Kelly?"

Kelly turned around in the desk chair. The base squeaked with age. "Hi, Mom. What's up?"

Mrs. Waters came into the room and shut the door. She clutched a piece of paper in her hand. Sitting on the sofa, she leaned forward, her elbows propped on her knees. "We have a problem." She held up the piece of paper as if presenting evidence.

Kelly took a closer look at it and winced. It was midsemester grades. Crap. Suddenly, several missed assignments ran through her head. Chapter seven in geometry. A failed pop quiz in Spanish 2. An unfinished assignment in history. Hopefully those missed and failed assignments would only add up to a C. She had to get at least a C to pass.

It was just that she'd been so stressed lately, what with the breakup. She hadn't felt like studying or doing any homework. It didn't seem like that much at the time, but now she wondered if her lack of ambition had finally taken its toll.

"How are the grades?" Kelly asked.

Mrs. Waters inhaled through her nose and then looked down at the paper. "You're failing Spanish and geometry and you're in jeopardy of failing history, too."

Kelly's face instantly reddened in embarrassment and shame. It was *that* bad? Her Spanish teacher was the only one who'd recently pulled her aside about her grades, but her history and geometry teachers hadn't said a word. Of course, her geometry teacher had suggested she find a tutor. Kelly had forgotten about that.

"I'll make the missed assignments up," Kelly said. "And I'll ask my teachers if I can do anything for extra credit. They're usually pretty good about that stuff."

Mrs. Waters shook her head and looked at the grades again. "You promised me you'd do your work the last time we had this conversation."

Kelly bit her lip. "Mom. Please let me try harder! I'll get a tutor for geometry, and history and Spanish will be a breeze."

Her mom crossed an arm over her chest. "If it was a breeze, then why didn't you do it the first time around?"

Kelly shrugged. She didn't have a good excuse for that. She couldn't say she'd slacked off because of a breakup. "Stress," she finally said, hoping that would suffice.

"You have three weeks to prove to me that you can bring your grades up. I expect to see some improvement."

"You will. I promise." Kelly jumped up and wrapped her arms around her mom's neck. "You're the best."

"You probably won't be saying that if you don't do your homework."

"No. I will."

Mrs. Waters nodded and left the room.

Kelly went back to the email to Drew.

Tell you what, I'll play poker tonight if you help

me with my geometry. Let me know. I'm in way over my head and I desperately need your help.

~Kelly~

♥ ♥ ♥

Alexia threw the dirty, wet sponge in the bucket of water beside her when she heard her cell ringing in her bedroom. She tiptoed over the newly clean bathroom floor so as not to smudge it.

She grabbed her cell off her dresser and flipped it open. "Hello?"

"It's your favorite person in the world."

Alexia smiled, clutching the phone harder. "Ben. Hi."

"So, what are you doing?"

"Well, I was just finishing cleaning the bathroom floor."

"Are you serious?"

"Very."

"That doesn't sound like fun."

Alexia sat on the edge of her bed and brought her legs up, crossing them Indian-style. "It's not, but someone has to do it."

"I guess. So listen, what are you doing after you clean the bathroom floor?"

"Not sure yet. I should maybe vacuum."

"Uh, no. You should get out of the house and go to a movie with me."

It'd been a few weeks since Alexia and Ben had their first kiss. They hadn't kissed since then, mainly because 1) Alexia was afraid that even though her first kiss hadn't been so bad, her second might be disastrous, and 2) she didn't want her friends to find out about Ben yet. Part of her worried that Kelly would see Alexia and Ben together as a direct violation of the girl dating rule. Ben was Will's twin brother. It would almost be like she was going out with Will.

"Come on," Ben said, "say yes."

What were the chances that she'd see one of her friends at the theater? Sydney was at home. Alexia knew that because she'd just talked to Sydney not that long ago. Kelly was catching up on homework, and Raven was working.

"What would we go see?" Alexia asked. Besides, even if she did see someone, she'd tell the truth: that she and Ben were just friends. He hadn't officially asked her to be his girlfriend.

Yeah, that's exactly what Raven said about her and Zac, and you got on her case about it, she thought. Alexia groaned at her internal critic. This was different. She wasn't going through a breakup, so the rules didn't completely apply to her.

"We'll see whatever you want," Ben said.

"What about *Kiss and Tell*?"

There was a long pause, then, "Well, if that's what you're into . . ."

"I'm kidding!"

Ben let out a prolonged sigh. "Thank God. I wasn't going to say anything, but I really didn't want to see that movie."

"Not a fan of love stories?"

"Not on the silver screen, because nothing is that perfect."

"How about *When They Collide*?"

"I like humor," Ben said. "How about the seven o'clock show? I'll pick you up?"

"That sounds good. See you then."

♥ ♥ ♥

Laughter filled the movie theater all around them. *When They Collide,* a comedy about a man and a woman butting heads in the corporate world and then falling in love, was hilarious.

As she and Ben walked out, people recapped their favorite scenes, repeating the funniest snippets of dialogue. On the sidewalk, the amber glow of streetlights lit the way as they headed for the car they'd parked on a side street.

"I had fun," Ben said, bumping shoulders with her.

"Me, too."

He grabbed her hand, threading his fingers with hers. A smile graced her face as Ben's thumb ran up and down the side of her hand. How was a gesture so small so thrilling?

When they reached Ben's car, he unlocked the passenger door first and held it open as Alexia climbed inside, out of the cool breeze. Hands trembling with excitement, she folded them into her lap, not wanting Ben to see. He'd probably think she was an inexperienced dork. Maybe he held hands with a lot of girls he took out on dates. Did he take out a lot of girls?

Engine now running, the heat blasted out of the vents, warming Alexia's face. She turned to Ben and caught him staring at her, the car still in park.

"What?"

"I like you," he said, the candor surprising Alexia, even coming from Ben.

The smile on her face turned nervous. "I like you, too."

"So if you like me, and I like you, why aren't we officially together?" He grinned. "I want you to be my girlfriend, Alexia."

Alexia's mouth dropped open and she quickly snapped it shut.

His girlfriend?

Did she hear him right?

"Say something," he coaxed, reaching across the center console to take her hand again.

"I'm just surprised."

"Is that good or bad?"

"It's good," she clarified. "I . . . uh . . ."

The well of excitement in her chest made it hard to breathe. She looked over at Ben in the driver's seat. This was what she'd been waiting for. The last two years, her friends had had boyfriends and she was always single. Up until this point, she'd worried she'd always be alone and she'd graduate from college sans boyfriend. Either that, or she'd have to settle for someone she didn't really, really like.

But she liked Ben, if the butterflies in her stomach were any indication.

"Okay," she said, thinking only of the moment and nothing in the future, namely, what would her friends say? Would they shun her now because she had a boyfriend and they didn't? She didn't want to lose what they had now, all of them together, hanging out.

"Okay what?" Ben asked, looking diffident.

"Okay, I'll be your girlfriend."

"Yeah?"

"Yeah."

Leaning over, he threaded his fingers into her hair and kissed her, sealing the deal.

I have a boyfriend!

TWENTY-FOUR

Rule 4: *You must forget The Ex's birthday. Forget that he was born.*
Rule 18: *Do not ask anyone what your Ex is up to. Who cares! Your only concern should be what you are up to.*
Rule 20: *You have twenty-four hours to mourn the loss of The Ex. After the twenty-four hours, no more tears.*

One hour on Monday. Two hours on Tuesday. Thirty minutes on Wednesday.

Mmm, Wednesday was a good day at least, Sydney mused.

Three hours on Saturday.

The list went on and on, way past twenty-four hours. She'd probably mourn the loss of Drew for the rest of her life. Twenty-four hours wasn't enough. A lifetime wasn't enough.

She ticked off the days on her desk calendar with a finger stopping on March eighteenth.

Tomorrow is Drew's birthday, she thought. No, I'm not supposed to be thinking about it. I'm supposed to be forgetting it.

She opened her desk drawer, grabbed a tiny jewelry box, and flipped open the lid. There were only three things on the inside: a bracelet her mother had given her on her tenth birthday, a heart-shaped locket handed down to her from her grandmother, and a ring. A guy's ring. The one Sydney had bought months ago for Drew's birthday. She ran her finger around the cool white-gold band as if circling the edge of a wineglass to make it sing.

What was she going to do with it now?

Maybe she should get rid of it. After all, if she was going to follow Rule 4 and forget Drew's birthday, having the gift she'd bought for just such an occasion really defeated the purpose.

But not yet, she thought numbly. I don't want to get rid of it yet.

A part of her, deep down inside, hoped that she'd need the ring in the future. That maybe there was a little chance they'd get back together. And then she'd regret getting rid of the ring.

"Sydney!" her dad called from the kitchen.

Sydney slammed the lid of the jewelry box closed and deposited it back in the desk drawer. "Coming."

In the kitchen, Mr. Howard pulled open the dishwasher and started stacking several bowls on top of the counter. "Help me unload, please?"

Sydney started with the plates, since they were easiest. "Mom coming home today?"

Mr. Howard slid the bowls into the cupboard. "No. But I'm sure she'll be home in a few days." He stopped long enough to look at Sydney and smile a closed-lip smile. Sydney knew what he was thinking. He missed Mrs. Howard, and a few days were probably going to turn into several days.

They finished emptying the dishwasher. Sydney excused herself and headed into her bedroom. She picked up her Breakup Code journal and turned to a fresh page, flopping down onto her bed. She settled in on her stomach, her legs bent at the knees.

There were so many things running through her head, things she wanted to get out, but she didn't know where to start. She uncapped her pen and started doodling. Swirls turned into her name as she wrote it over and over again, and then she was writing *Drew + Sydney.*

Grumbling, she dropped her forehead to the page with a thump. It'd been three weeks since Craig's party at the abandoned barn. Three weeks since Drew took care of Sydney and practically stayed the night with her. The whole thing had only made the breakup worse. She couldn't stop thinking about how sweet and protective he'd been. Or how gentle he sounded when he'd said he loved her.

She'd almost rather have none of Drew than just a little bit, which is exactly what she'd had that Saturday night. He'd been there for her as if they were still together. He'd taken care of her, made sure she got home and into bed as promised, but he was gone when she got up, having slipped out sometime in the night. When she called later in the afternoon to thank him, he'd been aloof. Did he regret staying with her?

At least they hadn't gotten into a huge argument. They were always fighting when they were together and the arguments came more often than "I love you," but she'd made herself believe they were just in a "phase." That they'd get over it.

But they hadn't, and here they were: Done. Finished.

If the breakup was good for anything, it was that it showed Sydney some of her faults. She probably would have broken up with herself because of the way she was acting near the end. She'd taken Drew for granted.

It wasn't just about keg parties or being more outgoing. They were two different people now. Unfortunately, Drew had been the first to figure it out, while Sydney had been in the dark. She'd tried to hold on to something that wasn't even there anymore. She'd fooled herself.

"Dinner's almost done," Mr. Howard called, the smell of simmering taco meat wafting out of the kitchen.

"Okay."

Sydney grabbed her pen again and started writing, just to get her thoughts out. Her mother used to keep a journal when Sydney was younger. Mrs. Howard would sit in the chair in the corner of the living room that looked out over the backyard. The chair was in the same spot, dust collecting on the beige upholstery. It didn't move and no one used it.

I'm sorry, she wrote in her journal. *I'm sorry for not seeing. For not listening. I'm sorry for taking advantage of you and your good nature. I'm sorry for the things I said and didn't say. I wish I could go back.*

Reading it over, she nodded to herself. It sounded good in her mind, truthful. It was almost a release getting it on paper. Was this what her mother felt, writing in her journal so long ago?

What would Drew think if she read it to him? She didn't want to use it to get him back, she just wanted him to know what she was thinking and feeling. So that maybe he wouldn't feel so bad about breaking up with her. It would be her way of telling him how much he meant to her *and* that she was ready to let him go. Well, *almost* ready to let him go.

It could be a birthday present. Instead of the ring, she'd give him this on open-mike night.

Was she crazy for wanting to humiliate herself in a public venue? Yes, she probably was.

"Dinner's done," Mr. Howard said.

"I'm coming." Sydney capped her pen and shut the notebook on it, marking her spot so she could pick up the journal later.

♥ ♥ ♥

The next day, in order *not* to think about Drew and his birthday, Sydney got up early, packed a backpack, and headed out to Birch Falls Park with her mother's digital camera.

It was one of those late winter days when the sky was clear and the sun was shining. In direct light, it almost felt like spring in the above-freezing temps. Thank God spring was just days away. Sydney couldn't wait to get out of her winter clothes.

She parked in the front lot of the park and got out of the car with her backpack. She'd used the digital camera a few times since fetching it from the attic. She couldn't find the user's manual, so she didn't know much about the camera's features. The important thing was she knew how to turn it on and how to take a picture. That was really all she needed.

There were a few cars in the parking lot but no one in sight. Most likely they were on one of the ten different trails that ran through the park. Sydney had been on all of them with her mother.

Keeping on the narrow, paved walkway, Sydney headed toward the start of her favorite trail, the Lost Lake Trail.

The path was clear, but wet from the melting snow. Sydney's Columbia hiking boots made slapping noises in the shallow puddles.

On each side of the walkway were woods, the ground covered in patches of snow and piles of crisp leaves. A fat black squirrel darted beneath one of the wooden benches as Sydney stepped on a twig.

Squirrel, Sydney thought. *I saw a black squirrel the day Drew and I officially broke up.*

She sighed as the old pain from that day came flooding back. She was done crying, but the ache in her chest whenever she thought of Drew was still sharp.

I don't ever want to look at another squirrel again, she thought.

But then she brought up her camera, hit the ZOOM button twice, and snapped a picture. The screen on the back of the camera brought up the shot. She'd caught the squirrel bringing something to its mouth with both hands. It almost looked like it was praying.

"That's actually not too bad," she said to herself.

"What's not too bad?"

Sydney shrieked and whirled around. Kenny, a guy from school, stood behind her, his chest rising and falling quickly as if he'd been running. Sweat beaded on his temples. His cheeks were red.

"Hey," she said. "You scared me."

"Sorry." He shrugged and then repositioned his baseball hat on his head so that the brim was in back. "I thought you heard me run up."

Sydney looked past Kenny to the paved trail winding through the trees. Sometimes Drew came out here and ran with Kenny. Part of her was hoping she'd see him come up.

"I'm by myself," Kenny said. He put his hands on his hips.

"Right. I was just"—She stopped herself before she sounded silly. Kenny was no idiot. He knew she'd been looking for Drew. "How is he?"

"Drew? He's"—Kenny ran his shirtsleeve over his temples to soak up some of the sweat—"he's okay, I guess. You know Drew. He's not all Dr. Phil with his emotions."

Sydney smiled and nodded. She shifted her weight from foot to foot. There were a million other questions she wanted to ask him, but she hated to sound so nosy. And it wasn't like it was any of her business what Drew was up to. There was also the possibility that she'd just annoy Kenny with the grilling, and if she annoyed him, he'd probably complain to Drew about it.

What would her friends do in this situation? Raven would just smile and flirt to get the answers she wanted. Alexia wouldn't ask at all. And Kelly . . . she'd come up with a way to ask without actually asking.

Come on, Sydney. You're the smart one. Think of something.

"So," she began as her mind tried to grab for something clever, "what have you been up to?"

Kenny was with Drew all the time. Maybe she could glean something from his answer.

"Just hanging out," he answered. "Mostly it's just been me and Todd and Drew and Kelly. You know."

What about Nicole Robinson? Sydney so wanted to ask. She parted her lips, ready to blurt the question out before she could think better of it, but then she looked down at the camera in her hands. It signified something new in her life, something that was just hers. And right now, the thought of hiking through the woods and taking pictures like she and her mom used to do, sounded more interesting than discussing high school gossip.

She cared if Drew was seeing Nicole Robinson, but caring wouldn't get her anywhere. It would just cause her more stress, and she'd come to the park to enjoy herself.

"Well," she said, "I should let you get back to your run."

Kenny nodded. "Yeah. Still have a mile left to go." He raised his arms above his head and stretched. "See ya round." He tipped his head good-bye and jogged off down the pathway.

Sydney brought up the camera and snapped a photo. The result popped up on the screen. The sun shined muted rays through the bare tree branches so that it looked like Kenny was running toward some sort of heavenly light.

"Beautiful," Sydney said under her breath. She still had room for fifty more pictures on the camera, and she couldn't wait to fill up the memory card.

TWENTY-FIVE

Rule 22: *You can never follow The Ex nor ask his friends to put in a good word for you.*

The next weekend, Sydney was pretty much doing the exact same thing she'd been doing the weekend before: nothing. Unless you count driving around aimlessly as productive weekend activities. Just what was she supposed to be doing on a Friday night anyway, as a single girl? She'd spent the last two years of her life planning her weekend around someone else and now that it was just her, she felt kind of lost.

She'd already tried the party route. It'd been fun, hanging with people outside of school, but the drinking was now definitely on her never-do-again list. If she had such a list. She usually didn't do things she'd regret since Drew had always been her sounding board, telling her if her ideas were good or reeling her in when she went crazy. Like that time she decided she was going to take horseback-riding lessons and had to start *now*.

"You're afraid of horses," Drew had reminded her. "And the lessons are expensive."

"But . . ." she'd said, because she really wanted to ride a horse, maybe bareback on the beach somewhere.

"Why don't you think it over for three days. If you're still interested, then do it."

He'd been right, actually. A few days later, the idea didn't seem so bright.

Now she had no sounding board. She had no Drew. Would she ever get over him? Probably not, but she was trying to move on and her friends had helped her with that, along with The Breakup Code. It was nice to have some guidance, and it helped get her mind off Drew when she focused on following The Code.

Sydney turned into Scrappe and parked. She was about to get out when she noticed Drew's truck drive by.

Drew.

Where was he going? What was he doing now on Friday nights if he wasn't hanging out with her? As far as she knew there were no parties going on. Not that she was in on the party loop or anything.

Sydney jumped in her SUV and left the parking lot of Scrappe going the same direction Drew was. Curiosity was probably going to drive her mad or get her into a whole load of trouble, but rationality was not with her at the moment.

Drew was two cars ahead of her by the time she got onto the street, which was probably a good thing. He wouldn't be able to see her as easily.

He turned up ahead onto Hilldale, and Sydney slowed, turning behind him. His brake lights glowed red in the early evening dusk as he pulled up to the curb and parked. Sydney grimaced, hoping he didn't notice her driving by as he got out of his truck. Thankfully, his back was to the road.

He was at Kelly's house, probably hanging out with Todd. Todd was all right but could get obnoxious.

Maybe she should drop in to visit Kelly.

No. That would be too obvious. Besides, it wasn't right to use her friend like that. Not that she didn't want to see Kelly or hang out with her. Sydney picked up her cell from the passenger seat and dialed Kelly's number

Mrs. Waters answered the phone. "Hello?"

"Hi, Mrs. W, it's Sydney."

"Hi, are you calling for Kelly?"

"Yeah."

"Hold on a minute." A few muffles sounded as Mrs. Waters shifted the phone from her ear and yelled through the house for Kelly.

Kelly picked up on another extension. "Hello?"

"It's me."

"Oh . . . Syd, hey."

"What are you doing tonight?" Sydney slowed for a stop sign. "You want to hang out?"

"Actually . . . I'm doing something with my brother tonight. He asked me to come to a party for the basketball team."

"Oh." So that's what Drew was doing. "Is it a huge party?"

"Nah. It's at Matt's house. I guess his parents are going to be there and everything, so . . . "

"Drew will probably be there."

"Yeah. He's here now, with Todd."

Sydney bit her bottom lip. "Hey, can I ask you a huge favor?"

"Sure."

"Will you . . . uh, keep an eye on him for me. I mean, you know, just . . ." Oh, what was she saying? She was starting to sound pathetic. And obsessed. Like a crazy ex-girlfriend who couldn't get over her ex-boyfriend. Which she totally was, but now Kelly knew . . .

"I understand, Syd. Sure. I'll keep an eye on him, but I doubt he'll do anything."

"I know. And it's not like I have any claim over him now. I just don't want him hooking up with random girls. You know? He deserves someone great."

Kelly laughed lightly. "I know."

Taking in a breath, Sydney said, "Well, I should go. Have fun."

"Yeah. I doubt it. When do I ever have fun with my brother?"

"Then why are you going?"

There was a long pause before Kelly answered. "I don't know. Just to get out, I guess. But, hey, we should do something tomorrow. Want to go get coffee or something?"

Would she? Hell, yes. "Yeah. I'll invite Alexia, too. We're supposed to hang out. What time?"

"How about two? Meet me at Scrappe."

"K. See you then."

Sydney flipped her cell closed and realized she was still sitting at the same stop sign. Before hitting the gas, she dialed Raven's number. Maybe she was available.

I sure hope so because I do not want to go home to another night of silence.

♥ ♥ ♥

Raven grabbed her cell out of her bag and left Horace's garage, the sound of drums and guitars fading out as she shut the door behind her. "Hey, Syd," she said after seeing Sydney's name on the caller ID.

"Hi. What are you doing?"

Raven kicked at a rock with the toe of her boot. "Oh, nothing."

"Good, I'm coming over."

"Wait. I'm not there."

"Then where are you? And how can you be doing nothing if you're not even home?"

Raven groaned with indifference. "I'm at a friend's house."

"What friend?"

"A friend friend."

"That doesn't make any sense."

"Yes, it does."

Sydney gasped. "You're at a boy's house, aren't you?"

"No."

"Liar! Who is it?"

"It's not like that." Raven shifted, hugging her free arm around her waist. The night was still and the rainbow thermometer on Horace's garage door said it was forty-eight degrees, but Raven was only in a thin T-shirt and her flesh popped with goose bumps.

"It's Horace," she finally said, "and we're just friends."

"Horace McKay?"

"Yeah."

"Oh. Well, that's cool. What are you guys doing?"

The entrance to the garage opened and Horace poked his head out. "We're ready when you are."

"Okay," she said to him, then turned back to the phone. "I'm helping him with his band. I'm . . . uh, singing."

"Wow. Seriously?"

"Seriously."

"You always did have a great voice, Ray. You're having fun?"

Was she ever. Singing with the band was a huge rush. Like jumping off a cliff. Not that she'd ever jumped off a cliff. But if she had, she imagined it'd be as exciting as singing with live music thumping all around her.

"Yeah." She smiled to herself. "I'm having tons of fun."

"You sound like you're glowing." Envy edged her tone.

"I've always loved music."

"It's more than that."

Raven leaned her back against the garage wall. "I guess it's because I'm doing something for myself, instead of for a guy."

"Or maybe it's because you've found a guy you really like."

Raven's cheeks burned with guilt. It was a good thing she was on the phone. Sydney wouldn't have missed the blushing. "We're friends, Syd," she repeated, though she didn't sound very convincing.

"Yeah," Sydney said. "Just friends. So listen, Kelly, Alexia, and I are going to Scrappe tomorrow at two. You want to meet us there?"

"Sure."

"Cool. Talk to you later."

Raven hung up and was heading inside when her cell rang again.

"Now what?" she muttered, thinking it was Sydney again, but no, it was her mother. Raven checked the guys out through the door window. They were still waiting for her.

"Hi, Mom," she said.

"Hi, sweetie. Where are you?"

"A friend's house. We're practicing for band." She wasn't exactly lying after all.

"Oh, that's nice to hear! I'm glad you're getting serious about band. It's an important school activity—"

All Raven heard was "Blah. Blah. Blah."

"I know," she said vaguely. Usually her mother's conversations revolved around what she thought was good for Raven. So answering, "I know," was always a safe bet, even if she wasn't listening.

"When will you be home?" her mom asked at the same time Horace strummed several chords on his guitar. "What was that?"

"Nothing," Raven said, moving away from the garage. "It was nothing."

"Was that a guitar?"

"No."

"Raven!" Hobb yelled out the door. "Come sing your little heart out!"

"Sing?" Ms. Valenti said. "Who was that?"

"No one." Raven waved Hobb away as she went farther down the dirt driveway, past the cars. She was almost to the road now. No way was her mother going to hear the guitar playing.

"Raven Marie. What is going on?"

"Mom." Raven took in a breath. Should she lie?

"Are you playing in some sort of garage band?"

Raven let the silence answer for her.

"Come home right now."

"Mom."

"No. You get home this very minute. I want to talk to you."

"No."

"No what?"

"No. I'm not coming home this very minute." She clenched her jaw, feeling anger rise in her gut. "I'm going to practice with the band first and then I'll be home."

"I don't want you wasting your time in some garage band, Raven! You come home right—"

Raven flipped the phone closed on her mother's screeching voice then turned it off. She was going to be in a world of trouble when she got home, but she'd figure it out then.

TWENTY-SIX

Rule 28: *Do not lie to your girl about The Ex, even if it breaks a rule.*

"You ride with Drew," Todd said as he rushed around his bedroom digging through the piles of dirty clothes on his floor.

"Todd," Kelly said, glancing quickly at Drew as he leaned against the dresser, which, if Kelly had to guess, was empty since it appeared *all* of Todd's clothes were on the floor. "Why don't we take my car and we can pick Emily up on the way?"

Last weekend, while Drew helped Kelly with her geometry, he'd asked her to come to the basketball team's annual party. She'd been adamant about not going since he was Sydney's ex-boyfriend and that just seemed wrong. But really, she'd be going with her brother, and Drew would just be riding along. That is until Todd decided to change the plan.

Todd stopped digging through clothes long enough to send his sister a disgruntled look. "No freakin' way. It won't be a date if my little sister is driving."

"I don't think it's a date anyway. Who would want to date you?"

"Ha-ha." He pulled a navy blue T-shirt out of a pile and inspected it. "Emily wouldn't have called me specifically to see what I was doing tonight if she didn't want me."

Kelly snorted and stole a glance at Drew. Drew smirked, shaking his head. Kelly had been close to turning down this invitation, but now she couldn't wait to go. She hadn't been out to a party in months. It wasn't Will's scene. Kelly liked going just to dance. She didn't need to drink or gossip or anything like that, she just needed to work to the music in order to have a good time.

Todd pulled his T-shirt off and threw on the blue one. "Just ride with Drew. What's the big deal?"

She wasn't exactly sure what the big deal was. Something told her showing up at a party with her best friend's Ex wasn't a good idea. Not that there was anything to be guilty of—they weren't going on a date—but what would it look like to everyone else? People talked in Birch Falls.

"I don't mind you riding with me," Drew said, stuffing his hands in his jeans pockets.

"See?" Todd straightened, running a hand through his messy hair. "Besides, this crap shot was the one that invited you in the first place."

"That is true," Drew said, smiling.

Kelly sighed. "Fine. Let me go get my coat."

Todd raised his arms in the air. "Hallelujah! She's finally listening to me."

"Shut up, Todd!" she hollered as she headed down the hallway.

♥ ♥ ♥

The thump of music could be heard out in the driveway as Kelly got out of Drew's truck. There were already several cars parked in the driveway and along the side of the road. Lights lit all the downstairs windows of the Victorian-style house and some of the smaller basement windows.

Drew got out and came around the front of the truck to meet Kelly. "Ready?"

"Yeah."

They walked up together, passing a few girls who were leaving. The girls looked at Drew, smiling flirtatiously until they noticed Kelly with him. Then their faces fell and whispers started between them.

Drew and I are just friends, she thought. I have nothing to feel guilty for.

Mr. Turner, a fifty-something man with thinning hair, opened the door after Drew knocked.

"Come on in, Drew," Mr. Turner said, pulling the door back. "Everyone is downstairs."

"Thanks."

They passed Mr. Turner, and Kelly fell behind Drew, letting him lead the way. They went into the living room, down a hallway, and then rounded a corner to the basement steps.

The taupe carpet was plush beneath Kelly's flats. Music filled the stairwell and got louder the farther they went down. When they were past the overhang of the wall, the temperature rose a good five degrees. It was hot and muggy from so many bodies. Kelly looked out over the basement and was surprised to see a moving mass of people. She didn't think it'd be so packed.

When they reached the floor, Kelly pressed into Drew as a couple tried to get past her up the stairs. Drew leaned over. "You want to get something to drink?" he shouted.

"Yeah."

Drew took her hand and pulled her through the dancing crowd. They emerged on the other side of the basement where cool air spilled in several open windows. There was an L-shaped sectional couch in the corner, a huge entertainment center directly across from it.

Music played through the surround sound while the LCD TV hanging on the wall displayed a moving image of an ocean complete with palm trees and a hammock. It was like one of those living screen savers.

A game of cards was in play on the square, glass coffee table. Through an arched doorway, Kelly saw a pool table and a guy she recognized from her math class lining up a shot.

"Come on," Drew said, nodding toward another room of the main basement. There was a bar along one wall where an older woman filled glasses with ice and soda. "Hi, Mrs. Turner," Drew said.

"Oh, Drew! How are you?" Mrs. Turner brushed hair from her eyes then unscrewed the cap on a two-liter Pepsi.

"I'm fine. Thanks. Can we just have some water?"

"Sure." Mrs. Turner handed over two bottles.

"Thanks." Drew handed a water to Kelly. "Want to sit down?"

She nodded and he led her back to the main room to the couch. Drew and the other guys did their handshake thing as Kelly made herself comfortable on the end of the couch. She fidgeted with her jacket, pulling it around herself to hide her stomach. This did not feel like a skinny day for her.

What did she have to eat yesterday? Turkey sandwich . . . a plum . . . oh yeah, a bowl of ice cream. The latter probably didn't complement her thighs.

Maybe she needed some exercise.

She leaned over toward Drew. "I'm gonna dance."

"Okay," he said as she got up.

Tentatively, she approached the throng of dancers looking for someone she recognized and could sidle up to. There were a few girls she recognized from some classes, but no one she knew well.

Then she heard her name shouted over the din of the music, followed by a shrill finger-in-the-mouth whistle.

Craig Thierot.

"Hey!" he shouted, coming up alongside her. "Dance with me?"

"Yeah." She started swaying her hips, arms hung in the air. Craig got in close but kept his hands off her, opting instead to hook his index finger around hers. She hung her head back and laughed as he twirled her around.

It'd been a long time since she got out and danced at a party. This was not Will's sort of thing and "dancing" to him was a formal, slow dance. Something you had to take lessons to learn.

Craig grasped her hand tighter, sliding his other arm around her back as he dipped her. She screeched as she tossed her head back, the ceiling suddenly straight above her, and then Drew popped up in her line of sight.

"Mind if I cut in?" he said, giving a sideways grin.

Craig hoisted Kelly back up. "That's cool, dude." He let Kelly go and melted into the crowd, finding another dance partner easily.

A fast pop song came on next and instantly the mood in the room shifted as did the pace of dancing. Drew took Kelly's hand. She started bobbing her head in time to the quick beat, her feet moving beneath her. Drew followed her lead as Kelly swung their hands up in the air along with everyone else.

He laughed as she shouted, "Woo!" and made a circle around him wiggling her hips.

This was so much fun! How long had it been since she'd had this much fun? Like, months! Ever since she started seeing Will. His idea of fun was sitting at home making US history flashcards.

By the time the song was over, sweat beaded on Kelly's forehead and she swiped it away. Drew grabbed her hand and pulled her off the dance floor, thrusting a bottle of water in her hand.

"That was fun," he said, grinning at her.

"Totally." She downed a gulp of water and her stomach growled. "Is there food here? I'm starving."

"Just chips," Drew said, looking apologetic. "But we could go get something. If you're hungry."

"I'm starving, but I don't want you to leave the party or anything."

Drew shook his head. "It's cool. I came, I made an appearance. Now I'm ready to go. Come on."

He grabbed her hand and pulled her toward the stairs.

♥ ♥ ♥

You deserve the best, but I gave you the worst, Sydney wrote in her Breakup Code journal. *You were always looking out for me, but I never paid enough attention to realize it.*

The ringing cell pierced the silence in Sydney's bedroom and the whole damn house. She rolled off her bed, grabbing the cell from atop her dresser. The lit screen said LISA.

"Hey."

"Hi, Chut," Lisa said. "What's up?"

Sydney tried not to cringe at the nickname. "Not much." She resettled on her bed, uncapping her pen. She drew a star on the open page in her notebook then ran over the bold black lines again and again. "What's up with you?"

"I was just at Matt's party . . . for the basketball team."

"Oh." Sydney drew another star, bigger than the last. "Was it fun?"

"It was okay. I saw Drew there."

Sydney stopped doodling. "Yeah?"

"Yeah. And he was there with someone."

Wasn't he going with Todd and Kelly? Had plans changed? "Who was he with?" Silence fell on the line. "Lisa?"

"He was with your friend. Kelly."

Sydney let out a breath of relief. "Oh. Yeah. I know. I just talked to her not that long ago. She and Todd were going with Drew."

"Well, she and Drew just left together, without her brother. And . . . they were dancing together. Like all over each other."

Sydney's heart sped up in her chest. "But . . . "

"I'm sorry. I thought you should know."

"You're sure it was them?" Sydney shut her pen in her journal and got up, pacing the floor.

"Oh, yeah. I'm sure. Drew's hard to mistake."

"Okay." Sydney suddenly felt numb all over. "Thanks, Lisa."

"Don't thank me. Call me later, okay? We'll do something."

"Sure. Bye." She disconnected and continued pacing her room. Kelly wouldn't do anything to jeopardize their friendship. Would she? There had to be some sort of mistake or explanation. Drew and Kelly were friends. They had been for a long time. Sydney met Drew through Kelly.

Sydney dialed Kelly's cell number and Kelly picked up on the second ring.

"Hi," Sydney began, wondering how to approach this conversation without sounding like a bitch or an obsessed ex-girlfriend. "So, did you go to the party?"

"Yeah," Kelly said, sounding a little bit breathless.

"Did Drew . . . uh, dance with anyone?"

"No." A door slammed somewhere nearby and then a car engine started up. "My Chemical Romance" blared when the CD player started up. "Sorry. Hold on," Kelly shouted. The music faded in the background.

"You with Drew?" Sydney asked. Had Kelly been lying about the dancing? Or was Lisa? Why would Lisa lie?

"Yeah," Kelly said. "We're going to get something to eat."

"Is Todd with you?"

Kelly groaned. "No. He ditched us for Emily Sutton. Can you believe that? Emily is an idiot, don't you think?"

"So it's just you and Drew?" Sydney clutched the phone in her hand. She had nothing to be angry about, did she?

"Yeah. Is . . . that okay?" Kelly asked softly.

Sydney squeezed her eyes shut and counted to ten. Was it okay? Should she care? Yes, she cared, but maybe the right question was: Did she have a right to care?

"Sure. That's fine. I don't care," she finally said. "Just call me later. Okay?"

"I will. Bye."

Sydney flipped her phone closed but continued pacing the bedroom. Was Kelly lying? Had they been dancing all over each other? Did Drew even dance?

Sydney tried to shake the anger rolling in her gut. She just needed to calm down. There had to be a reasonable explanation. Until then, she had no reason to doubt her best friend.

TWENTY-SEVEN

Rule 11: *You must never date your girls' Exes.*

Alexia looked over at Ben sitting on her living room couch. She was still amazed that she had a boyfriend. It'd taken so long that she'd begun to question her date-ability. Like maybe there was something wrong with her and she'd be single for the rest of her life.

It probably helped that Ben was so outgoing and forward, unlike her. He'd been so goofy right from the start that she felt comfortable around him and didn't clam up as usual.

Maybe that'd been her problem all along. She just needed to meet someone who was comfortable with himself. Ben was definitely secure with who he was.

"What?" he said, catching her staring.

"Nothing." She looked away as her cheeks turned red.

Ben scooted down the couch and rested his head on her shoulder. "Pet me, love," he said, snuggling into her.

She laughed and ran her fingers through his messy hair. "So what are we doing tonight? You want to watch a movie?"

He sat up. "Well, there's this party for the basketball team. I want to make an appearance at least. We could watch a movie then head over there?"

Probably someone she knew was going to be there and she didn't want her friends finding out about Ben yet. How could she tell them when they were all going through breakups? Her being the only one with a boyfriend right now would separate her from the group. Instead of it being four single friends bonding and hanging out, it'd be three single friends and one with a boyfriend.

"I don't get into parties," she said, hoping that would be excuse enough not to attend.

"It's not one of those parties. It's for the basketball team. The coach is probably there and Matt's parents. It'll be cool. I promise." He grinned, showing all his teeth.

"Nah. I don't think I want to go."

The grin slid away. "Something wrong, Alexia?"

"No. Why?"

Brow furrowed, he rubbed his bottom lip with his index finger, thinking. "You know, now that I think about it, you avoided me all week at school. And whenever I suggest going out into public together, like somewhere where we'll be seen, you talk me out of it."

Did he know she was keeping him a secret?

"Well, I'm just a very . . . introverted person."

"Bullshit," he said softly. "Tell me the truth."

"Uh . . ."

He crossed his arms over his chest, kicking one leg over the other knee, waiting. "Is it because I'm so handsome? You're afraid of mass hysteria among the female population?"

She giggled nervously. At least he was still joking with her. That was a good sign except, something told her when she admitted the truth, he wouldn't be in the joking mood any longer.

"It's because of my friends," she said, then everything poured out in one long, run-on sentence. "So for now," she finished, "I want to keep this . . . us . . . between us."

With a sharp intake of breath, he stood, towering over her while she remained on the couch. "No," he said.

"What?" She got up. "What do you mean, 'no'?"

"I'm not some dirty little secret, Alexia."

The natural grin he always wore was gone, replaced with something close to embarrassment.

"You're not," she said, frantic. "I just don't want to hurt my friends."

"But you'll hurt me?" The corners of his eyes crinkled with confusion. "I don't get it."

Quick, think of something! Alexia thought. He looks like he's about to run and you'll lose the only boyfriend you've ever had. And in record time, too! Raven couldn't even top this!

"Listen, Ben," she began, guilt edging her voice, "I didn't mean to hurt you. It's just . . ."

"What?"

"Just give me a few days. Okay?" She wrung her hands. "I'll tell my friends that we're together."

"Take as much time as you need." He grabbed his coat off the couch. Shrugging into it, he looked over at her. "Call me when you tell them."

"Wait. You're leaving?"

He stopped, hand on the front door. "Yeah. I'll see ya later, okay?"

"Ben?"

He stepped outside, closing the door softly behind him. Alexia ran to the front window and watched him climb into his car. She hoped he was kidding, that he'd get back out of his car and laugh hysterically and she'd laugh, too. But no, he started up the engine and drove away.

"He was serious," she muttered.

Suddenly she knew or at least had a better understanding of how her friends must have felt when their boyfriends broke up with them. Alexia felt like she had to fix it or go somewhere and be proactive about it, but there was nothing to do but to watch Ben drive away. That was the worse feeling of all, like you were helpless, like everything was out of your control.

But that wasn't true exactly with Alexia, because she could fix this, unlike her friends. Their boyfriends had broken up with them. There were no second chances or invites to call later when they figured it all out. But Ben had extended a second chance, and Alexia had to take it.

But not yet. Alexia's friends were important to her. This wasn't about Ben, he was making it about him. She just wanted to keep her friends *and* have a boyfriend. That was possible, wasn't it?

Her friends hadn't been very good about juggling both, but Alexia was determined to try. The plan, at least in her mind, had been to wait until her friends went through The Breakup Code and were finally over their exes. Then she'd tell them about Ben. But not before then.

Kelly laughed, forgetting that her mouth was full of taco salad. She threw her hand over her mouth as the hysterics continued. Across the table, Drew's eyes were watering, tears streaming down his face.

"I have pictures," he said, wiping his face.

"No way! I want a copy. Todd would never be able to pick on me again if I had a picture of him in girl's underwear."

"You could use it as a threat. Tell him you'll post it all over the school," Drew said, dipping a fry in ketchup.

"Totally. Of course, I'd have to hide the picture in a safe deposit box, since he'd probably tear my whole room apart trying to find it."

"That's true."

"Does he know you have pictures?"

Drew nodded. "He tries to find them every chance he gets."

"I bet he never played another game of Dare after that."

Drew popped the fry in his mouth. "Nope. I'm the reigning champ and probably will be till the day I die."

Their server, a twenty-something woman with extremely long blonde hair, came up to the table. "Can I get you guys anything?"

"No, thanks," Drew said. "Kel?"

"I'm fine." She smiled.

"Okay. I'll get you your check." The waitress flashed a smile at Drew, clearly interested in more than serving him dinner. Beth—that's what her nametag said—had been flirting with Drew since they came into Striker's an hour ago. Either Beth sensed that Drew and Kelly were just friends, or Beth didn't care.

Kelly was waiting for her to ask Drew for his phone number. If Drew went up to the register alone, maybe that's when Beth would make her move.

Beth was so not Drew's type. Sydney was short, dark, and had a fiery personality. Kelly always thought they'd made a great couple. Beth was none of those things, at least from what Kelly had observed while being there.

"Here you go," Beth said, laying the bill on the table facedown.

"Thanks." Drew flashed his drop-dead-because-I'm-gorgeous smile and Beth nearly did. Except Kelly suspected Drew had no idea how his smile affected people or that he *was* so damn gorgeous.

"I'll be right back." He grabbed the check while reaching for his wallet with the other hand. Kelly turned in the booth to watch him saunter up to the front counter. Beth was there waiting, conveniently.

She tapped several things in on the touch-screen register. Drew handed over a twenty, which Beth held on to for several seconds as if prolonging his stay. She handed his change over, then, eyes darting around, she asked him something. Drew paused, smiled, then nodded toward Kelly.

Beth's face fell. "Oh," she said, nodding.

What was that all about?

Drew grabbed two mints from the crystal bowl by the register and came back over to their table. "Here. I got you a mint," he said, tossing the red-and-white-striped candy on the table.

"Thanks, but I'm not a huge fan of mints. You keep it."

Drew frowned. "Oh. Yeah . . . Sydney . . . she likes mints. I guess it was habit, grabbing them." He scooped the mint up and stuffed it in his pocket. "Sorry."

"It's no big deal." Kelly stood, putting her coat on. "So, did the waitress hit on you?"

He laughed. "No. She asked if you and I were together."

"Oh? What did you tell her?"

"I said yeah." He shrugged.

Kelly's mouth dropped open. "You did what?"

Frowning, Drew leaned over. "It's no big deal, Kel. I didn't mind paying. You can pick up the bill next time."

Kelly relaxed and shook her head at her own stupidity. "I thought . . . I mean . . . the way the waitress had been acting . . . I thought she had asked are we together, like boyfriend and girlfriend."

Drew scrunched up his nose. "You don't think that's what she really meant, do you?"

Before Kelly could answer, Drew shrugged. "It doesn't matter either way. Come on." He threw a five-dollar bill on the table. "Let's go."

She followed him outside, unable to ignore Beth staring. Like it was Kelly's fault Drew wasn't into her.

Whatever.

In the truck, Kelly shivered, the cool air of night having crept in while they were eating. Drew turned the engine over and blasted the heat. By the time they pulled up in front of Kelly's house, the cab of the truck was a good eighty degrees.

"Well, thanks for taking me to the party and out to dinner."

Drew shrugged, propping his arm over the back of her bucket seat. "I had fun."

"Me, too. Oh, and hey, you have to get me a copy of that picture of Todd."

"Will do."

Kelly reached for the door handle, but Drew put his hand on her forearm. "Wait." She stopped. "Kel . . . that thing . . .

in the diner . . . " He shifted, setting both hands in his lap. "Would you, uh, want to do this again? With me?"

Kelly swallowed hard. Sometimes, like now, Drew's eyes unnerved her. "Like, as friends?"

He turned sideways in his seat. "No."

Now her mouth was bone-dry. Swallowing was impossible. "Uh . . . Drew . . . " He was asking her on a date. Kelly had wanted to hear something like this from Drew years ago, before Sydney, before he spent two years dating her best friend. It was too late now, though.

No matter how much she liked him then, now it was too late. She couldn't have him, she couldn't hurt her best friend. But more important . . .

"Drew, I know you broke up with Sydney for whatever reasons, but I think you still love her. You guys were perfect for each other and no matter how much we get along or have fun, you're thinking about her."

The mints proved that and the comment about doing math with Sydney . . . not that she was going to point it out specifically and embarrass him.

His flicked his gaze down. Kelly finally felt like she could breathe.

"So are you turning me down because you don't want to hurt Sydney, or because you think I belong with Sydney?"

"Both."

"Do you think we should get back together?"

"Do you want the truth?"

He looked up again. "Yeah."

"Then, yes. I think you miss her but you don't want to admit to it."

Shifting again, he turned to the driver's-side window, propping his elbow on the door rest. "We just weren't getting along anymore."

"Did you try to get along?"

He shrugged. "Maybe I jumped ship too soon."

"She misses you, too, you know."

"I know."

The front door of Kelly's house opened and Todd stuck his head out. "What the hell are you doing out there?" he shouted. "Emily dumped me!"

Drew grunted, shaking his head. "We told him, didn't we?"

Kelly laughed. "Yeah. I'm not letting him live this one down, either."

"Well, you should go wipe his nose. He's probably crying like a little girl."

Kelly nodded, pulling the door open. "Thanks, Drew. Really."

"You're welcome." He gave her a sheepish smile, the one Kelly knew he reserved for the people closest to him, the *real* smile. "See ya later."

Nodding, she shut the door and watched him drive away.

TWENTY-EIGHT

Rule 23: *I know you can't wait for this moment: If you come face-to-face with The Ex, you must let him know what he has lost by flirting with him, touching him, and doing whatever the situation calls for.*

The Thursday before open-mike night, Raven still hadn't figured out what she was going to do. Defy her mother? Or quit the band? She shook her head at her own thoughts as she headed toward third hour.

Footsteps fell around the corner of the next hallway. Raven slowed. The heavy boots on the tile—*dum, dum, dum*—told Raven exactly who it was. Not only that, but she could sense Caleb was nearby, like a deer might sense some moron trudging through the woods. Instinct told her to run, run far away!

She hurried, trying to get into the next hallway before Caleb saw her.

"Raven! Wait a sec!"

Too late. Raven cringed. Should she pretend she hadn't heard him? Keep going? Disappear inside the bathroom? Maybe she should run right out the door and never look back.

Caleb was like a thorn in her side now. She was almost embarrassed that she'd gone out with him at all.

"Hey," he said, slipping in front of her before she had the chance to run. "I got you something." He pulled a rose from behind his back.

"What's this for?" she said.

"It's an apology."

Was he serious? Had she somehow stumbled into the fourth dimension? Because this was not the Caleb she knew. The Caleb she knew didn't apologize for anything. He probably didn't even know the meaning of an apology.

"Caleb—" This was really not a good time for him to play her. She had been in a bad mood since her mother forbade her to sing with Horace's band.

Singing and hanging out with those guys had been the one good thing she had done since Caleb broke up with her. She looked forward to every single practice she could sneak in, but now she hadn't been over there in almost a week and it was starting to get to her. She missed Horace and Dean and even Hobb. She missed singing.

It was this bad mood that propelled her to do what she did next.

She took the rose from Caleb's hand. "Thanks, baby," she cooed just like she used to when they were together. Giving the rose a customary sniff, she got in close to him.

Running a hand down his arm, she flicked her eyes up. His lids were at half-mast as he slipped his arm around her shoulders and tugged her into him. She snuggled up and tilted her head as if waiting for a kiss.

Caleb leaned over, and just as he went in for the lip-lock, Raven turned her face away. "Sorry," she said, tapping the rose against his chest, "but you broke up with me, remember?" She arched a brow. "Then humiliated me in front of the whole school by kissing some random chick. Take your rose and shove it, Caleb, 'cause us breaking up was the best thing that ever happened to me."

With that, she swiveled on her heels and walked away.

♥ ♥ ♥

That was like a breath of fresh air, Raven thought. She slouched in her chair as she waited for the final bell to ring and her US history class to begin. Or, really, for Horace to show up and take the seat next to her.

Less than a minute later, he walked in the door, his brown leather boots scuffling across the floor. He smiled when they locked eyes and he made his way through the aisle of desks over to his.

"Hey, Ray," he said, turning sideways in his seat. "Are you still grounded?"

"Yeah," Raven said, rolling her eyes, "but I'm working on my mother. I just can't promise anything." Dread filled her stomach even thinking about it. "Working" on her mother wasn't going to get her anywhere, most likely. Her mother was stubborn as a mule when it came to the things she thought were "good" for her daughters.

"Open-mike night is this weekend. We really need to practice at least once before the show," Horace said.

"I know." Raven tapped her pencil against her book. "Maybe you should find someone else." It pained her to say the words aloud. She didn't want them to find someone else. She wanted to do it, and the thought of letting another chick take her spot made the dread turn into a hard lump of envy.

"No way," Horace said, and Raven settled with relief. "We want you. Your voice is perfect for the songs."

A smile pulled her lips tight. She was probably glowing right about now. "But what if I can't get away?"

"We'll figure something out," he said, sounding sure of it.

Raven, though, was having a hard time believing him.

♥ ♥ ♥

"If it makes you that happy, you have to do it," Alexia told Raven later that day at lunch. "You'll always regret not trying."

Raven popped the tab on her can of Coke. "But what am I going to do about my mother?"

"You can lie," Kelly said, ripping her turkey sandwich into tiny little bites.

"Like what?" Raven asked. "Tell her I'm studying at the library?"

Sydney snorted. "I don't think that'll fly."

Everyone turned their attention to Sydney. She'd been grumpy all week. Raven figured it had something to do with Drew and the breakup, but Sydney wasn't confessing anything.

"Right." Kelly nodded. "You could tell her you're at my house studying for a huge history test."

"You can use me, too," Alexia said. "Just let me know before, in case your mom calls or something."

"Thanks, but even if I do get away to practice, my mother's still going to find out eventually. I mean, we're playing at the open-mike night at Scrappe. My mom's going to be there, and then I won't just be grounded, I'll be locked in my bedroom forever with SAT workbooks and college applications."

Alexia popped a chip in her mouth and crunched it up. "But if it's important to you, you have to do it. That's what my mom always says. You can't let something pass by because you don't have the courage or because someone says you can't. You'll regret not doing it and then what?"

Raven nodded, letting Alexia's advice sink in. Playing with Horace and the band made her happy, but it'd make her mother furious. What would her dad do? If anyone could understand her love for music, he could. And he might just be the only person who could talk Raven's mother out of the grounding.

Raven knew that the best time to catch her dad was on a Friday afternoon. He worked six days a week, sometimes twelve hours a day, but he always took Fridays off. He always said it was his favorite day of the week. There was something hopeful about Fridays.

Now he sat across from Raven at a red-flecked table in Striker's. He was the only one in the whole place who wore a full suit, a silk tie, and dress shoes that were shinier than the chrome appliances in the diner's kitchen.

Mr. Andrews pushed his wire-framed glasses back up the bridge of his nose and looked at his daughter. "So what's going on, Raven? Talk to your daddy."

Raven hadn't called him "Daddy" since she was in seventh grade, but he always referred to himself that way and she never corrected him. She took a drink from her chocolate shake then twirled the straw through the thick drink.

"Mom grounded me because I was singing with a band."

Mr. Andrews inhaled deeply and crumpled a napkin in his large hands. "You know how your mother views music and bands."

"I know."

He shook his head. "Raven, I loved music when I was your age and I wanted it more than anything. Your mother gave me a chance with it and I failed. She doesn't want to see you fail. I don't want to see you fail."

Raven's dad had been out of their house for so many years now that he'd developed a separate scent from Raven and her mother and Jordan. His was deeper, muskier, like woodsy chocolate. She smelled it now and suddenly realized how much she'd missed him. The fault for their recent silence couldn't rest entirely on him. She could have called him, too. When she asked for his help, he was always there. Like now. He would push aside any business he had to help his daughters.

"Dad, I need to do this." She shoved her milk shake aside. "This is important to me—and how in the world am I going to learn anything if I'm not allowed to try? You and Mom can't always protect me. Please tell her to let me go to the school's open-mike night and sing."

He picked up half of his BLT and took a bite. He wiped his hands on a napkin and chewed up his food before answering. The wait was nearly unbearable.

"Listen, I'm not going to tell your mother what to do. If she thinks what she's doing is right, then I have to respect that." He leaned forward conspiratorially and lowered his voice. "But let it be known that if I listened to what everyone else said, I wouldn't be where I am today." He sat back and winked at her. "Now finish your milk shake."

Raven took the glass between her hands and smiled. She knew exactly what she was going to do.

TWENTY-NINE

Rule 1: *You must not email or IM The Ex ever again. Take his name off your email list.*

Sydney spent the next twenty-four hours before open-mike night burying herself in preparation. Focusing on it helped keep her mind off Drew and Kelly.

Crap, you just thought about them again.

Okay, so maybe her mind wasn't completely on open-mike night.

So far, she hadn't heard anything else about Kelly and Drew hanging out together. Sydney was beginning to feel like a paranoid idiot. At least she hadn't acted on her anger and paranoia. That had to count for something.

Now she went into the computer lab at school and started up a computer. She had to make flyers for the fund-raiser tomorrow night. The flyers were a last-minute advertising venture. She was going to pass them out at some of the downtown stores.

The event was coming together nicely. The back room at Scrappe was filling up with homemade goodies—cookies, brownies, fudge—and she and Alexia were making chocolate candy later. Dr. Bass, long before she became a successful psychologist, made candy on the side for extra income. She had molds, double boilers, everything the girls would need.

Raven and Kelly were doing no-bake cookies, which they'd picked because neither of them knew much about baking.

The performers' schedule had been full since Tuesday, and there were more people on the waiting list. Sydney was supposed to go on at 8:15 P.M. She was thinking about bowing out, though, and letting someone else—i.e., someone with actual talent—have her spot.

Reading poetry in public, especially amateur poetry, was like putting your soul in front of the firing squad. And would Drew be able to appreciate what she was doing? Would he even care? After all, she was reading for him, so he would know how much of a great guy he was, even if she didn't let him know it while they were going out.

It'd been days since she talked to him last. She wasn't randomly calling him anymore to bug him or hear his voice mail. She was actually really proud of herself. It was almost as if she was finally moving on.

Maybe she was. Had it been The Breakup Code? It helped having something to focus on. The journal really, really helped. No wonder her mother used to spend so much time journaling. It was a huge release, yelling, whining, pouting to the journal pages, and she didn't have to regret spewing her emotional insides afterward because no one was listening.

But tomorrow night, practically the whole school would be listening as she recited a poem. It was both exciting and nauseating, but she'd never backed down from anything.

The flyers done, Sydney hit the PRINT button and the printer whirred to life. While she waited, she opened up a Web browser and checked her email.

You have 1 new message.

Probably from Alexia or something.

She clicked on the link and her inbox opened up. She read the sender name . . .

Drew Gooding.

Her heart literally skipped in her chest then slammed against her rib cage, beating like a frenzied drum. It was just an email from Drew. She'd opened her email a thousand times before and seen his name there in her inbox.

But this was different. It was different because they weren't together anymore. Because he hadn't emailed in weeks. And she hadn't initiated this. He had.

Clicking the subject line to open the message, Sydney bit her bottom lip and took in a deep breath.

> *Hey Syd,*
>
> *I wanted to call, but I wasn't sure if you'd feel like talking. This way, if you want to ignore me, you can just hit the delete button.*
>
> *I guess I just wanted to see how you've been. I'm not asking you for anything. I just want to talk.*
>
> *—Drew*

Like she'd ever ignore Drew. Not now. Not ever. Yes, she'd been heartbroken about him breaking up with her. Yes, she'd been angry when he hadn't immediately returned her phone calls. But he had been her best friend at one time—actually, he still was.

There were only a few people in this world who knew Sydney inside and out. Drew was one of them. He'd always been a decent guy, even when he was breaking up with her. That's why she'd fallen in love with him in the first place.

She hit the REPLY button on the email and typed in a message, then read it back.

"No, that sounds needy," she muttered, hitting the DELETE key and holding it down. She rewrote the email like ten times before she came up with something that sounded upbeat but not too upbeat—and not desperate.

Drew,

Of course I'd want to talk to you. Come to the open-mike night tomorrow night at Scrappe. Be there by eight. We'll talk then.

Sydney

She didn't want to think too hard about this. She didn't want to get her hopes up, but right now she felt breathless and a little light-headed. If Drew wanted to talk, what did that mean?

♥ ♥ ♥

Alexia stirred the second pot of melting chocolate while Sydney squeezed melted red chocolate into heart-shaped molds.

"So how are things?" Alexia asked. "With the breakup? The Code?"

Sydney shrugged. "I think I've broken, like, every rule."

"Sydney! Are you serious?"

"Unfortunately. It's not as if I set out to break the rules. It just happened. But I really like the journal. It was a good idea, Lexy."

Alexia shut the burner off on the stove and poured the chocolate into a plastic squeeze bottle. "What about Kelly and Raven? Have they said anything to you?"

"No. You'd have to ask them."

"So basically what you're saying is The Code was for nothing? If you broke all the rules . . ."

Sydney licked chocolate from her finger and then washed her hands. "No. That's not what I'm saying. I think . . ."

She turned the faucet off and stared out the darkened window. Her lips parted as if she was about to say something and then thought better of it. "Never mind. I don't know if I can explain it well, but I think The Code worked. Okay?"

Alexia set the squeeze bottle aside and propped her hands on her hips, her hair shifting around her shoulders. "But you broke the rules. That means it didn't work."

Sydney rolled her eyes. "You're overanalyzing again." She filled up another chocolate mold, then, "Well, that should be enough chocolate. Can you bring this stuff to Scrappe tomorrow? I still have flyers to pass out tonight."

"Yeah. I got it."

"Thanks." Sydney grabbed her purse and coat. "Call me later, okay?"

"Sure." Alexia walked Sydney to the door, said good-bye, then went searching for her parents. She found both of them in the den. The ceiling light blazed, the desk lamp was on, and the curtains were drawn back. Her parents always liked surrounding themselves with light. They said it was good for the mind, especially during the winter months.

"Hey," Alexia said, dropping into one of the red upholstered chairs. "What are you guys doing?"

"Final revisions on our book," her dad said. He licked his finger and flipped through several pages. "It's due Monday, so we're in crunch time."

"And what are you doing?" her mother asked.

Alexia made a fist and rested her face against it. "Nothing. Sydney just left and I'm waiting for the chocolate to set."

"How did the candy turn out?"

"Fine."

Dr. Bass grabbed his ceramic mug. "I need more coffee." He looked to his wife. "You, honey?"

"No, thanks," she said as she came around the desk and sat across from Alexia. When her husband's loafers squeaked on the hardwood floor in the hallway, she turned to her daughter. "Everything okay?"

Growing up with two psychologists, Alexia was used to talking to her parents about how she felt. However, she was also accustomed to both of them trying to analyze and treat her. It could get annoying, and the older she got, the more she censored what she said.

Still, this whole thing with The Breakup Code and Ben was weighing on her. All she'd wanted was to help her friends and bring them all back together. They *were* hanging out again but had she really helped them?

If they were all breaking the rules, then things weren't really going the way she'd hoped. And in her own love life, she'd only managed to screw things up with Ben. If she couldn't help herself, how could she help her friends?

She'd failed them.

Maybe her mother would have some advice for her. After all, the coping list they'd had her make when she lost her cat had worked wonders. They probably knew something she didn't about the process.

"Remember the coping list you guys asked me to make when I lost Gypsy?"

"I remember." Her mother nodded and crossed one leg over the other.

Alexia explained how she'd created The Breakup Code for her friends, using the coping list as a model. "At first I thought it was going well, but now it's not working right because they're not following the rules exactly."

"Honey," her mother leaned forward and clasped her hands together, "that coping list . . . it was never entirely about following the rules."

Frowning, Alexia said, "What do you mean?"

"Coping lists are meant to be distractions."

"What?"

"That's what coping lists are. If you're focusing on the list, you're not dwelling on the pain or frustration. It's used for depression, death, quitting addiction. It's common among people who want to quit smoking. But I've heard of it used for all sorts of things."

"So you were tricking me when I lost Gypsy?"

Dr. Bass scrunched up her nose. "No. Of course not. It's not trickery, it's basic psychology."

Alexia pursed her lips. It did make sense. When she had to go to the doctor's office as a kid and get a shot, before sticking her, the doctor asked what her favorite cartoons were. As she listed her top three, the doctor poked the skin at her bicep and, surprisingly, it hadn't hurt as much as she thought it would.

"Are your friends getting over their exes?" her mother asked.

Alexia shrugged. "It seems like it."

"Then, honey, your Breakup Code apparently worked."

THIRTY

Raven was already shaking and the band wasn't scheduled to go on for another hour. Scrappe was packed, and people were still lining up outside waiting to pay the five-dollar cover charge. Whatever kind of advertising Sydney and the rest of the student council had done, it'd worked. It was almost a miracle. Raven had no idea there were so many people living in Birch Falls.

"Here you go," she said, handing an older couple change from their twenty-dollar bill. "Let me just stamp your hand and you can head in."

She rocked the SCRAPPE stamp across a rainbow inkpad and pressed it onto the woman's hand, then the man's.

The stamp had been custom-made by one of Ms. Valenti's vendors. No way would anyone be able to replicate the stamp and bluff their way in without paying the cover charge.

A thirty-something woman came forward in line holding the hand of a ten-year-old girl, her face practically glowing with excitement.

"You excited to see the show?" Raven asked, taking the ten-dollar bill from the mother.

The little girl nodded. "I came to see Horace."

Her mother smiled, shaking her head. "My daughter has a little bit of a crush."

"Mom!"

"Oh, sorry." Mom gave an apologetic shrug. "I just think it's cute."

The little girl let go of her mother's hand and crossed her arms over her chest. "I do not have a crush."

"I wouldn't blame you if you did," Raven said, grabbing the girl's hand to give her a stamp. "I think Horace is a pretty great guy."

The girl looked away sheepishly. "Yeah. He is cool. How do you know him?"

Raven wanted to say she was singing with the band, but she didn't want to jinx it, or worse, have it get back to her mother somehow. Instead, she settled on, "He's a good friend of mine."

"My brother is friends with him," the girl explained. She puffed out her chest. "He comes over all the time."

"Cool."

The mom held out her hand for a stamp. "My son plays the bass guitar in that band Horace is in."

"Oh! Hobb?"

"Yeah, I guess that's his nickname." She smiled, then, "I just know him as Sean."

Raven blushed, having forgotten that "Hobb" was a nickname he'd acquired in the seventh grade because of his hobbit-like feet. "Sorry," she said.

"No. I think it's cute." Apparently, Hobb's mother thought everything was cute. She turned to her daughter. "Ready?"

The girl nodded again, the embarrassment from seconds ago having disappeared to make way for the renewed excitement. "Do you know what time Horace will be on?"

"Eight thirty," Raven said.

"If you see him, will you tell him Sugar Pop said good luck? He'll know who I am."

Sugar Pop? Raven wondered.

She just nodded, then took money from the next person in line. "I'll tell him."

Sugar Pop beamed. "Thanks."

The student council had decided to decorate for the open-mike night to make it feel like a big celebration. There were gold lights strung up around the ceiling, windows, and performance area. Lisa's mom had made centerpieces for all the tables using glass holders, fake ice cubes, and gold lights on battery packs. It'd been Sydney's idea to get two Glade PlugIns so the scent of fresh coffee mixed with the scent of pumpkin spice.

"Syd?" Lisa said. "Please tell me you brought paper plates for the baked goods?"

"Oh, yeah. They're in my car. I'll go get them."

"Thank God," Lisa muttered, hurrying off to tend to something else.

Sydney pulled her car keys out of her pocket and headed through the back room, avoiding the front entrance. Three girls unwrapped the goodies, getting them ready to set out. Sydney said hi as she passed, then headed through the exit door.

As she rounded the corner toward the parking lot she saw Drew, his height putting him above most of the car roofs. Her heart responded before her brain did, thrumming in her chest as if she were an amateur in the relationship department and this was her first crush.

But then a girl came up alongside Drew and they stopped in the middle of the parking lot. At first Sydney thought it was Nicole Robinson because of the strawberry-blonde highlights in her pulled-back, messy ponytail. Then the girl shifted and Sydney saw her face.

It was Kelly.

Sydney moved back, hiding around the corner of the building. She couldn't hear what they were saying from this distance, but Drew couldn't stop smiling and fidgeting. And then they hugged. Sydney's stomach knotted with anger, with jealousy, with disappointment.

But mostly anger.

She made a fist, car keys digging into the palm of her hand as she left her hiding place and stalked through the parking lot.

Kelly was *so* dead.

"I'm not expecting anything," Drew said. "She might not want to work things out."

"I don't know," Kelly said, leaning against her car door. "I think she loves you enough to try anything to make it work."

Drew hung his head, fidgeting with the zipper on his jacket. "I've really missed her. I could barely make it through a whole day without wanting to call her for something. I even made this list of excuses to use when she answered."

He laughed, smiling to himself. "Anyway, I just wanted to thank you. For everything." He shuffled over and wrapped Kelly in a hug. "You're a good friend."

Friend. She'd had her chance to be more than friends with him, but she couldn't. Not ever. For one, he was too good a friend, and two, she couldn't hurt her best friend. Sydney meant more to her than any guy. All three of her friends did.

"Good luck," Kelly said, giving Drew a sisterly pat on the back.

"Thanks." He pulled away, shoving his hands in the pockets of his cargo pants. "I better get inside. She said be there by eight. I don't want to screw up already."

"Break a leg," she said. He grinned, heading off to the front of the store.

Kelly grabbed her purse from the backseat of her car, then, after slamming the door shut, hit the LOCK button on her car remote. She headed to the aisle of the parking lot, noticing a figure walking purposefully through the cars.

"Hey, Syd!" Kelly raised her hand in a wave.

Except Sydney didn't wave back, she just clenched her jaw, making her way toward Kelly.

Wow. She looks pissed, Kelly thought, and the words tumbling out of Sydney's mouth next only clarified the observation.

"You . . . you . . . argh! I can't believe you!"

Alexia hurried through the growing crowd to the front door and tapped Raven on the shoulder.

"What?" Raven asked, making change for a customer.

"I just heard someone say they saw Sydney and Kelly arguing out in the parking lot."

Raven looked up. "Really?"

"I think we should go out there."

Raven scanned the faces in close proximity. "Hey, Lisa!" she called. Lisa came over, a clipboard in her hands. "I have to go. Can you take over the front door?"

"I still have tons of things to do and—"

"It's really, really important. Please?"

Lisa rolled her eyes. "Fine." She took the SCRAPPE stamp from Raven's hand and helped the next customer.

"Let's go," Raven said, pushing her way out the door.

♥ ♥ ♥

Alexia could tell Sydney was pissed just by looking at her. Heat turned her cheeks bright red. Her hands were in constant motion and her nostrils flared.

"What's going on?" Alexia said as she and Raven came between the argument.

Sydney thrust an accusing finger at Kelly. "She's seeing Drew!"

"What do you mean 'seeing Drew'?" Raven asked, keeping her voice calm and neutral.

"Going out with him! Dating him! Hello!"

"Calm down, Syd." Alexia rested a hand on Sydney's shoulder. The touch seemed to bring her back to reality, and she pursed her lips.

"I'm not seeing Drew," Kelly said, her voice hitching. She looked like she wanted to cry. "I'm not hiding anything about my love life. Unlike someone I know."

Raven frowned. "What do you mean?"

Kelly nodded at Alexia. "Is there anything you've been keeping from us?"

Alexia grimaced. "I've been dating Ben!" she blurted.

"Will told me," Kelly added.

Raven turned to Kelly. "What were you doing talking to Will? That's in violation of, like, all the rules."

Sydney propped her hands on her hips. "You've been breaking rule twenty-seven for God knows how long."

"What's rule twenty-seven?" Kelly asked.

"Don't form any new crushes."

Kelly furrowed her brow. "Who have you been crushing on?"

Raven spread her arms out. "Like I can control something like that! It's a dumb rule anyway."

"You think it's dumb because you broke it," Sydney retorted.

"You guys!" Alexia stepped in the middle. "Listen to us. We're arguing over boys and who broke what rules? I created The Code to help you and bring us all back together, but since we're here, arguing with each other, I guess it didn't work at all."

Everyone fell silent and looked at the pavement. Alexia hugged her arms around herself.

"I wouldn't say it didn't work at all," Raven said. "I'm over Caleb. Totally."

Alexia looked up.

Kelly nodded. "I'm over Will."

"I'm over my old relationship with Drew. I was starting to move on, and then he emailed me." She couldn't help but grin.

Raven lifted a brow. "He emailed you?"

Sydney nodded. "It sounds like he wants to talk . . . but . . . "

"He does," Kelly said. "That's what we were talking about just now. You. I was wishing him good luck. We're just friends, Sydney."

"I know." Sydney kicked at a rock on the pavement. "I always knew that. I was just . . ."

"Totally still in love with him," Raven supplied. "Which makes you sort of crazy."

Sydney snorted. "Ha-ha. But you're probably right."

"I'm always right." Raven squared her shoulders proudly.

"That's a funny one," Kelly said sarcastically, pulling her coat tight around her midsection.

They all laughed, then Sydney turned to Kelly. "I'm sorry for accusing you of anything."

Kelly shook her head. "Don't apologize. I can see how it might have looked to you, but just know, I'd never, ever, do anything to hurt you."

Sydney wrapped her arms around Kelly's neck. "I know. I should have trusted you." Over Kelly's shoulder, she motioned to Raven and then Alexia. "Come over here. Get in."

Raven and Alexia sidled up and Kelly and Sydney pulled them into a group hug.

Alexia smiled, relief running through her. They were her best friends. After all, if they didn't have each other, then they didn't have anyone.

"We're sorry," Kelly said. "You were right. We were arguing for nothing."

"I just . . . I want us to be best friends again and not let boys come between us. I suggested The Code to help you guys get over your exes. I thought it would bring us closer together."

"It did." Sydney smiled across their tight group hug. "In some weird way it worked."

"I got over Will," Kelly said. "And I was able to hang out with you guys while doing The Code."

"It helped me, too," Raven added.

Sydney ducked her head. "It helped me, even if Drew and I *are* still talking."

They pulled apart. Alexia debated telling them how and why The Code worked, that it was a diversion tactic. But it didn't really matter how or why it worked, only that it did.

"So, are we all okay?" she asked.

They all looked from one to the other.

"I'm good," Raven said.

"Me, too," Kelly said.

Sydney smiled. "I'm okay, except for the fact that I'm supposed to go on in fifteen minutes and read my amateur poetry."

"Poetry?" Raven asked.

"I know. It'll be lame. But I have to do it."

"We'll be there for moral support," Kelly said, the parking lot lights turning on behind her.

"Definitely," Raven said.

Alexia gave Raven a reassuring squeeze. "*You* have us, too. I just hope your mom doesn't lock you in your bedroom for eternity after this."

Raven snorted. "Yeah. Me, too."

"Ready to humiliate ourselves, then?" Sydney asked.

Raven shook her head. "But I guess at this point I can't really chicken out, so let's go!"

THIRTY-ONE

Rule 26: *You cannot kiss any boys for at least three months after the breakup.*

Sydney clutched the poem in her hand, the paper now crinkled and moist from her sweating fingertips. She swallowed, throat raw from the heat inside Scrappe. She stood off to the side of the performance area waiting for Doug Mulne to finish his stand-up comedy act. He was good, too, the whole crowd was laughing. Sydney would get up there with her dramatic, depressing poem and either put everyone to sleep or drive them out the door.

Doug thanked the audience and walked offstage as Ms. Valenti went up, the performing schedule on a clipboard in her hand.

"And now I'd like to welcome Sydney Howard reading a poem called 'I Wish.'"

If you're going to chicken out, now's the time to do it, she thought.

But she didn't, she couldn't. She walked over to the microphone and unfolded the paper.

Taking a breath, she looked out over the crowd, scanning the faces. It seemed like hundreds of people were staring back at her. She couldn't remember what Scrappe's customer capacity was, but it had to be full. She searched the room for Drew. She just wanted to see a familiar face. She found him near the back, his electric-blue eyes standing out of the crowd. He grinned and lifted a few fingers in an uncertain wave.

Sydney smiled, the fear taking a backseat to the desire to get these words out.

She started reading.

"I wish I could take it back,
The things I said,
The things I did,
Maybe we'd still be you and me.
We went together,
You and me,
Like rain and rainbows.
But then we were
Just you, just me,
And maybe that's what you wanted,
To find yourself.
To be yourself.
I respect that,
But I still love you.
I still love you and me.
I wish I could take it back."

When she finished, the whole place went silent and no one moved. The instinct to run coiled in her calves until her mother stood up from her table and started clapping. Then

Kelly and Alexia and Drew clapped and the whole room stood up, hands coming together.

Sydney exhaled, relieved. "Thank you," she said into the microphone and stepped down, threading her way through the crowd over to her mother. "What are you doing here?"

"Your father and I had a long phone conversation last night in which he chastised me for not being home and spending more time with my only child." Mrs. Howard took a deep breath. "I realized he was right. So here I am. Perfect timing, too. That poem was beautiful."

"Thanks."

"I used to write poetry in my journal when I was your age." She rolled her eyes. "Well, I still do, actually."

Sydney wasn't sure what to make of all this. It'd been so long since her mother did anything in her free time that involved Sydney. Would it last, this epiphany?

As if reading her daughter's mind, Mrs. Howard said, "I took a week of vacation so we can hang out, and after that I'm going to try and cut my hours."

Sydney raised her brow. "Really?"

"Really." Mrs. Howard wrapped her arms around Sydney. "I love you, honey."

"I love you, too."

"Now," Mrs. Howard pulled back, "I think there's someone waiting for you in the back. How about you go talk to him, and I'll meet you at home?"

Sydney stole a glance across the room at Drew. She desperately wanted to go over there, give him a hug, and beg him to take her back, but she'd have to settle for talking.

"Thanks," she said to her mom. "I'll probably be home around eleven."

"Take your time," Mrs. Howard said.

Nodding, Sydney slipped into the crowd and made her way to the back corner.

♥ ♥ ♥

Raven could count on two hands the amount of times she'd ever thrown up. She was about to have to move on to her toes because she'd already hurled in the bathroom. She felt beyond nauseous now as she waited offstage for the last performer to wrap up.

"You'll do great," Horace said, putting a reassuring hand on her shoulder.

"Yeah, but my mom "

"As soon as she hears your voice, she'll realize you were meant to do this." He smiled and came around in front of her. "Ray, I have faith in you. I know you can do this."

"Unless my mother pulls me off the stage."

"We'll form a human barricade."

She snorted. "Oh, by the way, this little girl at the front door told me to tell you Sugar Pop said good luck."

Color flared on his cheeks. "Oh, right. She's Hobb's little sister. I, uh," he shifted his eyes down, "call her Sugar Pop."

Raven laughed. "I thought it was cute."

He shrugged again. "Go ahead, tell me it's lame."

"No. It's cute."

"Well, thanks for sparing me the ridicule."

The crowd clapped as two comedic freshmen left the stage area, bowing as they went. Raven's nausea flared again as performance time neared. Her mother went to the microphone and announced the band.

"Please welcome the next act, an amateur band called . . ." she looked at her clipboard, "October."

They'd all decided on the band name last night after an hour's worth of debating. And the brilliance of the name went no further than Dean seeing an old calendar hanging on the wall, forgotten since the month of October, which Hobb decided would be the name of their first album. If there was an album.

"I can see it now," Hobb had said, spreading his arms out as if reading a headline. "The debut alternative band October hits the Billboard charts with their groundbreaking album, *Forgotten Since the Month of October.* It's sheer brilliance."

"Is that you talking," Horace had said, "or the headline?"

"The headline."

Raven couldn't help but laugh now as she thought about it. She'd had fun last night, although the only reason she was there practicing with the band was because she'd lied to her mother and told her she was studying with Horace at the library.

Hanging out with Horace, Dean, and Hobb was fun, and playing with the band was exhilarating. If only she could persuade her mother to believe it was a worthy hobby.

The guys went onstage and positioned themselves behind their instruments, Horace on the guitar, Hobb on the bass, and Dean behind the drum set. Raven waited offstage just as they'd planned, so her mother wouldn't know she was singing until she actually *was* singing.

Horace started the song off, his guitar riffs pulling the audience in, fingers flicking the pick over the strings. Dean and Hobb came in next, and Raven ran up, taking the mike in her hands.

She avoided looking over where she knew her mother was. If she was going to storm the stage, Raven didn't want to see her coming.

The mixture of the guitar strings, the bass chords, and the drums thumping behind her had Raven's adrenaline pumping through her veins. She forgot about the nausea and the fear of her mother.

Time to jump in.

Raven parted her lips and sang. She closed her eyes, belting out the moody lyrics, tapping her foot in time with the drums. There was no audience, no mother, just Raven and the music, everything coming together perfectly.

The song built, emotion and excitement rose in Raven's gut. This is what she wanted to spend the rest of her life doing. Living a month without this kind of excitement would be like living a life without air.

She needed this.

When the song ended, Raven glanced over at her mother, afraid to see anger and disappointment, but instead she saw a smile on her mother's face and maybe even mistiness in her eyes. And standing right behind her was Raven's dad.

"Wooo-hoooo!" he yelled, fists flailing in the air. His ex-wife shot him a glance, but he just kept shouting.

Ms. Valenti shook her head as if amused and came onstage to announce the next act. But before she grabbed the microphone, she hugged her daughter and whispered, "I've never seen you look so beautiful as you did up here onstage. We'll talk about this at home." Then she said into the mike, "Give it up for my daughter and the band October!"

The applause was thunderous, claps mixing with hollers and whistles. Raven couldn't help but smile as Horace grabbed her hand and winked at her. She closed the distance between them, sliding her hands up his jaw, pulling him over.

And then she kissed him.

♥ ♥ ♥

"Hey," Drew said when Sydney reached him.

"Hi. Happy belated birthday, by the way."

He grinned. "Thanks."

"Here." She pulled the ring she'd bought him from her jeans pocket and handed it over. "I know we're not together anymore, but I bought it months ago and it wouldn't be right to give it to someone else."

Twirling the ring in the light, he read the inscription. "To the day I die."

"It's still true," she said. "I'll always love you in some way, whether we're *in* love or not."

"I'll always love you, too." He slipped the ring on his middle finger. It fit perfectly. "I liked your poem."

She met his eyes. "Yeah?"

"I liked it enough to want to kiss you right now."

She giggled. God help her, she giggled. How long had it been since she'd lowered herself to giggling? Probably two years. Since she and Drew started seeing each other. There was something about him now that made her feel girly and carefree.

"So, are you? Going to kiss me?"

"That depends on whether or not you want me to kiss you."

"You always did plan too much," she said, and leaned in.

"I did," he whispered, his minty breath fanning across her face. "And you were always too impatient."

"I was." It was time to be completely honest with herself and Drew. She had a lot of things to work on, obviously, but she was willing to change if it made their relationship stronger and made her a better person. But the most important thing was that being single had showed her who she was and what her flaws were. As much as she hated to admit it, being without Drew had been good for her. She was Sydney now, not Sydney *and* Drew. She was her own person.

"So," Drew said, running his fingers across her jawline.

"So . . ." she echoed.

The audience went wild as the band October hit the high note of the song. Sydney thought this moment couldn't be more perfect, here now with Drew, with Raven's awesome voice sounding around her.

God, she'd remember this for a lifetime.

"Just kiss me already," she said.

And he did.

Alexia was running on pure adrenaline. It seemed to be in the air tonight like laughing gas, muddling her brain, moving her feet beneath her. Maybe what she was about to do was crazy, but she had to do it. Sydney read her poem in front of everyone, spilling her innermost thoughts through the microphone, and Raven sang her heart out while facing the wrath of her mother.

In the spotlight now, Alexia turned to Ms. Valenti and motioned toward the microphone. "Mind if I make a quick announcement?" She wasn't even sure if he was here, or if he'd even care now, but she had to get it out there.

"Sure." Ms. Valenti stepped aside.

Alexia went to the microphone and took it in her hands. The stage lights seemed to bake her freckles, beading sweat on her forehead. She tried to ignore the knot in her stomach and the hundreds of eyes trained on her.

"Hi," she said, her voice sounding too loud through the speakers. "Um . . . I just wanted to say . . ." She was probably committing social suicide but who cared? "That I *really like* Ben Daniels and . . ."

Someone sidled up next to her. She glanced over as Ben took the microphone in his hands. "And I just want to say that I really, *really* like Alexia Bass. I like her more than banana splits and sunny days and Yo Mama jokes."

Alexia laughed with the audience. Someone started stomping as if they were at a basketball game, cheering on the team. The rest of the crowd joined in and yelled, "Kiss her! Kiss her!"

Ben wove an arm around Alexia's waist, put his other hand behind her head and dipped her, planting his lips on hers as the crowd roared.

Alexia was pretty sure this was the best night of her life.

Kelly cheered with the rest of the crowd as Ben kissed Alexia onstage. "Woo!" She screamed, clapping above her head. This sure was one night to remember.

When she was old and gray and her body was too wrinkly and run-down to fit in a nice pair of jeans, Kelly would look back on this night. Maybe she didn't have a boy like her friends, but that, actually, was good. She'd been chasing after Will so long she'd forgotten who she really was. It was time to get in tune with Kelly.

When she knew herself again, she'd know who the perfect guy was. And maybe, if she stopped looking so darn hard, the perfect guy would find her.

THIRTY-TWO

Rule 25: *Do not ever think that you will never meet or love a guy the way you liked or loved The Ex, because you will—just give yourself the chance by letting The Ex go.*

"So we're all in agreement," Alexia said, "that we are done with The Breakup Code? And that it's time to lay it to rest?"

Raven stopped scrolling through her iPod, wound the earbuds up, and slipped it inside her bag. "I'm in agreement. I hope I never need The Code again."

"So you and Horace are doing good?" Sydney asked, before chomping on a few pretzel sticks.

Raven waited to answer while Alexia's mom set a tray down on the coffee table with four glasses filled with soda. "There you go, girls," she said. "If you need anything else, let me know."

"Thanks, Mom." Alexia took a glass for herself.

After Dr. Bass's footsteps disappeared into the kitchen Raven said, "Yeah, we're doing more than good. It's a little scary, actually. But, hey, it's only been two weeks."

Kelly grabbed a handful of pretzels from the bag on Sydney's lap. "Why is it scary?"

"Because," Raven shrugged, "I really, really like him and I don't want to screw it up. You guys know how I am."

"But you can change," Alexia said. "Besides, Horace is actually a good guy."

"Okay. Okay," Raven said. "Enough of me. How are you and Ben?"

Alexia's face lit up and she looked away. "We're fine."

"Ohhh!" Kelly widened her eyes. "By the look on your face, you're more than fine!"

"Our Alexia is finally in love," Sydney said.

"Stop, you guys!" Alexia thumped Kelly with a throw pillow. "I'm not in love just yet, so calm down."

Sydney laughed, drawing their attention.

"And what about you? How are you and Drew?"

With a demure expression she said, "We are so good that I'm in agreement that I'm through with The Breakup Code. I don't think I'll need it anytime soon. Drew and I are better than we've ever been."

"She's definitely in love," Raven said. "Look at how googly-eyed she is."

"Shut up!"

"Kelly?" Alexia said. "Are you in agreement? Should we lay The Code to rest?"

Kelly slipped her worn four-leaf-clover rubber band off her wrist and set it in the shoe box they'd deemed The Code Casket. "I may be the only one of us still single, but I'm in full agreement that we put The Code away for safekeeping. I'm never going back to Will Daniels. I will never, ever sacrifice myself to please a guy. That's definitely the number one thing The Code taught me."

Sydney threw her clover rubber band in The Code Casket. Raven threw hers in, too. Alexia put a copy of The Code inside the box and shut the lid. "Ready then?" she asked, glancing from one girl to the next. Sydney and Raven both nodded.

Kelly hesitated. She was over Will. She was excited about being single, but that didn't stop her from worrying that she'd never find someone new. That she would never love someone as much as she'd loved Will.

Still . . . The Breakup Code had worked. She wouldn't need to use it anymore.

"Kelly?" Alexia said.

"I'm ready."

"Wait, wait," Sydney said. "Let me set up the camera. This is an important snapshot. A picture to remind us of the day we were no longer heartbroken. Don't you think?"

They all nodded.

"You three crowd around The Code Casket," Sydney instructed as she jumped up with the camera. She hit a few buttons, checked the angle in the camera's screen, then set it on the coffee table. She ran over and got in next to Kelly. "Three seconds."

"All together," Alexia said.

"As Women of The Code," they said in unison, "we hereby lay The Breakup Code to rest."

The camera flashed.